# FOREVER BABY

A FOREVER NOVEL

# ELLIE WADE

# dedication

*If you have ever struggled with insecurities or questioned your worth, this book is dedicated to you. I want you to know that you are enough just the way you are.* ♥

# contents

# prelude

"Seriously, Mom! This is so ridiculous! Nothing is wrong with me. I don't want to go see Dr. Thomas. He is a complete idiot." The anger inside me threatens to explode. I lean my head against the car window in defeat, watching the cookie-cutter houses in a subdivision pass by on this now all too familiar route to see my therapist Dr. Stupid-Ass Thomas.

"Honey, I know you don't want to go, but your father and I think it is important. Can you please try to be cooperative today?" my mom asks in a sincerely concerned tone.

"Mom, it's not that I don't try. I have nothing to say. Why can't you understand that I'm fine?"

"Well, sweetie, your actions say otherwise, and I want to make sure you're getting the support you need before you go off to college. I worry about you, and I don't want you to make any decisions that could hurt you in the long run."

I am so sick of this spiel. I have heard it many times over the last few years.

My mom is worried about—*how does she put it?*—my self-worth. She feels that I don't value myself the way that I should, and because of that, I will make bad choices to fit in, but I honestly don't see her side. I am happy with my life. I feel like my mom has emotionally switched places with me, and she is hell-bent on causing teenage drama. *I think that's supposed to be my job.* She loves to create drama where there is none. She's always eager to jump in and save the day when, in fact, there is nothing that needs to be saved. I know the nurse in her wants to fix any problems that she perceives need to be fixed. I wish she would understand that I'm not one of those problems.

"Do you sit around at night and imagine these so-called decisions? Last time I checked, I'm doing pretty well. Do you want me to let you know what other kids my age are doing? Will it make you feel better to know that I'm not whoring around or popping acid like candy? I get good grades. I am a good person, Mom. Why don't you have any faith in me?" I'm close to yelling now, but it's true. I could partake in many activities that would, indeed, be harmful to me, but I choose not to. Besides what my parents imply, I don't want to grow up to be a loser.

"Please don't be like that, Olivia. You know I only want the best for you. I know that you are a good girl, honey, and I am so proud of you.

Your father and I are worried that when you go off to college without the support system you have here, you might make decisions that could be detrimental to your future."

"If I promise not to tattoo my face or start shooting up heroin the second I get to college, can we forgo this appointment?"

"Very funny, Olivia."

"Well, that's about as much credit as you're giving me," I say dryly. "Seriously, Mom, what do you think I'm going to do? I don't understand. You are making a big deal out of absolutely nothing."

"Sweetie, you are a beautiful, smart, and kind person, but you don't see it, and that worries me."

I know my parents think that something horrific must have happened to me at some point in my life to cause me not to value myself as much as I should. Okay maybe they are right to think I have some self-esteem issues, but I think a lot of people do. We don't enter this world as beacons of wholeness, eager to take on the each day with our self-confidence. I personally believe that we are born as blank slates, and our worth comes from others—at least initially—until we are strong enough to value our own opinions over those of the people around us.

*Does one have to suffer through a tragic upbringing to have self-esteem issues? No, I don't think so.* I was never abused, neglected, or molested. My life's tragedy isn't worthy of an *Oprah Winfrey Show* special. My life has been the opposite of a tragedy. I have been loved as much as I think a set of parents can love their child. I have been very wanted, so much so that my mother underwent years of fertility treatments to finally conceive me. I don't know. Maybe this is part of it—my insecurity to be everything my parents dreamed I could be, to be worthy of their struggle. They have never led me to believe that I am anything but worthy. Nonetheless, the ever-present voice is in my head, reminding me that I'm not quite enough.

I cannot pinpoint a series of shameful experiences in my past as the cause of my insecurities. In fact, there is not even one. I honestly believe that small moments in our lives mold us into the people we are going to be. These fragments in time are so inconsequential that they don't even have staying power in our memories. Perhaps, a girl in Sunday school class didn't like my dress or a glitter project that I had poured my five-year-old soul into, and when I shared that particular experience with my mother, it was brushed off with a hurried smile as she stressfully made dinner after a hard day's work. Small moments like that could have filled up pieces of my being with emptiness, slowly chipping away slivers of my spirit. It could be that some people are prewired to need less validation from others than I do. *I'm not sure.* Regardless of the reason, I do not value myself as much as I should, and I am aware of it. Unfortunately, I can't change my personal self-worth.

Although I have tried, I can't trick my mind into believing something that I don't.

The moral of this story though is that it doesn't matter. It's okay that I am not exploding with self-confidence. I would venture to say that most people aren't. I am still a whole person, and I am happy with my life. I am certain that I won't make detrimental choices the second I am out from under my parents' roof to—*what? Fit in? I'm not that pathetic. Why can't Dr. Thomas or my parents understand this? Why can't they understand that this is who I am, and I'm okay with it?* I know all of this interest comes from a good place where my parents are concerned, but I'm beyond annoyed.

"Mom, how many more of these so-called therapy sessions do I have to go to?"

With a hint of resignation in her voice, she says, "I don't know, Olivia. I'm trying here, okay?"

"I know you are, Mom, but I'm fine. I'm happy. Please believe me."

"I want you to have someone to talk to if there is anything you need to work through, you know?"

"While I appreciate that you care, please believe me that I am good, Mom. I'm good."

"If you are so great, then why did you end it with Ryan?"

I let out a deep sigh. "Mom, we have gone over this. It just wasn't there anymore. We are better off as friends."

Ryan has been my best friend since I was ten, and for the last four years, he was my boyfriend. My parents think that I ended it because I didn't think he would stay with me throughout college and that I wanted to beat him to the punch. The truth is, I ended it because I didn't see him as anything other than a friend in my future.

"Eastern?"

I groan. "Mom!"

My parents are upset that I didn't apply to their alma mater, the University of Michigan. Instead, I applied to a smaller college located ten miles away from it. It had nothing to do with me thinking I couldn't get into U of M. I knew I could have, but the prospect of spending my adult life paying off student loans was enough to scare me away. I know it's a great school, but I want an education, not a lifelong debt sentence.

"Volleyball?"

In as calm of a voice as I can muster up, I say, "Mom, we have been over this. I didn't want to play anymore, and that is it. There is no underlying reason. Just stop it."

"But you were so great, honey. You could have gotten a scholarship."

"I'm not going to keep rehashing every decision that I've made with you. I have reasons for everything I do. Please, just stop."

We drive the rest of the way to the office in silence. My mom sighs, and I can sense the defeat in her posture. Hopefully, this will be my last session. I know she worries about me, and she probably always will.

Apparently, the only way to prove to her that I am a well-adjusted person is to make it through college without doing something idiotic. I think I can handle that.

# chapter 1

Three Years Later

I stare in amusement at the sight of one of my sorority sisters in a wedding dress with her long blonde hair dangling toward the floor while she's doing a keg stand.

Ten or so drunk frat guys in ties and untucked dress shirts are standing around her, cheering and yelling, "Five! Six! Seven! Eight!"

*I wonder how long she'll be able to chug down cheap beer while upside down before she throws up all over that secondhand gown.*

My eyes move to the handsome, tall guy holding up one of her legs. He winks at me and flashes his all-American boy smile. That adorable boy is one of my best friends, Nolan. I'm not surprised that he's right up in this comical keg stand action as he always manages to be the life of every party.

"Nine! Ten! Eleven!"

Just like that, beer sprays out of the sides of her mouth, like a shaken soda can exploding. She signals to be let down. The guys guide her feet to the ground, and I watch her wipe her face as she stands.

"Weak," says the voice next to me.

I turn to my best friend, roommate, and sorority sister, Cara.

"Totally," I agree. "I can do fifteen seconds, and I hate beer!"

"I know, right? Lame."

At that moment, Britney Spears and will.i.am pound from the speakers, and Cara grabs my hand.

We wind our way to the makeshift dance floor as we both shout in unison, "It's Britney, bitch!" Our love for Britney is one of the many things Cara and I share.

The Italian restaurant has been converted into a bar for the evening. Our sorority and Nolan's fraternity rented it for our year-end Wedding Social. This is the exact reason I joined the sorority three years ago—for the awesome parties. Sure, I know that sounds bad. I guess I was supposed to join for sisterhood and the great philanthropic work, but I didn't. Yes, it makes me feel good to rake leaves for the elderly every fall and to run a canned food drive on campus. And, of course, I love all my sorority sisters—well, most of them—but the reason I pay incredibly high dues every semester is for the parties.

The college Greek community invents reasons to have parties, and those dues allow us VIP access. We attend a smallish college in Michigan in a city named Ypsilanti (pronounced *ip-si-lanti*). I not only go to college here, but I also live here year-round. Eastern Michigan University is widely ignored because it's in the city next to Ann Arbor, where the almighty affluent and prestigious University of Michigan resides. To be fair, parts of Ypsilanti are kind of dumps, so I can see why some would ignore it, but I love it. Without a plethora of choices for evening entertainment, Greek life is that much more beneficial.

Everyone here is dressed for a wedding. And no wedding celebration would be complete without a lucky (fake) bride and groom. At last month's sorority meeting, we had a long debate about who would be the bride. I, for one, wanted nothing to do with that position. *Who would want to hang out all night in an itchy, heavy wedding dress? No, thanks.* My simple above-the-knee black halter dress is ideal for me. Cara is dressed in something that could have just come off the runway. She's wearing a one-shoulder asymmetrical mint green dress with feathers and sequins. If it ended any higher on her thighs, it would be considered indecent. On anyone else, this dress would come off as ridiculous, but on Cara, it's crazy hot.

It was completely my luck to befriend the supermodel of EMU. She's tall at five-ten, but she usually stands taller because she insists on wearing four-inch heels. Model thin, she has dark, round eyes, full lips, and chestnut hair that falls to the small of her back. She is the most beautiful person on campus, and luckily for me, she is even more so on the inside—making her my perfect partner in crime, my BFF.

I met Cara freshman year. We lived in the same dorm, and we became inseparable out of random luck and convenience. She has an older cousin who resembles me—well, sort of. We both have blonde hair and blue eyes. Besides those two attributes, our appearances aren't all that similar. But in the world of fake IDs, it is close enough. Armed with her cousin's ID and Cara with her older sister's ID, she and I became barhopping regulars as freshmen. However, in all honesty, I don't think the bouncers at the local twenty-one-and-over establishments really studied my license too closely because they were too busy ogling Cara's flawless body. Cara and I have definitely been making the most of our college experience.

Eyes closed, I raise my hands in the air while waving my hips to the music when strong, warm hands wrap around my waist, pulling me close. A tall, hard body grinds behind me to the repetitive bass. I don't have to turn around to know that it's Nolan. I can smell his deliciousness—a combination of cologne, body wash, and a scent that is solely his. I always tease him and say that he smells like bottled hotness.

"Hey, beautiful," he says, nuzzling into my hair.

"Hey. You finished staring down the bride's skirt?" I yell over the music with a smirk.

"Yeah, she disappeared into the bathroom, probably throwing up. Too much upside-down cheap-beer chugging will do that to a bride."

We laugh.

Cara leans into us. "Hey, Livi, I'm heading to the bar. Want a drink?"

"Vodka and cranberry, please?"

"Nolan?"

"Heineken. Thanks, Cara. Put it on my tab, okay?"

"Sure thing." She grins and saunters off.

Nolan always pays for our drinks. I used to try to stop him, but I got sick of fighting about it. Now, it's the way it is. He comes from money. His dad is an exceptionally successful businessman, and Nolan is provided with endless funds to use, no questions asked. So, it's not really a hang-up for me anymore. I put my foot down on other stuff, but drinks are not worth the argument.

Despite working my ass off at a local Mexican restaurant, I struggle to pay for my portion of the rent in the slightly ghetto apartment that I share with Cara. I'm not bashing the place. I love living on the second floor of our large white 1920s-character home. But to say that we have a bum who periodically snoozes in our side yard would not be an exaggeration. Once, we came home late after a party, and a very inebriated girl, who we did not know, was in our kitchen making macaroni and cheese. We let her finish, and then she passed out on our couch. She was gone when we woke up the next morning. One would think we would have started locking our door after that incident, but we didn't.

Nolan twists me around, so I'm facing him. My arms go around his neck as we grind to some Usher.

"Hey, you want to go soon? We have a big day tomorrow," he says, giving me his melt-my-heart smile.

"No way! This is our last hurrah! Cara would kill me if I left early. We can sleep on the plane. Plus, you know the end is my favorite part."

I give him a cheesy grin, and he laughs.

"Okay, you're right."

I do love the end of all college parties. There's nothing better than jumping around the dance floor with a bunch of intoxicated, happy people while singing the lyrics of classics, like "Pour Some Sugar on Me"—*I'm hot, sticky sweet, from my head to my feet, yeah*—and "Sweet Caroline"—*Sweet Caroline...bum...bum...bum, good times never seemed so good.* I don't know what it is about being drunk, but it makes all music recorded when I was in diapers or before very cool, like, seriously cool—like, get-drunk-and-scream-the-lyrics-at-the-top-of-my-lungs-while-jumping-up-and-down-with-hands-raised-in-the-air cool.

The night winds down, and I am completely happy. Nolan is standing to my right, and his strong hand is wrapped around my middle. Cara is on my left, and my arms are out to my sides, circling around their backs. We are a collective mass of bodies, swaying in a harmonious circle of sweaty, very drunk people while belting out the lyrics to "Piano Man." This is my favorite part of the evening.

The air is unseasonably warm for an end of April evening. The tepid breeze blows my long blonde locks away from my back as we make our way the four blocks from the social to Abe's Coney Island where the chili cheese fries can only be described as a plate of yummy goodness sent from heaven, especially when they are consumed at two o'clock after a night of drinking. A block into our journey, I hear a group of guys yelling compliments—or more like, slurring drunken catcalls—having something to do with a hot ass. I look back to see Cara's reaction to the scene, and I'm surprised to find her a block away, still outside the bar entrance. She's laughing with a guy, one of her ex-boyfriends, I think. I scan the area behind me, not seeing anyone else, but the wobbly idiots are still hooting and hollering.

I face front again when Nolan says, "You know they are yelling at you, right?" He has an uncanny ability to know my thoughts without me verbalizing them.

"I doubt it," I say, forcing a laugh, as I roll my eyes.

"Why do you keep doing that?"

"What?" I answer in the best innocent tone I can muster up.

"You know what. Stop it. You know how beautiful you are."

Playfully punching him in the side, I tease, "You are just saying that because you love me."

"I do love you, but that doesn't change the fact that you are beautiful, Liv."

He takes my hand in his, and we continue our way to the restaurant. I take my free hand and wrap it around Nolan's forearm, leaning my head on his bicep, as we walk in silence. Nolan has always made me feel special. For some reason, when he says it, I believe him, but it never takes long for the doubts to creep back.

"Wait up, bitches," Cara calls out. She jogs up beside me, hand in hand, with one of her exes.

"Hey, Tony," I greet her counterpart for the evening.

He gives me a sly head nod. If I remember correctly, Cara's fling with Tony only lasted a couple of weeks. I never liked him anyway. He's too cocky.

I peer up quizzically at Cara, and she knows what I am asking. She responds with a slight shake of her head, which is all I need to know. Tony is not going to be hanging around after tonight.

Nolan interrupts our silent conversation. "Sorry, Cara. The chili cheese fries aren't going to wait forever."

# chapter 2

I study my reflection in the mirror after finishing my makeup. I pulled off a decent appearance, considering the little sleep I'd gotten last night. We hung out at Abe's, laughing until very late—or very early, depending on how you see it. It was a great conclusion to my junior year.

I hear Nolan's voice in the next room. *Crap.* It must be time to go already. I come out of the bathroom a little frantic, checking my list to make sure I packed everything.

"Livi, you know they do have stores in Spain," Cara says.

I look up from my list to see Nolan and Cara examining me from the kitchen, their lips slanted upward with sly expressions plastered on their faces. I know they're inwardly laughing about my obsession with lists and my subsequent anxiety about forgetting items on said lists. Nolan and I are heading to Seville, Spain, for the summer as part of a foreign exchange student program. We'll be studying Spanish at a local university there.

I ignore their snickering. "I know, but there is nothing wrong with making sure I have everything."

With a mock heartbroken expression and pouty lips, Cara pleads, "Well, you know you could always cancel and stay here with me." This line has become her mantra over the past few months.

I frown as I walk over to Cara and give her a big hug.

She squeezes me tight. "I am going to miss you. What am I supposed to do all summer without you?"

"Cara, it's only a few months, and you'll be busy with work and creating your signature tan. Plus, you do have other friends, and you are coming to visit at some point. The summer will go by quickly, I promise!" I exclaim reassuringly.

A knock at the back door sounds, followed by a singsongy, "Hello," coming from my mother.

"Mama!" I say as I lean in, comforted by my mom's firm hug.

I'm happy to see her, if only for a few minutes. It wouldn't feel right to head to another continent without a farewell from my parents.

Releasing my grip from my mom, I twist and fall into a hug with my dad.

After kissing my head, he says, "Ready, sweetheart?"

"What? Max didn't want to be here for your send-off?" questions Cara.

My older brother, Max, and Cara have a love-hate relationship. Max loves Cara—at least, he lusts for her—and she pretends to hate him. I'm pretty sure she relishes the attention that comes with his crude advances.

"He is in L.A., but I'm sure he would be more than happy to visit this summer to keep you company," I say, winking.

"Ugh. No, thank you. The only good thing about you leaving is not having visits from him," Cara states with an inflated note of disgust in her voice.

I chuckle and face Nolan. "You ready?"

After one final hug with Cara, Nolan grabs my bags, and we head out the back door, followed by my parents.

Cara yells after us, "You better text me constantly, Livi! I want all the juicy details!"

I laugh and agree. Knowing that I will be in another continent later today is both thrilling and terrifying. I'm not much of a traveler. I can count on one hand the amount of states I've seen. Thinking about what it will feel like to be in a whole other country is mind-blowing.

Touching my mom's arm, I say, "No worries, Mom. Seriously, the details won't be that juicy."

My parents drop us off at the airport with hugs and kisses and promises on my part to call or email often. After Nolan and I work our way through the lines of impatient people at the check-in counter and then security, we make it to our gate right as the airline attendant announces that boarding will begin.

Nolan and I take our seats in first class, of course, thanks to his last-minute upgrade of my ticket. He orders us drinks as soon as we sit down. He knows how much I hate flying—well, the idea of flying since I've never actually flown anywhere before, but I've worked myself up with the terror of it all.

He takes my hand. "Liv, it'll be fine. You know it's safer to fly than drive, right?"

"Yeah, so they say," I say dryly. "Whoever *they* are."

I lean into Nolan's shoulder. He holds my hand and tells me ridiculous stories to make me laugh despite my fear as the plane ascends. Once we're in the air, the anxiety lessens as my excitement grows. *I cannot wait to get to Spain.*

Nolan squeezes my hand in assurance. "Love you, sweets. This is going to be so kick-ass."

I smile warmly at him, adoring our long-standing habit of using sickeningly sweet pet names for each other. "Love you, too, hot stuff. This is going to be pretty awesome, isn't it?"

Nolan is one of the most important people in my life. As much as I love my family and Cara, Nolan is the person who centers me. He can read me, and he simply knows what I need. To have someone who truly listens and understands is priceless. I am beyond lucky to have such a caring person in my life. Our relationship isn't romantic—usually. We have had a handful of drunken kisses but nothing out of control.

I met him the first day of my freshman year. He was in my Spanish 101 class. Of course, I noticed him immediately upon entering the class. It would have been hard not to. He's gorgeous with his short, beautifully messy golden-blond hair, bright emerald eyes, defined jaw, and killer smile. His body isn't too shabby either. He's tall and lean with defined muscles.

He's majoring in international business, and I'm majoring in bilingual Spanish education. We've taken Spanish classes together every semester. It has worked out to his benefit because he's copied most of my homework assignments. He doesn't take learning Spanish too seriously, and I think he's only taken the courses to please his dad, who insists the extra language will help him in the business world.

We hit it off that initial day, and I knew Nolan was best-friend material from the first time I invited him out with Cara and me. He didn't change around her, like every other guy does. I've lost many potential guy friends and boyfriends after introducing them to Cara. They immediately stop thinking with their brains as another one of their body parts takes over, and they forget I'm even there. I guess that's one of the downfalls of being best friends with the hottest girl at school. Nolan was different though. He didn't make me feel any less important when we were around Cara. Her appearance didn't seem to affect him, like it does with the rest of the male population.

Nolan's lack of interest in Cara might be due to the fact that he has a girlfriend in Miami where he grew up. He has been with Abby since his senior year of high school, but I really don't understand their relationship. He doesn't see her much, except when he goes home for the holidays. She's visited Nolan a few times, but my time with her was limited. The time I did spend with her, in all honesty, wasn't pleasant. She doesn't seem to like me much—maybe because Nolan and I are so close—so she and Nolan tend to do their own thing when she visits. She's pretty with a short blonde bob, brown eyes, and a heart-shaped face, but her personality doesn't match the outgoing charm of Nolan.

Nolan let me know about her on our first study date during the second week of school, so we have only ever been friends. I'd be lying if I didn't admit to initially fantasizing about us being more. I mean, he is a walking god of gorgeousness. I quickly got over that hope though, and I am happy to have him any way I can get him.

Some might find our closeness odd, but it works for us. I need Nolan in my life. I couldn't imagine the past three years without him. He is always there for me, listening and giving me strength when I need it. I hit the jackpot when it comes to friends—this I know.

After many laughs, a sandwich, and a nap while snuggled next to Nolan, we're descending. We grab our luggage from baggage claim, and then we're met by a crowd waiting on the other side of customs. Among the group, I see people reuniting with hugs and kisses and anxious faces of those waiting for loved ones, and then I see a young woman who seems to be around my age. She's holding up a sign that reads, *Olivia Marshall.* I let go of Nolan's hand and walk over to her.

The girl holding the sign introduces herself as Nadia, my new roommate for the summer. Nadia is pretty with copper highlights woven through shoulder-length brown hair, light brown eyes, and a warm smile. She greets me with a big hug and a kiss on the cheek. She signed up to host an exchange student for the summer through the university, and then I was placed with her. I will be living with her and her brother. Their home is close to the university, so I won't have a long commute to class.

I scan the group until I find Nolan. He's smiling and talking to his new summer roommate, a guy who appears to be around the same age as Nolan. He's about a foot shorter than Nolan, and he has black hair that is slicked back and tan skin. He emits a friendly vibe. He isn't what I would call good-looking, but he seems to be pleasant from the exchange I see between him and Nolan.

I walk over to let Nolan know that Nadia and I are leaving.

Nolan introduces me to his roommate, Pedro, and then leans in to give me a kiss on the cheek. "Call me when you're settled in."

Pulling my luggage behind me, Nadia and I make our way out of the airport. "Olivia, I am so excited you are here. We are going to have a great summer, truly." The warmness in her voice eases all the apprehension that courses through me.

"Thanks. I am so happy to be here. You can call me Liv or Livi if you want," I say as we trek through the parking structure toward her vehicle.

I sit in the front seat of Nadia's metallic blue Nissan Maxima as we head toward my new home for the summer. She hasn't stopped talking since she started driving. I'm happy that I can understand her Spanish, and I almost as easily respond correctly. All my hours of studying this language over the past three years have paid off. She is fluent in English as well, but she knows the point of studying abroad is for me to improve my Spanish speaking. While listening to Nadia excitedly yammer on, I can tell that I'm going to love her. Also a twenty-one-year-old, she attends the college where I'll be enrolled come Monday.

I'm exhilarated while peering out the window, watching Seville pass by me. From what I can see, it's a lovely place, very picturesque and vastly different from Ypsilanti. Many of the buildings seem to be older and made of stone. We drive by many narrow cobblestone side streets. The buildings and houses stand side by side, sometimes appearing to be connected. Each colorful building blends into the next as we pass.

Seville—or *Se-bi-ya*, as pronounced in Spanish—is a magnificent place. It's large but with a quaint, romantic feel. Driving me around the city, Nadia points out a few popular tourist attractions—the Cathedral, Palace of San Telmo, Guadalquivir River, and the Metropol Parasol— and she gives me a brief summary of each. I really enjoy seeing the Torre del Oro, which translates to the Tower of Gold. It has a fairy-princess vibe.

Nadia promises to give me a more detailed excursion later as she passes the university. The University of Seville is a long two-story stone structure surrounded by a tall wrought-iron gate. It is located on a cobblestone street in the Casco Antiguo district set in the center of Seville on the east bank of the Guadalquivir River. This area is considered the old quarter of Seville. The school has an antique grandiose elegance to it, reminding me of a palace, like the one belonging to the royal family in England. Everything I have seen so far has been nothing shy of stunning, all containing the old-world charm. It is surprising to me that such a populated city can maintain a charming appeal.

Nadia turns onto a road across from the university and makes her way through a maze of narrow cobblestone streets. On either side of the street are two- and three-story buildings, all made of cream-colored stucco. Wrought-iron hanging baskets are suspended below the windows, most filled with flowers. In a few of the open spaces between the buildings, I can see tall palm trees.

After winding her way through a few one-way streets, Nadia parks the car on the side of the road and gets out. Despite the few minutes it took to navigate through the tight streets, I can tell that we are still close to the school. She helps me with my bags, and we make our way around the corner to a little stone square patio situated in the center of three buildings. Each building is aligned with a side of the tiled square patio. Each building's entrance is facing the center where a palm tree and a few flowering plants are growing.

Nadia stops in front of the door belonging to the building at the back end of the square. She places her key in the thick wooden door that's discolored from years in the sun. On each side of the door is an antique-looking flower hanger bursting with tiny purple flowers. I am in awe as I step toward the door that Nadia is holding open with a welcoming grin.

It is hard to believe that twenty-one-year-old siblings live here. It's such a far cry from the homes that surrounded me in Ypsilanti. I recall taking note that most of the buildings we passed were beautiful as well. *Maybe this is the norm here?* I haven't stepped foot into the house yet, but the expectations I had for this country have already been exceeded.

When we walk through the front door, we're standing in a large open space containing the living room and dining area. The marbled floor is a brownish-orange ceramic tile. The décor is very eclectic. The fabrics and materials used are all different and not the least bit cohesive, but it seems to work. The rooms have a comfortable, youthful quality.

"Our parents bought it for Carlos and me to use throughout college," she says matter-of-factly as we walk through the open space.

"Wow, that's nice."

"Yeah, well, it works out for them. We wanted to be close to the university, and later, when we are finished, they can rent it out."

"Why did you sign up to take in a foreign exchange student?" I ask, curious.

Nadia exudes happiness. Bubbly and sincere, she responds, "I thought it would be fun. Growing up with a twin brother, I always wanted a sister. I have been surrounded by boys my whole life. It was always just Carlos, his friends, and me. Plus, we have an extra room, so I thought, why not? You know?"

"Yeah, cool. I grew up with only a brother as well, so I understand."

"Carlos is out playing basketball with the guys. You will meet him later tonight. He is super easy to get along with if you blow off everything he says and don't take anything too seriously."

I let out a chuckle. "Okay, I will remember that."

I follow Nadia as she guides me through the house on a quick tour. Past the open living room area on the main floor are three doors. The door on the left leads to the kitchen, the one on the right enters a study, and the middle goes into my bedroom. To the right of the entry door is an open staircase that winds up to the second floor. That floor houses a bathroom and two larger bedrooms, one belonging to Nadia and the other to her brother.

Nadia helps me drag my luggage to my room situated at the far end of the living area between the kitchen and the study. My room is moderately sized and contains two twin beds with a nightstand between them. Along the back wall of the room are two large closets. At the end of the room is another door that opens to my own bathroom with a shower.

"So, Olivia, you can get unpacked, freshen up, and then we're going out!" Nadia beams with excitement.

I peer at her with a confused expression. "We're going out?"

"We're going clubbing! It's your first night here, and it's a Saturday! All of my friends are dying to meet my new American sister!"

"Oh, okay...yeah, that sounds great!" I say, thinking how tired I am. *Oh well, it's nothing that a shower, a killer outfit, and some alcohol won't cure.* "Do you mind if I invite Nolan?"

"Of course not! Give him our address, and tell him we'll leave for the club around ten." She reaches in and gives me a hug. "I'm so glad you're here. I think you will love it. I'm going to start getting ready. Let me know if you need anything, okay?" She walks out.

I grab my cell phone. I decide to first text Cara and my family to let them know that I arrived safely and that my new roommate is super nice. Then, I text Nolan.

*Me: Hey! You up to clubbing tonight? Nadia insists! ;-) xo*

*Nolan: You kidding? Abso-fucking-lutely! We're in Spain!*

I laugh out loud at his reply because Nolan is always up for a night out.

*Me: Sweet! Be here at ten!*

I text him the address.

*Nolan: I miss you already! See you soon! xoxo*

Heading to the shower, I can't help but notice the nervous butterflies flitting around in my belly. I can't pinpoint the source of my apprehension. It could be excitement. It has been a long day, and my exhaustion could be clouding my brain and blurring my emotions into confusion.

Nolan and I have been talking about this trip for a year. I am finally here, and my trip of a lifetime has started. *Am I nervous that it isn't going to be everything I dreamed of? Will it be more?*

Willing myself to keep my unease at bay, I step into the hot stream of the shower, letting the spray take away my reservations and the grimy sensation that comes with a long day of traveling. I remind myself that I am not here alone, and all of the unknowns, the things I can't plan or predict, will be faced with Nolan at my side. I hold on to that thought, and the butterflies calm.

# chapter 3

I check myself out in the full-length mirror hanging on the bathroom door, admiring the new dress that Cara insisted I buy for the trip. It is pretty damn sexy, if I say so myself. It's short, fitted, and strapless with an iridescent shimmer of purple and black. Like usual, I keep my makeup simple, applying only a light shimmery eye shadow and mascara to make my deep blue eyes pop and some light pink lip gloss. I curl my hair, creating long spirals that fall just above my bra line. As I'm putting on my strappy black heels, I hear Nolan's voice, followed by Nadia's laughter, in the living room.

Nolan turns his head when I enter the room, and he stops chatting with Nadia. He walks my way and wraps his arms around my back, fully surrounding me in a big hug. I'm lifted off the ground as he kisses my cheek.

"You are stunning." He nuzzles his face below my ear.

"Thanks. You clean up nicely yourself," I say as he sets me down.

He is striking in his fitted jeans and white button-up shirt.

As we go out the door, Nadia leans in and whispers in my ear, "Your boyfriend is delectable!"

I giggle, knowing exactly what she means. "He's not my boyfriend. He is my best friend."

"Oh my God, really? Interesting," she says with a mischievous smile.

I laugh. "Don't get too excited. He has a long-term girlfriend back in the States."

She sighs as she closes the door. "Figures."

We arrive at a club named El Q, and the three of us head in.

Nadia grabs my hand and pulls me through the crowd. "Come this way. My friends got us a table!" she yells to Nolan and me as we weave our way through the packed club.

This place is unlike anywhere I've ever been to. It's huge, and the giant dance floor takes up the entire first level with outlying tables and leather chairs lining the walls. Behind the dance floor at the end of the club is a stage with dancing bodies showcased by floor-to-ceiling windows overlooking the city of Seville. The backdrop of city lights is stunning.

Wrapped around the dance floor are three levels with balconies visible to the floor below. Each level is filled with round tables surrounded by black leather booths. All the tables are full with people laughing, dancing, and drinking. Although smaller than the grand floor on the main level, additional dance areas are on each level as well.

I am giddy as I take it all in. *The college clubs have nothing on this place. I definitely have to bring Cara here when she comes to visit.* Nadia finds her friends at a table located on the main floor toward the end by the wall of windows. I wonder how they secured this great spot. Nadia introduces Nolan and me to everyone. About ten people, a mix of guys and girls, are sitting around the large table. They are all very welcoming, but it's so loud that I don't catch most of their names. Nolan orders a bottle of Grey Goose vodka with some chasers for the table.

My first night in Spain does not disappoint. The music is great, and I have so much fun dancing with Nadia and her friends. Nolan, of course, makes friends, and he is joking with everyone at the table. He's totally in his element. My head starts to feel fuzzy, and I can't remember how many drinks I've had. Nolan always makes sure to keep my glass full, and while it's a kind gesture, it's occasionally a hazard.

He grabs my hand and pulls me out a couple of feet past our table into the sea of dancing bodies on the main dance floor. Wrapped around each other, we sway to the music. Nolan lifts me up and holds me against him with his hands under my behind. I secure my legs around his middle with my arms around his neck as I rest my head on his shoulder. We dance in this embrace for several songs. I feel relaxed and completely happy as I snuggle into Nolan's neck.

I pick up my head and look into Nolan's eyes, and before I know what's happening, Nolan's mouth is on mine. On instinct, my mouth opens to allow his tongue to entangle with mine. I suck on his tongue, tasting alcohol and mint. I hear him groan as he deepens the kiss, removing one of his hands from my behind and placing it on the back of my head. He buries his fingers in my hair and pushes my head firmly toward his. We kiss with a sense of need and urgency. My heart is racing when he pulls away abruptly.

"Jesus, Liv, I'm sorry," he says through labored breaths. He removes his hand from my hair and runs it through his own with obvious frustration.

I loosen my legs from around him and drop them to the floor. Extending my grasp behind his neck, I lean back in and kiss him on the cheek. "No worries, babycakes." I lay my head back down against his chest and close my eyes, allowing my breathing to calm.

It's not the first time that Nolan and I have kissed. It has happened a handful of times over the past three years, usually after we've been drinking. We always apologize, and then we are back to our normal routine.

Nolan's labored breaths settle as we continue to dance. Resting against him, I take in the music while his strong arms hold me tight, pulling me against his body. When I glance in the direction of our table, my gaze locks with a pair of mesmerizing dark eyes. For a moment, I'm frozen in this intense stare with an unbelievably gorgeous man. I blink and force myself to peer behind me, wondering if he's observing someone else. I don't see anyone taking notice. I turn my face back to him, and once more, I am met with his concentrated stare. *Yes, his eyes are definitely locked on me.*

I am still not able to pull my gaze away from him, and I feel this luring draw to him. I don't recognize him from earlier even though he is standing by our table. He's tall and tan with a face to write home about. He has a strong jawline that exudes rugged manliness, but at the same time, he has a soft, youthful quality. I have an intense urge to feel his skin under my fingertips. His hair is dark brown with faint golden highlights illuminated from the club lights dancing over his face. His regard is powerful, penetrating every thought and sensation running through me. Everything about him—from the way his hair frames his chiseled jaw and intense eyes to the way he's standing with his hands in his pockets while leaning on the wooden beam, watching me as if he can read my every thought—is disarming.

I experience a sense of complete exposure while I'm utterly aroused at the same time. My heart begins to race, accompanied by an uncomfortable throbbing sensation below my waist. I'm drawn to him by such a fierce force that it feels real and tangible. It's as if an invisible rope is wrapped around my middle, and he is reeling it in.

Nolan's voice breaks my trance. "Hey, love, you okay?"

I release the breath I am holding, and I blink, breaking my connection to this stranger. I face Nolan and then back to the man again. He's still staring at me.

"Um…yeah. I need to use the restroom," I stammer as I loosen my arms from Nolan's neck, letting them fall to my sides.

I hear Nolan saying something to me, but I don't catch what it is, and I don't stop to ask as I walk through the crowd to the other side of the club.

*What the fuck was that? Who is that guy? What was that?* I continue to weave through the throng of sweaty bodies. I'm completely perplexed as I get to the restroom. Completely hot and bothered, I wet a towel and dab my face and chest. *Pull yourself together, Olivia. Jesus.* I take a few moments to steady the rapid pounding in my chest. When I've regained my composure from my sudden loss of sanity, I exit the restroom.

Nolan is leaning against the wall, facing the restroom, when I exit. "You okay, babe?" He gives me a concerned grin.

"Yeah, I'm fine. I think I'm just tired," I reply as he grabs my hand and leads me toward the front of the club.

"Well, it is four in the morning. It's been a long day. Nadia went to hail a couple of cabs out front."

"Okay." Remembering my purse, I try to see across the club to our table. "Did you grab my purse?"

"No, I'm sorry. I didn't."

"No problem. Go ahead. I'm going to go grab it, and I will be right out." I can see the questioning expression on Nolan's face. "I'm fine, really. See you in a second."

I quickly walk toward our table, now void of patrons, and I get a glimpse of my black sequined purse that fell onto the floor under the table. Retrieving it, I begin to depart, and I see him. My chest expands with a sensation I haven't felt often—deep desire and attraction. My senses return, and I take in the surroundings past my tunnel vision, focusing on him. I stand immobile, unable to pull my eyes away. As quickly as my body flooded with desire, it leaves, only to be replaced by a different emotion, one that is not nearly as welcome.

# chapter

4

*What is this reaction? Sadness? Can I really say that I am experiencing sadness? The idea is ridiculous. Jealousy? Maybe. Disappointment? How can I be disappointed about something that never was?* My chest is full of an uncomfortable pressure as I stand, frozen, gawking at the hot guy who I had a brief visual connection with moments ago.

His arms are around another girl, and he is whispering something in her ear. She throws her head back in laughter, and I can't stop the stab of jealousy running through my veins. *What is my problem?* This whole scenario is irrational. In my head, I know it is. It doesn't make any sense, yet I can't pull my eyes away. I watch as he runs his hands slowly down her sides and around to her back, pulling her in close as they dance. I stay there, wondering who he is. *Who is this eye candy of a man that has me so befuddled? I don't do this. I don't stand around, ogling guys who happen to be attractive. What right do I have to feel jealous over someone I have never spoken to?*

I feel a hand wrap around my arm, and it breaks my daze.

"Hey, are you okay?"

I can hear the concern in Nolan's voice.

"Yeah, I'm fine. Let's go."

He takes my hand, and we head for the exit. I haven't even been in Spain for twenty-four hours, and I am going mental. I blame it on the exhaustion or the alcohol or both.

The moment I open my eyes, my thoughts go to last night. I lie in bed, still confused about the weird stare-down with the god of sexiness—no, the god of hotness. *Hmm…no, I can't think of a word to adequately describe his level of deliciousness, but, man, I've never had a reaction like that to anyone.* My mind travels to the subsequent gawking incident, and I still can't fathom why that affected me as it did. I experience a twinge of sadness, knowing I'll probably never see him again.

The flashing of my phone catches my attention. Reaching for it, I find a text from Nolan.

*Nolan: Hey! You feeling okay? ;-)*

*Me: Yeah. I'm not that bad. Must have been tired. Had fun though!*

*Nolan: Me, too! That place was the shit! We'll have to go again!*

*Me: Totally! We'll have to take Cara and Abby there when they visit!*

*Nolan: For sure! What are your plans today? It's our last free day. ;-)*

*Me: Not sure. Let me get my ass out of bed. Will text you later. xo*

*Nolan: Sounds good. Talk to you later. xoxo*

I plug my phone into the charger and head to the bathroom, smiling. I'm glad that all is normal with Nolan and me. I knew it would be, but I'm relieved anyway.

After a shower, I throw on some shorts and a fitted T-shirt and leave my room. A guy is sitting on the couch, eating a bowl of cereal, as he watches soccer. He has a slim build with caramel brown eyes and short brown hair with copper highlights.

He briefly breaks his attention from the game. "Hey," he says before returning his interest back to the TV.

"Hi," I say and go into the kitchen. I realize he must be Nadia's twin, Carlos. I met him last night at the club, but I didn't make the connection during our introduction.

I grab a bowl of cereal and go out to the couch to join him. We eat and watch soccer in silence for a while.

He breaks the quietness. "So, did you have fun last night?" He smirks.

I ignore the innuendo, wondering what the scene between Nolan and me must have looked like. "Yes, that place was so unlike anything back home."

"What are the clubs like in the States?" he asks through a mouthful of cereal.

"The places I've been to are smaller, not as fancy, a little simpler." *And ghetto*, I think, but I'm not sure how to translate that.

"Yeah, our clubs are definitely not simple. Did you like it?"

"Oh my God, it was awesome. I can't wait to go back."

Carlos laughs. "Well, you'll get your chance to go there and to a lot more like it. Unfortunately, we go to those places a lot. Nadia insists."

"You don't like clubbing?"

"No, not really. I'm not a dancer. I enjoy drinking and all, but I'd rather do that here with the guys or at a smaller bar."

"Why don't you go to smaller bars then?"

"We go to those, too, but Nadia kind of runs the show, and she loves clubbing. Also, my friends, Andres and Hugo, like hanging with the chicks at the clubs, and afterward, if you know what I mean." He winks obnoxiously at me.

"Uh, yeah…remind me who those two are when I meet them, so I know to stay away," I say.

He laughs. "Will do. You met Andres and Hugo. They were there, but I'm sure you met a lot of new faces. You probably don't remember. You'd be wise to stay away from them. I'm surprised they didn't hit on you last night. It was probably because you were attached to Nolan. Having a *friendship* like that will come in handy here if you want to ward off too much attention from other guys."

"Why did you say *friendship* like that? Nolan and I are really just friends. He has a girlfriend."

Carlos laughs. "Does his girlfriend know about your *friendship?*" His eyebrow rises in question.

I am slightly offended. "Nolan's girlfriend knows about me. You'll see. She'll be here in a few weeks." I scrunch my lips and lower my eyebrows, making my best I-am-serious face.

He raises his hands in surrender. "Hey, whatever. I don't care what you do." He smirks and continues watching soccer.

As I stare at him, I can see the obvious similarities between him and Nadia. He's the complete male version of her. My attention turns to Nadia coming down the stairs from her room. I talk to her about the day and find out that we're having a lazy Sunday. She suggests that Nolan and I go walking around town. I'm excited to explore the city that will be my home for the next three months.

It's hot and sunny. I decide to change into a light blue sundress and comfortable strappy sandals, and my hair is in a messy bun to keep it off my back. I'm waiting at the fountain in the Plaza de España. Nadia suggested I meet Nolan there since it's walking distance from the house, seeing that it is next to our summer university.

I see Nolan approaching in his loose cargo khaki shorts and fitted white T-shirt. I can see the outline of his muscles through his shirt. As always, he is adorable.

He flashes me his stunning smile. "Hey, beautiful. You ready to see some of the city?"

We walk hand in hand through the Plaza de España complex, which is truly breathtaking. Stunning brownstone buildings sit around the edge of a vast semicircle. We amble across a gorgeous Venetian-style bridge with stunning ceramic balustrades. The bridge over the canal follows the curve of the buildings, creating a pathway between the buildings and the plaza. Numerous intricately designed bridges allow the buildings to be accessible over the moat. Many tiled alcoves dot the plaza walls, each nook representing a different Spanish province. The striking ceramic tile tells the history of that area of Spain. I don't know if I've ever seen a more beautiful man-made place.

After walking around the plaza for over an hour, exploring every alcove and taking in as much beauty and history as we could, we decide to meander through the cobblestone streets and scope out a place to eat. We stop at a little restaurant for coffee and a late lunch. We're seated at an outside table situated on the stone patio. Each table has its own white umbrella blocking the sun.

Lunch is delicious. Nolan and I share a common Spanish meal—a large plate of paella that is made of rice, seafood, and vegetables. I sip my cappuccino as he sips his espresso, and we fall into a comfortable conversation. He reminds me that Abby is coming to visit in two weeks. I'm hoping that Abby and I hit it off on a more positive note.

After our meal, Nolan grabs a taxi to go home, and I walk the short distance back to my place. I am anxious to get back to the house and get everything in order for class tomorrow.

The house is empty when I get in. *I should call home.* Spain is six hours ahead of Michigan, so my parents will probably be getting back from church around this time.

My mom picks up after the third ring. "Livi, love! How is it? Tell me everything!"

I sure lucked out in the mom department. She and I have always had a close relationship. She has a tendency to worry a bit too much. That led to a few disagreements when I was in high school. But she only worries because she cares. I've always told her most of the details about my life. She is understanding and empathetic, and she consistently gives great advice. She's supported me through all my dramatic girl issues during my tween and teen years.

I tell her about everything I've encountered since arriving yesterday. She listens with interest, and before hanging up, I promise to call again soon.

Next, I call Cara and tell her about the awesome club Nolan and I went to last night and the mystery man who took my breath away.

The interest in her voice is almost tangible. "Tell me more! I told you there would be juicy details!"

I chuckle. "That's all there is to tell unfortunately."

"So, let me get this straight. The hottest guy you have ever seen engages you in a stare-down contest, and that's it?"

"Yeah, that's it."

"Come on, Livi! Why didn't you follow through? You didn't go talk to him, wave, or acknowledge him somehow?"

"I told you, when I went back, he was dancing with someone. What was I supposed to do?"

"Hmm…" she says out loud. "There is more to this story that you are not telling me."

I revisit last night, and the entire evening plays through my mind like a movie on fast-forward. I pause and try to imagine what Nolan and I looked like while dancing and kissing. *Ugh, the kiss.* Of course Mr. Hotness did nothing more than stare. *What choice had I given him?* To a stranger's eyes, I'm sure Nolan and I looked like we were together. *Maybe he didn't see the kiss?* I don't know when he first saw me. Regardless, straddling Nolan as we were dancing probably seemed intimate to any outsider.

I sigh. "Nope, that's all, Cara. It just wasn't meant to be."

"Okay," she says with deliberate slowness, obviously not content with my explanation. "Well, maybe you will see him again, and if you do, you need to at least introduce yourself."

"I will," I say, knowing the chances of seeing him again in a city this size are quite low.

She hasn't purchased her plane ticket yet, and I let her know when Abby is coming because I want Cara to visit at the same time.

"You know Abby doesn't like me, and I could use my partner in crime while she is here."

Cara reassures me, "It has nothing to do with you. She is just a bitch."

"Yeah, but it would make me feel better if you were here."

"Okay, I will talk to Jimmy tomorrow and see if he can schedule someone to cover my shifts while I am gone."

Jimmy is Cara's boss at the Italian restaurant where she is a server. I know this won't be a problem. Like most men, Jimmy would do anything for Cara.

Before I let her go, I promise to keep her posted on all future juiciness.

Going through my textbooks in preparation for tomorrow sounds like a good idea. I grab my Spanish textbook from the end table and open it to the first chapter. In bed, I lie on my stomach, propped up on my elbows. While attempting to study the first lesson, the words blur together as my mind races, taking in everything from the past two days. The gamut of emotions that I'm processing is exhausting. What a crazy whirlwind. Leaving the known—Cara, my job, my apartment, my family, and my city— to come to a place where I won't even be speaking my own language deserves some pause.

Coming down from the anxiety of the plane ride to take in the beauty and newness of this awe-inspiring place is a process. I wonder if everyone who travels experiences this overwhelming sensation. It wouldn't surprise me if the people native to Spain take the beauty of their home for granted. *Maybe I take the scenery in Michigan for granted? I'm sure I do.* I question what it would be like to travel to other places. *Would each new place bring on powerful sentiments as well?* Spain has me enchanted, and I haven't even been here for forty-eight hours. One lonely, happy tear falls, landing on the bottom of the open page. Chuckling, I wipe it off. I am such a sap, but I am so grateful to be here. The whole experience has already blown any expectation I had out of the water, and I still have three whole months here.

During my freshman year, my communications professor had us complete a grateful diary. For the course of the semester, we were required to write down three things that we were grateful for every day. As part of our final, we were instructed to write a paper on the diary. Obviously, the ultimate goal of the project was to point out what a little bit of gratitude could bring to our lives.

That project impacted me deeply, and I vowed to keep up my grateful diary for the rest of my life, so the greatness would never be outshadowed by the negative. My vow lasted almost a week after the semester ended. Nonetheless, from time to time, I still think about that professor and how he helped me to see the power of being thankful.

So, today, I think of three things that I am grateful for at this very moment. First, I am grateful for student loans because they provided the funds to take this trip. Second, I am thankful that I live in a world where such diversity and beauty exist. Most importantly, I am grateful for Nolan for giving me the strength to face all my silly anxieties and for empowering me to try something new.

I wake up in a fog, lying facedown, with my face smashed against the pages of my Spanish book. I grab my cell and see that it's seven in the evening. I then hear music coming from the other side of my door. Peering in the mirror, I wipe off the smudged mascara and rub my cheek to smooth out the creases left by the crumpled pages of the book.

Sluggishly, I make my way to the living room and abruptly stop mid-step. My mouth falls open when I see *him*. He's sitting on the couch, strumming a guitar and singing. I jerk my arm out and push it against the wall in case I fall over from the shock of seeing him here in my house. *He's singing? Playing a guitar? Seriously?* I steady myself and watch him like a stalker. *What is it about a sexy man playing a guitar?*

He's wearing a tight black shirt that clings to his perfect body. I watch his fingers dance over the strings while the guitar rests on his thigh. Even his hands are turning me on, and I have to stop myself from imagining what they would feel like against my body.

When he tilts his head up, meeting my stare with his dark blue, almost gray eyes, it dawns on me that my mouth is still wide open. I think I see a faint smile cross his lips as he continues to sing. I pull it together and close my mouth, steadying myself so that I don't need the wall to hold me up. He doesn't seem surprised to see me. My presence doesn't appear to affect him as he continues to play.

I am glued to this spot as I assess the situation. Gorgeous Guy is sitting on the couch with three other guys. One is my host brother, and the other two—well, I know I met them last night, but I can't remember their names. One of them is also strumming a guitar, and all four are singing. It's a very sexy-sounding song, all in Spanish, and I've never heard it before. When the god with the dark blue eyes sings, his voice cuts through me. He has a direct line to the area between my legs. Images of throwing his guitar to the floor and straddling his hot body while I lick every inch of his toned, tan body race through my head.

*Wait, what the fuck is happening to me? Rational people do not react this way to someone they've never met, do they?* I know I've never felt this way about a man, especially from simply being in his presence.

I jump when Nadia speaks, "They're really good, right?"

Turning, I see she's standing next to me, and I nod.

"They get together and play all the time. They do a few gigs at bars around town, but basically, they play for fun."

"Who is the guy in the black shirt?" I ask, hoping she doesn't hear the breathiness in my voice as I glance at Mr. Blue Eyes.

"That's Andres, and the one to his left playing guitar is Hugo."

*Of course that's Andres.* Carlos's warning rings in my ears.

Hugo has longer, above the shoulder, tousled, dark blond hair and striking brown eyes. His face is covered with short stubble, and it gives him a hot bad-boy look.

"And the shorter one on the chair next to Carlos is Julio. Carlos and I have gone to school with all those guys since we were five."

"Oh," I say with unexaggerated interest.

The guys finish the song and begin joking among themselves. Nadia walks toward them, and somehow, I make my legs follow.

Andres speaks directly to Nadia, "Hey, we're heading over to La Jolla. Do you and your friend want to join us?" He doesn't even glance my way.

"Sure." Nadia beams. "You're up for a trip to a bar, right, Livi?"

"Um…yeah," I manage to squeak out.

Andres directs his attention back to the guys without acknowledging me.

I return to my room and put on my favorite skinny jeans, black boots, and a black tank top. I let my hair out of the messy bun and brush it out. It's wavy, kinky, and disheveled, but it appears almost as if I planned it. I snap a hair tie around my wrist in case I need to pull it up into a ponytail later. I reapply mascara and pink lip gloss, and then I make my way to the living room.

The bar is located right around the corner from our street, so it's a short walk there. Once inside, we grab a spot in the far corner and order a bucket of beer that is quickly delivered to the table. La Jolla is a simple bar with red leather bench seats and wooden tables. Music is playing, but no one is dancing.

Hugo hands me a beer, and we start chatting. He's a charmer and a very funny guy. I know he must be popular with the girls, especially with his creamy chocolate eyes begging to be noticed. He has a European bad-boy-rocker appeal going on, if that is such a thing. He makes sure I always have a beer in hand, and I have a feeling he has ulterior motives. Based on what Carlos said, I'm sure I'm correct in that assumption, but I'm grateful because the beer is helping me to relax.

I get the courage to peer across the table at Andres, and I'm met with his intense midnight-blue stare. I immediately turn away, blushing. *What the fuck?* I can't take that stare of his burning into me for longer than a second. As we all sit and chat, I don't attempt any more glances, but I can feel his gaze penetrating the skin of my face as the night wears on.

Everyone seems interested in me, asking questions about every facet of my life. It's nice that this group of people seems to genuinely want to get to know me—well, except for Andres. It doesn't slip by my attention that he hasn't asked a single question, and through my peripheral vision, I see him absently staring at his bottle or around the room when I speak. I'm left feeling confused and irritated. So, he's either staring daggers at me or avoiding me like the plague. *I don't get it.*

Hugo's voice breaks through my brooding thoughts. "So, beautiful American girl, tell us more about you. What is your family like?"

"They're wonderful. My parents are very supportive. My brother, Max, is three years older than me, and we're very close. We always have been. You'd like him."

"What is your brother like? Is he outgoing or quiet? You know, what is his personality like?" Nadia asks.

I laugh. "He's definitely not quiet. He is always the life of the party, like Nolan, except my brother is a little cockier than Nolan. He's a total charmer, especially with the girls."

"Is he cute? Does he resemble you?" Nadia asks with interest.

I pull my iPhone from my purse and pull up the most recent photo of him. I grin as I study the photo of Max and me at my apartment. After getting home from a club, Max's arms are wrapped around me, and he has a wide grin. I am laughing. I can't remember what about. It was probably at something crass that came out of his mouth. He is not one for subtlety.

Grinning, I hand my phone to Nadia. "I don't know. See for yourself. Growing up, all my friends always had a huge crush on him."

Nadia takes my phone and peers at the screen. "Yeah, he is pretty hot," she says with a mischievous grin. "He looks nothing like you though."

My pale skin and light features are a complete contrast with Max's darker complexion. Our blue eyes are similar, but they're a mere coincidence. My parents adopted Max when he was four, and I was only one, so he has been a part of all my childhood memories.

Hugo glances at the phone screen and gives an indifferent shrug.

I take a sip of my beer and then direct my comment to him. "I'd say you two are very similar in personality actually." I give him a teasing glance.

Hugo laughs. "I hope that's a good thing."

"Depends." I take another drink of my beer.

Carlos cuts in, "Hell no, it isn't a good thing, Hugo. She's saying you remind her of her girl-crazy brother."

"With your motives, I'd say that's definitely a bad thing, man. She's on to your game," Julio says.

"Hey, who said I have motives?" Hugo feigns innocence.

"Oh, Hugo, let it go. Olivia doesn't want anything to do with your slutty ways," Nadia interjects with a glare.

He holds his stare on her for a moment, but he doesn't respond to her comment.

"Well, I'm glad you're here for the summer. You seem cool," Hugo says to me.

"Thanks, Hugo. You seem cool, too." I grin and clink my beer bottle against his. "Cheers to a fun summer."

The conversation carries on around the table. Andres's whole vibe is disarming to me. One minute, he's staring at me with the intensity of a nuclear bomb, and the next, he's doing everything in his power to ignore me.

I thought I felt something at the club. *Could it have been all me? Am I reading into our stare-down that first night?* I must be.

I'm sure he has the choice of any girl in Seville. It has to be all in my mind. It's a downright shame that my intense attraction doesn't seem to be reciprocated. *Total bummer.*

# chapter 5

The next morning, I walk with Nadia to school. The university was founded in 1551, and it has a very historic feel. The school is located next to the Plaza de España where Nolan and I were yesterday.

In front of the languages building stretches a large, rectangular grassy yard with old, tall trees and trimmed bushes. Students are spread sporadically around the garden, standing and chatting in groups, studying in the grass, or reading near the trees. The bright green lawn area generates a feeling of community. I could see how studying under a tall oak would be peaceful.

Walking along the sidewalk snaking around the school, I notice stone statues alongside the building and gardens. It feels like I'm about to enter an art museum or ancient palace as I pass lampposts that guide me toward the language department. Immediately, I see Nolan inside the door, waiting for me next to the stone staircase. His face lights up, and he heads my way. When he reaches me, he grabs my hand and pulls me in for a kiss on the cheek.

"How was your night?" he asks.

"It was fine. I went out with Nadia and her friends to a bar down the street from their house. It was fun," I say. "How was yours?"

"It was good. I hung out with my roommate and some of his friends at the apartment. It would have been more fun if you were there," he answers with a sheepish smile.

"Ditto," I agree.

Nolan has a way of calming me. I know I would not have felt so awkward around Andres if Nolan had been with me.

Studying a language is not always fun. Nolan and I tested into the advanced Spanish class. Our instructor, Professor Gomez, is a short, round man with black hair and a beard. His dark brown eyes light up when he smiles, which is often. He's quite funny. He's one of those people you can't help but like. I know he'll make the summer classes more enjoyable.

We have two classes with Professor Gomez, separated by a break, and then Nolan and I head back to my house to study. Lying on my bed, we are sprawled side by side on our stomachs busy with translations homework. After the completion of our schoolwork, we enjoy a lovely afternoon siesta.

I awake to the sound of music trickling in under my bedroom door. My heart races, knowing who's playing the guitar on the other side of the door. My back is against Nolan's front. I can hear his soft breathing as I rotate to face him. "Wake up, sleepyhead."

Nolan opens his eyes and smiles. "What time is it?"

I grab my phone from the nightstand. "Six. Do you want to eat something before you go?"

Nadia's family has a lady, Marie, who cooks and cleans for them. She usually comes to cook a large midday meal for Carlos and Nadia, which Nolan and I apparently missed because of our nap.

"I can warm up Marie's lunch. I've heard her cooking is out of this world."

"Sounds great. Just give me a second to wake up," he says with a yawn.

I roll out of bed and grab my brush from the bathroom. Giving Nolan a moment, I tame my bed head with a few swipes of the brush and wipe the residual mascara from under my eyes. I exit the bathroom. "All right, lazybones. Let's go."

Nolan and I head into the kitchen, ignoring the four guys playing music in the living room. I warm up two plates and sit with Nolan at the breakfast bar. The music streams in through the thin swinging door separating the kitchen from the main room.

"They sound pretty good," Nolan says between mouthfuls.

"Yeah, they are. I heard them play yesterday. They're all friends of Carlos and Nadia. I guess they've gone to school together forever."

"Right. We met them at the club that first night. Cool guys," he says.

I'm momentarily surprised that Nolan seems to know more about these people than I do. He's such a people person. Of course he got to know them.

After placing our dishes in the dishwasher, I follow Nolan into the main living area. He takes a seat in the armchair, and the only empty spot left is on the couch next to Andres. I sigh as I sit down, feeling totally uncomfortable. Andres starts playing a new song. I recognize the guitar intro, but I can't immediately name the song. The music reminds me of something I remember my dad playing when I was young.

Andres starts singing. He sings of dreams, loss, and dust in the wind. I'm completely still. The hairs rise on my arms as goose bumps appear. Andres's voice is so hauntingly beautiful. It emanates sadness. He closes his eyes, and I not only hear his voice, but I feel it. The passion of this song, his voice, the words resonate down to my core. I am mesmerized as I watch him sing as if he's the only one in the room. An air of awkwardness passes over me. This experience brings a sense of intrusion along with it, like I'm invading a private moment. I know he is singing for everyone, but the way he sings this song leaves me feeling as if I were watching him without his knowledge. The way his emotions are pouring out through the lyrics, I sense that this song is personal for him, and I can't help but wonder who it is in regard to.

As Andres strums the last note, I realize that I have tears running down my cheeks. I quickly move to wipe them away. Andres opens his eyes and peers right into mine. My breath hitches, and I stare at him like a deer caught in the headlights, unable to blink or avert my gaze. I think I see a deep emotion in him, sadness or hurt maybe. I can't tell. The moment is fleeting. He blinks, and the expression is gone.

Nolan speaks first, "That was awesome, man. You're really good. How long have you been playing?"

Andres faces Nolan and clears his throat. "Like, ten years or so, I guess."

Hugo speaks to Nolan, "Our band, La Banda, plays at some local bars. You should come out some night. Plus, many totally hot chicks show up at these gigs. It's awesome if you're looking for that," he says, giving Nolan a knowing smirk.

Nolan laughs. "I think I'm set with the girls, but I'd love to hear you guys play sometime."

"Whatever, man, but I wouldn't be surprised if you changed your mind. Seriously, totally hot chicks, dude. You'll see," Hugo states.

Nolan laughs again. "La Banda, huh? I hope you weren't going for originality." The name literally translates to The Band.

The guys all chuckle.

Andres answers, "Nope, that we weren't."

Carlos adds, "It's easy to remember. You have to give us that."

My body is positioned toward Andres as I follow the conversation. My knee brushes against Andres's thigh, and I startle. Pounding emanates from my chest at the momentary contact between us. I see Andres's body stiffen slightly, but he makes no other indication that he noticed.

The guys are heading out to a bar for the night, and they extend an invitation to Nolan and me. I decline, giving some excuse about a headache and needing sleep. I desperately want to avoid the awkward silence going on between Andres and me. Without much effort, Nadia is able to convince Nolan to go out with them.

Nolan leans in and kisses my cheek. "You sure you're okay? I can stay here with you if you want me to."

*He's so good to me.* I give him a hug.

"No. Go and have fun. I'll see you tomorrow." I wave to everyone else and head to my room.

Falling to my bed, I exhale a deep breath. Having the house to myself is exactly what I need to process the thoughts bouncing around my head like an out-of-control pinball game. I need calmness to make sense of everything because all the confusion is causing me anxiety. I am unsettled when I need to be grounded to function.

*Why do I have this irrational desire that keeps me longing for Andres?*

Minutes pass by, and the chaos in my head isn't close to coming to any order. Maybe I don't need solitude. I should talk to someone. Normally, I would talk to Nolan, but for some reason, I can't or won't, and I don't know why. It just doesn't feel right this time. Cara is sound asleep back in Michigan, so that is a no-go.

*Okay, focus. What is bothering me? Andres in general? No—at least, I don't think so. Yeah, so he is not all that friendly with me. Am I upset because he doesn't talk to me? I don't know.* That makes me sound immature. He is not the first person in history not to like me. I can live with the fact that I'm not everyone's friend. That would be unrealistic anyway. *Can I live with not being Andres's friend? Yeah, sure.*

*I mean, no.*

*Yes.*

I guess he's not unfriendly to me. He's simply indifferent. The indifference is killing me. *How can he be so controlled around me when I feel anything but?* The stark differences in our reactions to one another is making me feel disconnected—and to be honest, a little crazy.

*Deep breaths.*

*What am I grateful for today? I don't know.*

My every thought goes to Andres from the way he looks to his voice to his smile and the way tingles run up my body when he laughs. *How can I be thankful for something I don't have? Is that what is bothering me? Yes, of course. I need Andres. I do.*

*No, I don't.* I don't need someone who doesn't want me. But I desperately want him to want me. I don't think I've ever wanted anything more.

*Why?* I barely know him and what I do know of him isn't the most appealing. He is kind of an ass—at least to me.

*A super-hot piece of ass.*

The only thought that comes with any clarity is that I need to get over this funk. I am here in this awesome country for three more months. I need to soak in as much of it as I can. Pining over Andres isn't going to help anything. *Why is it that the first time I feel such an intense attraction to someone, he has to be so unattainable and distant?* I have to figure out a way to be around him and not be so affected by him. He is obviously a constant in Nadia's life, so avoiding him isn't an option, but neither is feeling like this—so desperate.

I have to cast aside all the powerful sensations that come with Andres and become indifferent. I am no stranger to indifferent. I can do it.

I shoot Cara a text. I know she will be at work, but I need to send it nonetheless.

> *Me: Hung out with hottie again. Still no interest on his part.*
> *Whatevs. I'm over it. Moving on. #whoneedshim Miss you. xoxo*

I don't know if I feel better or worse as I read over my text to Cara. Seeing it in writing fills me with gloom because it feels more real, the idea that I must move on and get over this intrigue I have toward Andres. I let out a faint chuckle. This whole thing is absurd. Only I would need to recover from a relationship that never existed.

Cara and Nolan have always told me that I sabotage all of my potential relationships by being too distant or by creating issues to solve before the concern is even a reality. Part of me knows that problems in my previous relationships arise because I want to find a reason to end it before the guy finds one. I'm afraid to want someone and have them discover that I'm not who they thought I was, that I'm not enough for them. I've never experienced true heartache, yet I continue to do everything in my power to make sure that I don't.

I know it doesn't make sense, but for Andres I would try, regardless of how broken I was left in the end. I would try.

chapter
6

The next day mirrors the previous one with the exception that Nolan leaves right after our midday siesta. I hang out with Nadia until nightfall, and she won't take no for an answer when she insists I go out with her and the guys.

I see that my life here is going to be a hectic barhopping extravaganza. I can't say that my mom would be too pleased with how much I'm going out. *As long as I'm getting my homework done and learning something, it's all good, right?* The way I see it, I'm immersing myself in the culture. After all, that's why I'm here.

I really lucked out in getting Nadia as my roommate. Her daily routine of school, homework, and going out is right up my alley. Her love for getting dressed up and having a good time reminds me of Cara. I love it.

We head down the street to La Jolla again. I sit in between Hugo and Nadia and take part in friendly conversation, but the unease at the table—at least for me—is obvious. I have to wonder if anyone else notices that Andres and I never speak.

I'm annoyed. *Seriously, what is his problem with me? Would it hurt to make polite conversation? Remember, indifferent. You are indifferent. Let it go.*

I see a spark of recognition on the faces of Andres and Carlos as they sit across from me and peer over my shoulder. I turn my head to see a group of three, two guys and a girl, making their way toward our table. Nadia notices at this point as well, and she lets out a quiet sound of annoyance.

I tilt my body, leaning into her. "What?" I whisper.

"Nothing. Just not a fan," she whispers.

"Of who?"

"The girl."

I watch the girl shorten the distance to our table, and I can't help but notice the almost primal stare she is directing toward us—no, not us. Her stare is solely meant for Andres. I study his reaction to the approaching girl, who is obviously on the prowl. He seems unaffected by her cutting gaze.

"Hey, guys," the taller of the two men calls out, addressing everyone.

"What's up, Ricardo? Haven't seen you in a while," Julio replies.

"Yeah, it has been a while," Ricardo answers.

Greetings are exchanged between the newcomers and those at our table, and several conversations are going on at once.

Julio's voice rises slightly as he speaks over the friendly chatter, "Hey, guys. This is Olivia. She is living with Nadia and Carlos for the summer."

Ricardo and the second guy, who introduces himself as Christian, extend a warm greeting. The girl, who I now know is named Camila, gives a slight nod in my direction before she continues her conversation with Hugo and Andres. Ricardo and Christian pull up chairs to join us, and Camila squeezes in the booth next to Andres.

The night continues, and I learn that the three most recent additions to our table went to high school with the group, but they don't attend the same university now. Christian has scooted his chair, so he is directly facing me, leaning his elbow on the table, while engaging me in all sorts of questions. He is cute and very friendly. I am relieved to have someone take my mind off the hushed conversation between Camila and Andres. *Yep, I'm not a fan of her either.*

"So, Olivia, do you want to dance?" Christian asks.

I pause. *Do I want to dance with Christian? I don't know. No, not really.*

He seems like a great guy and all, but at this moment, dancing with him doesn't sound appealing. The quiet conversation between Andres and Camila stops. I remember my promise to myself. This is a chance for me to be indifferent and move on.

Exhaling a deep breath, I reply, "Uh…yeah, sure."

I look to Nadia, and she is smiling gently. I think she approves. She must like Christian more than she does Camila. That is a good sign.

Christian takes my hand and leads me to the small dance floor. As I follow Christian, I sneak a peek back at our table, and I am met with a familiar steel-blue stare. His eyes are locked on me, and the emotion they are emitting resembles anger. I question the irritation I see in Andres's posture when Christian pulls me into a tight embrace.

We aren't the only ones dancing, but the floor isn't packed with writhing bodies either. At first, our dance is nothing but awkward. My heart isn't in it. Christian is simply fun though, and he is a great dancer. We are dancing to an upbeat song, and he places his arm around the small of my back. Suddenly, he dips me, and my hair brushes the ground. I let out a small yelp, and he snaps me back up to him. I steady myself with my hands sprawled on his chest, and I laugh. Then, he is twirling me. With my arm in the air, he uses my hand to spin me in circles.

A slower song plays, and I catch my breath as I wrap my arms around Christian's neck. We dance in true middle school fashion. It is more my pace.

"That was fun. I have never danced like that." I chuckle.

Well, maybe I have danced like that with Max in our living room when we were kids, but I have never in public. I feel my cheeks stretch from the wide grin on my face, and I realize that it is the biggest genuine smile I have had while in the presence of Andres. The thought of him sends my gaze darting over Christian's shoulder to our table. I stiffen when I see that the spot previously occupied by Andres and Camila is empty. I pivot my head around to see the back of Andres as he leads Camila out the door.

I lean my head into Christian's shoulder and breathe, not wanting him to see the panic on my face. *So, Andres left with her. Just great.* I close my eyes, holding in the tears threatening to spill. I know I am being irrational and juvenile, but I can't help the pain coursing through my chest. Sometimes, our bodies feel what they are going to feel despite the logic of the situation. Rationally, I know that I have no reason to be upset. *So, he left with a girl. It's not my issue.* I've heard of his girl-crazy ways. Maybe I just needed to see it to move on.

Taking in a deep breath, I raise my head. "Do you want to go do some shots?" I ask Christian.

"Sure," he replies.

At the bar, Christian and I each do two shots. I refuse when he offers to buy me a third even though I really want to do so many that I pass out and sleep for a day. I thank him for the shots and excuse myself to go to the restroom.

*Ugh.* I stare in the mirror. *Why does this even bother me? It shouldn't, right?* Andres is just some guy who I didn't even know existed up until four days ago. *So, why is he under my skin?* There are plenty of other great people in Spain. *For example, Christian is nice and all. Do I desire to have anything with him? No, not at all. It's fine. I don't need a guy. I just need to get a certain one out of my head.* I am going to go tell Nadia that I'm leaving. I have had enough of the bar scene for one evening.

I start to head back to the table. Passing the blaring speakers, I barely notice what song is playing as I peer at the floor. Then, I sense him in front of me. I stop and look up, and I am locked into his blue gaze. My heart races. His penetrating stare steals my breath, and I am lost to him. His eyes radiate so much emotion, but it's an emotion that I can't place. The magnitude of unspoken intentions behind his determined look sends a chill down my spine.

He lifts his hand and runs the pad of his thumb across my bottom lip. "Dance with me," he whispers in his raspy, sexy voice.

I'm stunned. "Camila?" I mutter with a crack in my voice.

He has a fleeting look of confusion before he answers, "She left."

I gasp when he grabs my hips and pulls me toward him, stepping us back onto the dance floor. My automatic response to his touch—the way my arms wrap around his neck, like we're closely acquainted—is unexpected, but I'm sure the alcohol I've consumed aids it. His eyes bore into mine, and I see a deep-seated emotion. *Perhaps desire? Lust?*

We dance, allowing the music to dictate our movements. I'm completely oblivious to the fact that our group is probably watching us. They are sure to be interested in this new development. Concerns of how I appear to anyone other than Andres don't resonate anywhere near my conscious. The only thought in my mind is our rhythmic bodies in this moment. The rest of the world has fallen away, and all I see is him.

I am cognizant of all points of contact between us. I close my eyes and take in his scent—clean, manly, sexy. Before I know it, I'm burying my head in his neck and inhaling his irresistible fragrance from his collarbone to his ear. I hear his intake of breath. One of his hands rubs around and cups my ass while the other makes trails up and down my back, creating an eager shiver down my skin. He slides his knee between my legs, and I start to grind against it to the beat of the music. It's a seductive dance of sensation. His mouth slowly peppers me with supple, full kisses on my lips.

*I can't believe this is happening!*

The feeling of his soft lips is exquisite. In the deep recesses of my mind, the warnings about this handsome man strive to come to the forefront, but I force them back, not willing to lose this moment. Both of his hands run up and down my sides. He stops below my arms and grazes the sides of my breasts. I inhale sharply as a shudder runs through me.

His hands wrap around the small of my back, and he draws me even closer. He runs his fingers from my waist up to my shoulder blades and through my hair. Pulling our faces closer, he presses his lips firmly on mine. His tongue enters my mouth, and I greedily welcome it with my own. I groan as I feel everything below my waist start to pulse. His tongue explores my mouth with confidence. I've lost all logic and thought, and I am nothing but feeling and sensation. My whole body is humming. My chest pounds with exhilaration. My hands explore the strong firmness of his body with a needy intensity.

I continue to dance with him, straddling his leg, while our tongues aggressively explore one another's mouths. He tastes so good, and his kiss alone could put me over the edge. I've never been kissed with such abandon. It's reckless and delicious. Everywhere his hands touch leaves me warm, and I can still feel the sensation after they've moved on. We're a pair of hot, entangled souls with exploring hands, urgent mouths, and racing hearts.

"Fuck!" he yells as he quickly pulls away.

I'm still reeling from his touch. I try to get my bearings at the loss of contact when he grabs my hand and leads me out of the bar. We start walking down the road. It's gotten cooler, and I embrace the chill in the air as it soothes my overheated, sensitive skin. As we walk, I don't say anything. I don't know what to say. I'm still trying to figure out what the hell just happened back there and what is happening now.

We finally stop when we reach a park at the opposite end of the street. He sits on a bench and pulls me down next to him. We sit there for a minute as he rubs his thumb over my hand.

"I'm sorry. I had to get out of there. I almost lost control in front of everyone. I don't know what I am doing," he says, sounding frustrated.

I open my mouth to speak, but then I shut it, not knowing what to say. I'm still mystified. *How did we go from ignoring each other to making out in the middle of the bar?*

He continues, "I tried to stay away from you, but you're like a magnet pulling me in. Something tells me I shouldn't go anywhere near you, that I'll end up crushing you, but I can't stay away from you. I felt a fierce attraction to you at the club your first night here. It's something I've never felt before. You fascinate me. I can't stop looking at you or imagining what it would feel like to touch you. I've never been drawn to someone like the way I am to you, and that makes me want to stay away. I don't do relationships, Olivia."

He sighs and runs his fingers through his hair in frustration. "That's the problem. I don't do relationships. I was hoping that my attraction to you would go away, but I know it won't. Every time I'm around you, I want you more. I'm sorry for what happened in there. I really don't know what I was thinking. Fuck, I wasn't thinking." He pauses.

"I don't want to fuck things up and make it awkward for us to be around each other. Carlos is like my brother, and I'm with him and Nadia every day. It could get confusing. I don't know. I don't do this. Olivia, I have a lot of fucked-up shit in my life, and I don't think I can do the relationship thing. You know?"

*Relationship thing? What the hell is he talking about?* I finally get the courage to speak. "Um...I'm not sure exactly what relationship thing you're talking about. I've seen you the past four days, and we haven't even spoken, so I don't know why you're talking about a relationship."

A slight grin graces his face. "Fuck, I know. I must sound like a complete idiot."

*Man, he is so sexy.* I could listen to him speak for days. The way his native language rolls off his tongue is such a turn-on.

"I just know I can't stay away from you, but I don't know if I can give you more than a brief thing. I'm afraid that if anything happens between us and you want more...I'll end up hurting you, and that's when it will get awkward. Does that make sense?"

*Deep breath. Reality check. Is this conversation really happening?* I stare into his dark blue eyes that are burning with such intensity. They look to me in question, needing a response. *What do I say? The guy who I have been infatuated with since the moment I saw him feels the same about me?* In my head, I am jumping up and down, squealing like a girl, and doing cartwheels around the park. I have to focus hard to keep my erupting joy from showing all over my face. Now is the time to play it cool.

"Yeah, I totally get it. I'm not asking you to walk down the aisle with me tomorrow or anything," I say, teasingly. "I don't need anything from you. I'm only here for the summer anyway." I pause, staring into his eyes. I commit every inch of his beautiful face to memory. It's a wonder to be this close to him. His face is pure perfection.

He laughs, flashing his brilliant smile, and tingles run through my body again.

"Can I see you tomorrow?" he asks hesitantly.

The nervousness in his voice is endearing.

I smile shyly, and I freeze in place from his intense, expectant stare. "Sure."

I don't know what he qualifies as fucked-up, but I'll take my chances to spend time with him, to have him talk to me, to have him touch me for however brief this thing might be.

"I'll pick you up after school tomorrow. When do you get out of your last class?"

And like that, the edge is out of his voice, and it's as if he's having a conversation with a longtime friend.

"Two o'clock."

"Okay, two it is." He stands, pulling me up with him.

We start walking, hand in hand, toward my house. He doesn't say another word, and neither do I. I sneak a glance at him as he stares into the distance, and I can tell he's deep in thought.

When we get to the door at the gate, he tilts my head up and gives me a lingering kiss. "Until tomorrow then." He turns from me and walks away, hands in his pockets, without a backward glance.

I stroll into the empty house and make my way to the bedroom. I close the door and lean up against it. Part of me wants to do an obnoxious happy dance, and then part of me wants to pinch myself, so I wake up from this dream because it doesn't seem real. Nothing that I thought I knew is making sense now.

I fall onto the bed, and I try to process the evening. I was so sure that Andres couldn't stand me. I think back to his words.

*I can't stay away from you. You fascinate me.*

It doesn't add up. *Am I really that bad at reading people? And what does he mean by fucked-up?*

I hear Nadia and Carlos enter the house, and a knock at my door follows.

"Come in," I say as I sit up.

Nadia comes in and closes the door behind her. "What the hell was that?" she asks, putting emphasis on each word. Her face is a cross between confusion and excitement.

*My sentiments exactly.*

I stifle a giggle, taking note of her dumbfounded expression. "I don't know," I say honestly, shrugging.

She crosses her arms and continues to stare at me. "That answer isn't going to cut it."

"I don't know. I went to the restroom. On my way back, he intercepted me, and we started dancing. It got steamy."

A small chuckle escapes her throat.

I continue, "We left. We went for a walk. He said he likes me, but he doesn't want to mess anything up. He said he doesn't do relationships, but then he asked if he could see me tomorrow. That's all I know."

"Hmm...I love Andres. He's like a brother to me. But be careful. He's never been good with relationships, so he's right about that. Actually, he's never been in a relationship that I know of. He's been with girls, *lots* of girls, but not for very long."

I can't help but notice her emphasis on the word *lots*.

She gives me a heartfelt smile. "Even though I've known you for less than a week, you're my sister now, and I don't want to see you get hurt."

"Thank you. I'll be careful." Even as I say the words, I know they aren't true.

What I'm willing to do to be close to Andres is anything but careful. It is reckless, irresponsible, and senseless. But the desire to be close to him, to feel his hands on me again, to feel his lips against mine is so fierce that logic and care hold no place in my brain when it comes to Andres. None whatsoever.

# chapter 7

When I get to school, Nolan is waiting by one of the old lampposts at the building's entrance.

"Hey, you. How was your night?" he asks.

"Interesting. I have a lot to tell you actually."

"Yeah?"

"Yeah." I smile up at him. "I'll tell you at break."

Professor Gomez is lecturing about the importance that food plays into the traditions of the De la Garza family in the novel *Like Water for Chocolate*, our assigned reading this week. My mind actively wanders over the events of the previous night. I hear the professor, but I am not focusing on his words. My thoughts are immersed in the deconstruction and analysis of the past week's events.

Nolan slides his notebook onto my desk. On the top of the page, he has written, *Dish it.*

My lips rise up into a grin. Raising my head, I see Nolan's smirk, and his ensuing nod toward the notebook.

*Okay, fine.* I write, *I kissed Andres*, and then slide his notebook back to him.

He reads my response, and his left eyebrow rises as he hands his notebook back to me. He didn't write a response, but from his expression, I know that he wants details. I write down the bullet points of the evening.

*Danced with Andres at La Jolla. He kissed me, and he's picking me up after class today.*

Upon reading my note, he turns to me, looking confused. He mouths, *Really?*

*Really*, I mouth back.

After class, Nolan and I head to the campus café to get coffee, and I tell Nolan about the preceding evening in more detail. I begin with the uncomfortable silent treatment between Andres and me, and I end with Andres pulling me out of the bar after a moderately inappropriate display of affection on the dance floor.

"Wow, I didn't see that coming. I've never seen you two even speak," is his reply.

"I know. It was surreal for me, too. It definitely wasn't expected."

"So, you like him?"

"Yeah, I think so. I don't really know him well. We haven't had any real conversations yet. So, I guess we'll see." I omit my immediate nonsensical extreme attraction for Andres, if solely for the fact that it verges on bizarre, even to me.

"Cool." He looks down at his watch. "Hey, Liv, we better get to our next class."

After our second class, Nolan is adamantly illustrating a very vivid picture of an embarrassing encounter at his apartment. He was walking down the hall after his shower last night when he stepped on a centipede on the floor.

"Fuck, Livi, this thing was six inches long with a million legs."

"A million, huh?" I chuckle.

"A fucking lot, okay? I felt it slither under my toes! I screamed like a girl and jumped two feet off of the ground, dropping my towel. I didn't see where it had gone, and I wasn't going to risk seeing it again by picking up the towel. I was naked and making my way to the bedroom when Pedro comes around. He was probably seeing why I'd yelled. You should have seen his face when he all but ran into my naked ass."

I'm doubled over, laughing, with visions of Nolan and his nude face-off with the killer centipede. I straighten and notice Andres leaning against a tree in the garden with his hands in his pockets. He's looking at me with an inquisitive expression on his face. I immediately stop laughing. He takes my breath away.

*Breathe, Liv.*

Giving myself silent encouragement, I grab Nolan's hand. "Come on, scaredy-cat." I lead him to where Andres is waiting.

"Hi." I smile at Andres, feeling like a lovesick girl. *Geez, pull it together.*

Nolan greets Andres. They shake hands and exchange a couple of pleasantries.

Nolan bends down to kiss my cheek. "Call me later."

I smile as Nolan walks away. Andres has a fixed expression on his face as he watches Nolan. Andres grabs my hand and leads me away from the school and toward the road. We walk in silence, and I notice that we're headed for a motorcycle leaning on its kickstand on the sidewalk.

I stop abruptly. "Is that yours?" I ask, a slight shrill to my voice.

"Yes," Andres answers, sounding confused.

"Oh, no, I don't do motorcycles. You do know how incredibly unsafe they are, right?" I'm sure the expression on my face is one of complete terror.

I'm normally not a scared person. I mean, obviously, since I had a homeless man frequent my yard back home, and it didn't faze me enough to lock my doors. Something about certain modes of transportation, specifically planes and motorcycles, freak me out. I have visions of plummeting to my death from the sky or being propelled off a motorcycle into a tree. I know these fears are irrational for the most part, but seriously, it could happen. It has happened. I've seen the news stories. I just can't help my anxiety.

He takes a step to stand behind me. Encasing me between his arms, he pulls me toward him. My legs turn to jelly as he kisses my shoulder. Then, ever so sweetly, he proceeds to place little kisses in a line from my shoulder to my neck, ending at the base of my ear. My body shivers as he starts to nibble my earlobe.

In between nibbles, he whispers, "I will keep you safe, I promise."

I'm awoken from my sensual escape when his heated body steps back from mine. Following a startling smack on my ass cheek, I yelp and laugh. He grabs a helmet and hands it to me, and he's obviously very pleased with himself.

I'm feeling contradicting emotions, but against my better judgment, I put on the helmet and climb on. *You only live once, right?* That thought brings a smile to my face. I am going to text Cara about this later. She loves to obnoxiously hashtag *YOLO* after everything. It has become a running joke, causing her to do it more than necessary.

As we drive away, I wrap my arms around him, and his tight abdomen flexes under my grasp. I lean my head into his back and close my eyes while holding on as tightly as I can. I think he laughs as we merge onto the street outside of campus. We weave through the bumpy streets. I venture a peek, and I am utterly panicked as he swerves in and out of traffic, around potholes, and between cars. This would be terrifying in a car, and it is completely paralyzing on a motorcycle. Andres isn't wearing a helmet, and a million horrid images flash through my mind as I imagine the worst. I pray we make it safely to our destination.

The motorcycle slows as we bounce down a cobblestone street. We halt, and I open my eyes. We're parked in front of a gray concrete gate. Andres lifts me off the motorcycle and holds me to him. I'm grateful because I honestly don't know if I could stand on my own at the moment. My legs are still shaking as the adrenaline subsides.

With one arm circled around my back, holding me, he removes my helmet with the other. My hair falls from its messy bun. He places the helmet on the motorcycle seat and runs his fingers through my hair. I fix my eyes on his face and marvel at his full lips and perfectly smooth skin, and my breath hitches when my gaze meets his eyes. The prior ride of terror is all but forgotten.

"Come." He grabs my hand and leads me through the gate door.

I peer up at a tall house made of the same stucco material as the house I am staying in, but this one has varying shades of gray. He takes me inside and explains that he lives here alone. The house is three stories, including the rooftop deck. I learn that his dad is an architect and designed the whole thing. It's bare with no finishing touches—light bulbs without enclosures, cabinets without doors, a couple of walls without drywall, the wooden studs visible. He leads me up to the top floor to his bedroom and a wide-open outdoor living space. The rooftop balcony is half the house's width and overlooks the city. It's a breathtaking view.

"My father never finished the house."

"Why not?"

"After my mom died, I guess he couldn't. This home was their dream."

*Oh.*

Andres doesn't expand on the bomb he dropped, and I don't ask about it. He sits on the outdoor couch facing the backdrop of Seville. I sit next to him.

"Tell me about yourself, Olivia," he says as he tucks a strand of hair behind my ear.

"There's not much to tell. I have an older brother, Max. My parents are great. My mom's a nurse, and my dad's an electrician. I grew up in a small town in southern Michigan."

"What are you studying in college?"

Even such a simple question coming from Andres is a major aphrodisiac. I have come to the conclusion that everything sounds sexy in Spanish, especially in Andres's voice. I am finding that I don't even have to translate the Spanish to English in my head anymore before it registers. Other than when I'm talking to Nolan in English, I am constantly thinking and speaking in Spanish. I am even dreaming in Spanish, which always excites me when I awake.

"I'm going to school to become a teacher. I hope to teach the Latino children in Detroit. The whole Latin community and culture is very interesting to me." I blush.

He's staring at me with sincere curiosity.

I continue, "I go to Eastern Michigan University and live with my best friend, Cara, who's like a sister to me. You'll meet her. She's coming to visit in a few weeks."

Then, I stop, realizing I implied that he and I would be hanging out for more than today. He doesn't seem to notice my hesitation.

"What's your favorite color?" he asks.

"Hmm…digging deep now, huh?" I grin. "Actually, that question doesn't have a simple answer. If I had to pick a color to wear, it is black. I love all blues in general, and you can't go wrong with pink. Oh, I also love the oranges and reds of the leaves when they change colors in the fall." I pause. "Can I say all colors?" I look at him quizzically.

"Sure." He laughs. "Favorite food?"

"Mexican, hands down."

"Mexican?"

"Definitely." I smirk.

"Well, I will have to take you to some of my favorite restaurants and see if I can change your mind on that one."

"I doubt it, but you can try," I say in a tone indicating a challenge.

"What's your full name?"

"Olivia Rose Marshall. Yours?"

"You have a beautiful name. My middle name is Paulo, and last name is Cruz."

"Andres Cruz. That fits you."

His name sounds like one belonging to a movie star, and to be honest, he could be one. I still can't get over how attracted I am to him and that I am sitting in his house.

"What is your favorite thing to do?" he asks.

"Probably chilling with Cara and Nolan."

"Tell me about you and Nolan."

"I met Nolan on my first day of college. We had Spanish together. We've been friends ever since."

"You've never been more than that?" he asks, his face concerned.

"No, always only friends."

"You appeared to be more than friends at the club on your first night here."

*Oh, yeah, I guess he saw that.* "Um...that was a drunken accident. We don't normally go around and kiss each other. He has a girlfriend. We really are solely friends."

"But you hold hands? You seem very comfortable together, like there's more than friendship between you."

"We're close, very close. We've always been loving with each other. That's just the way we are, but it doesn't mean anything."

"It always means something, Olivia," he says.

"No, not with Nolan. Friends only, I promise." I smile reassuringly.

Andres's demeanor shifts, and he quickly changes the subject. "Are you hungry?"

"Um...yeah, a little." I realize I haven't eaten all day.

Andres leads me to the kitchen. "Well, I don't have much. I don't eat here too often. Is a sandwich okay?"

"A sandwich is great."

He opens the refrigerator, pulls out ingredients, and proceeds to make us each a ham sandwich.

He hands me a plate. "Your sandwich, madam." He winks.

*God, he is good-looking.*

We eat and talk some more.

I'm nervous when I speak. "What about you, Andres? Tell me about you."

"I don't have any biological siblings, but I've grown up with Carlos, Nadia, Hugo, and Julio. They're like family to me. My mom died when I was fourteen. She was the best in every way." His face lights up at the mention of his mom. "I was going to college for a while, but I needed a break. So, now, I'm not really doing much of anything besides the band. I want to go back to school at some point, but I need a while to figure out what I want."

"Where's your dad? He doesn't live here?" I ask.

"No. He couldn't stay here after my mom died. He has a small apartment about twenty minutes from here."

"Have you always stayed here alone?"

"Most days, yes."

"But you were only fourteen! A fourteen-year-old would never be allowed to raise himself in the States."

"This isn't the States. Plus, technically, I still had my father. It's not like I reported it to anyone. Livi, honestly, it wouldn't have mattered if he were here or not. It was probably easier with him gone. I stayed at Carlos and Nadia's a lot." Andres pauses thoughtfully. "He wasn't well. He still isn't. He hasn't been since my mom died." He places our plates in the sink. "Come on, let me take you home. I'm sure you have homework to do before we go out tonight."

"We're going out?"

"Yeah. We're going to Demo. It's a sweet bar. You'll like it."

*I'm sure I will*, I think as Andres takes my hand.

He leads me out of the house, and my skin hums at the contact of his touch. It's already so addictive.

After our terrifying ride back to my house, Andres helps me off of the motorcycle before he leans in and gives me a tender kiss. He pulls away, leaving me breathless. My lips tingle with the memory of his mouth on mine as I watch him swing his leg over the bike.

"I'll be back by ten, beautiful." He flashes me his gift of a smile.

I'm melting as he rides away.

I count down the seconds until tonight. Today's events and the time I spent with Andres was so comfortable, fun, and simply perfect. I have to remind myself that it wasn't a dream. It's hard to believe that we were practically strangers yesterday. *What a difference a day makes.* Prickles of anticipation race across my skin as I think about tonight. I can't even imagine the excitement that the evening will bring, and it can't come soon enough.

# chapter 8

Leaning against the wall, I sit on my bed as I finish the last of my homework. I look up to see Nolan watching me from the other bed.

"Are you finished with your translations?" I ask.

We're working on the subjunctive today, and to be honest, it sucks.

As Professor Gomez has said, *The subjunctive is not a verb tense, like past, present, and future. It is a mood.*

The subjunctive is widely used in Spanish but not in English, so it is difficult for my brain to grasp the concept. How do you translate a mood or know when the mood of the conversation requires a subjunctive verb? It's all very confusing.

"Close enough." Nolan smiles.

"Do you want me to help you?" I know that if I'm finding this difficult, Nolan certainly is.

"No, I'm good. I'm just thinking about how much I miss you already."

"What do you mean?" I ask.

"Well, I'm going to miss you this summer when you're off on your adventures with Andres," he says, a hint of sadness in his voice.

"Nolan, nothing is going to change. I'll still see you every day at school, and we'll still hang out. Plus, I don't know what's going on with Andres yet. It might not be anything."

Inside, I know Nolan is right. Things are already different.

"No, it is something. I haven't seen you act this way about a dude in, like—well, ever. I'm happy for you, sweets. I'll miss you, that's all."

I walk over to Nolan and sit on his lap. Wrapping my arms around his neck, I lean my head against his chest. "Nothing is going to change, hon. You're still my best friend. I might not see you as much as I want to, but I promise to see you as much as I can. Okay?"

Nolan doesn't say anything as he hugs me tighter.

After a few moments, I break the silence. "We are going to some bar tonight. Want to come?"

"I would, but I made plans with Pedro and some of his friends."

"Oh, that's great. Well, tomorrow then."

"Definitely. I better get going, Livi." He leans down and places a quick kiss on my forehead. "Have fun tonight."

"Thanks. You, too."

"Livi!" Nadia yells my name from the living room.

I walk out and see her standing with Carlos, Hugo, Julio, and Andres. He looks amazing. He's leaning against the living room wall, facing me, with his arms crossed. He's wearing a pair of worn jeans that fall seamlessly from his hips and a black button-up shirt that is untucked with the sleeves rolled to right below his elbows. The top two shirt buttons are undone, and I can see enough of his chest to make my heart stutter. I ache to run my hands under his shirt.

Andres observes quietly as Hugo and Julio affectionately greet me. After Julio releases me from his hug, I face Andres.

"Hey," I say, feeling strangely shy. I fidget with the snap on my purse.

"Hey," he says with a grin. He places a kiss on the side of my mouth.

I can smell mint as he lets out a breath, and my stomach tightens excitedly. I close my eyes as I relish in the feel of his skin against my cheek, a slight trace of stubble causing friction. He pulls away, and I exhale, opening my eyes that I'm sure are clouded with desire. My heart hammers in my chest, a steady rhythm that forms a melody, accompanying my powerful state of intoxication with Andres.

My shoulder is jarred forward as Carlos hits it on his way past us.

"Let's go," Carlos says.

Carlos, Nadia, Andres, and I jump into Carlos's car. Hugo and Julio follow behind us in another car as we head to Demo.

The bar has a very cool ambience, not at all flashy. It has one room with a stage where a band is playing at the far end. Wooden tables and chairs surround a small dance floor that is in front of the stage. We grab a table, and a bucket of bottled beer is delivered, a standing order indicating the frequency that the guys come here. Nadia and I each order mojitos. I can tell from the familiarity of the conversation with the waitress that the guys come here often.

Andres is calm and happy, joking with the guys. He's holding my hand under the table, and his thumb is running back and forth over my fingers, leaving me feeling completely elated.

Two girls walk over to our table and start talking with Andres. He politely answers their questions and then leans in to kiss my neck. I giggle. The girls get the hint and start talking to the other guys. Hugo is more than happy to accommodate the girls, and he invites them onto his lap. They eagerly accept the invitation. I see Julio glance at Carlos and roll his eyes. I laugh. I like Julio. He's funny and kind, and he doesn't take anything too seriously.

Carlos has grown on me, too. At first, I found him very standoffish, but I soon realized that he has a more serious and matter-of-fact personality. He doesn't sugarcoat anything or fake emotions that he isn't feeling. To be honest, it's quite refreshing when compared to Hugo, who dramatizes everything and is a constant flirt. Hugo is one of those people who is super excited to see everyone. You'd think that every person who comes up to him is his long, lost best friend. I get it. It's nice in a way that he makes people feel important, even validated, but I imagine it could get exhausting. No one can seriously be that happy, excited, or energetic all the time. Carlos's lack of interest in things that don't actually excite him is definitely a welcome change. Julio is the one who points all of this out, making fun of the situation, lightening the mood, no matter where we are. He's always good for a laugh, which I love.

Andres is just…yummy. *Sigh*. Besides Andres's obvious outer appeal, something about him is so attractive. He is so calm and collected most of the time, and I find it to be attractive. Additionally, he has this bad-boy-with-a-kind-soul allure going on, and it is completely irresistible. He also has a great sense of humor, but up to this point, I've been too nervous around him to appreciate it. More than anything, his heart is incredibly caring although guarded. The love and respect that he has for his friends is exceptional.

Ignoring the girls giggling on Hugo's lap, Andres whispers in my ear, "Dance with me."

*Oh, and then there is the dancing.* Nothing is more captivating than the way my body feels when moving against his.

I nod, and he leads me to the dance floor. I am again transported into a world of longing, sensation, and hormonal bliss as Andres's hands are all over me while mine are all over him. I rub my fingers through his messy hair as his lips meet mine. The exquisite feeling of his tongue exploring my mouth while his hands grasp my hair and pull me into his face leaves me feeling shaky and needy. I bite his bottom lip, and he groans into my mouth. On my leg, I can feel his firm desire through his jeans as he leans into me. He is such a sexy dancer. I never considered myself great on the dance floor, but with Andres, I don't even have to try. It's remarkable how my body reacts to him as we move to the music.

I remove my hands from his hair and run them under his shirt and over his tight abdomen, feeling his smooth skin and the ridges of his muscles. He lets out a sharp intake of breath, and he pushes me toward the corner of the dance floor. Without taking his mouth off mine, he guides me to the hallway leading to the restrooms. Pushing me against the wall, he grinds his hips into me, and I want to explode. The intensity has increased, morphing into a forceful, rough, passionate kiss that ignites all my senses. He kisses me hard, and his tongue licks me greedily. Tingles run through my body from my scalp to my toes. My hands are ravenous, running down and up his back and then into his hair, as I pull him closer to me. My fingers ache to feel every inch of him, and moving my hands under his shirt, I claw down his back.

We are suspended in this all-consuming kiss. I lose all concept of time when I am with him like this. He is my drug. He fuels my addiction with his mouth as he takes me to a new high. He pulls his mouth away and leans his forehead against mine, panting. I inhale sharply at the loss of contact.

"God, Liv, I want you. I want to take you to the restroom and fuck you so hard."

"I'm not objecting," I whisper through labored breaths. Surprisingly, I'm not uncomfortable with my admission.

Andres's arms straddle either side of my head, holding him up, as he sighs. He says, "No, beautiful, you deserve better than a restroom." He places a series of now sweet, soft kisses on my cheeks and on my forehead. Taking a step back, he takes my hands in his and places one kiss on each, never letting his captivating eyes leave mine. He leans into me and wraps me in his arms.

We stand in an embrace, my arms around his neck and his around my waist. He pulls me close and holds me while our breathing calms. I rest my head against his chest and listen to the sound of his heart. The sounds, smell, and feel of being this close to him are comforting and safe.

Eventually, Andres takes a step back. He lets out a sigh. "What are you doing to me?"

*My sentiments exactly.*

He grabs my hand and kisses it once more before entwining our fingers and leading me back to our table of friends.

Carlos smirks at me when we get back. "That was a long restroom break. It's about time you came back. We're ready to leave. I'm starving."

One of the girls who was drooling over Andres a while back is still sitting on Hugo's lap with her very eager tongue down his throat. The sight of them together makes me feel sick.

I can't help but wonder, *If I weren't here, would that be Andres's mouth readily accepting her tongue?*

I stand gawking, submerged in my negative thoughts, as the rest of the group gets up from the table.

Nadia returns her attention back to Hugo, who hasn't noticed that everyone is standing and ready to leave. "Hey, are you coming to get food with us?" Nadia asks in annoyance.

Hugo pulls away from the girl and looks up at us. "Nah, I think I'm going to go home with…" He turns to face the girl on his lap. "What's your name again?"

"Juanita," she answers.

"Yeah, I'm going home with Juanita. Catch you guys tomorrow."

Hugo faces back toward Juanita. She is all smiles, ready to accept his attention.

*Really?*

I see Nadia roll her eyes before pivoting on her heels toward the exit. I quiet the voice in my head that is reminding me that up until a week ago, that could have been Andres.

# chapter 9

The next day, Andres picks me up from class in his deathtrap of a vehicle. We then go back to my house. I study while he watches me. He rubs my back and my hair, making it very hard for me to concentrate. After I'm finished with my homework, I lie on my side, facing Andres. We're parallel to one another as I gaze into his eyes. He runs his strong hand up and down my arm, leaving me with tingly goose bumps. I take his hand and flip it over to look at the small star tattoo on the inside of his wrist.

"Do you mind if I ask you about your tattoo?"

A moment passes before he answers. "I got it to remind me of my mom," he says quietly.

"You don't like to talk about your family, do you?" I ask as I run my fingers over the silky skin of his wrist, tracing the points of the star.

He sighs, looking at his hand resting in mine. "I don't mind talking about her. It's just painful, so I don't really bring it up."

"Can you tell me a little about her? What is the significance of your tattoo?"

His stare focuses on the star, his eyes full with emotion. "Well, my mom was amazing…like, the best mom in the world." His lips press together into a sad smile. "All she ever wanted to be was a mom, and she made sure that I knew how much I was loved every day. She was always my biggest supporter and made me feel like I could do anything. While I was little, when she tucked me into bed at night, she used to tell me that she wished upon a star, and I came true. She said she thanked her lucky stars that she had been blessed with me. I got the star tattoo to remind me that even on my darkest days, I once had unconditional love and that I need to live a life that would make my mom proud. When you're hurting, it's so easy to give in to the darkness and become someone you don't want to be. I don't want that to happen to me. I admit that it's like I'm living in the dark most of the time, and I'm just going through the motions, but at least, I haven't lost myself completely to it. I could never do that to her."

"She sounds wonderful, Andres."

"She was. She was the best." He smiles sadly and strokes the back of his hand against my cheek.

"Are you and your dad close?"

Andres's body stiffens, and his calm, nostalgic expression instantly changes to hard coldness. His quick response lacks emotion. "No." His whole demeanor has changed.

I'm cautious as I continue, "Why not?"

"I don't like to talk about this stuff. It's not pleasant, and I have spent the last eight years trying to avoid this type of conversation. Let's just say that my dad hasn't handled my mom's death well, and because of that, we're no longer close."

"Okay, I understand. How should I act when I meet him?"

Andres rolls his eyes and lets out a quick laugh. "You won't."

"Um…okay," I say, feeling uncomfortable from my presumption.

"It has nothing to do with you. You are wonderful, but you'll never meet him. He's not a part of my life that I want you to be involved with. Okay?" He gently grabs my chin and pulls my mouth to his for a quick sweet kiss.

"Okay," I say, sensing that he's done with this conversation.

We spend the rest of the afternoon snuggled together on my bed. We explore one another with our hands and our mouths, but our clothes stay on. We kiss until my lips are raw and throbbing with pleasing pain. At some point, we fall asleep while entwined together. It's the best nap ever.

After dinner, we go to the movie theater. We see the new James Bond film, and although it's in English, I try to read the Spanish subtitles instead. I give up halfway through because trying to focus on anything while Andres is rubbing his thumb across my hand is idiocy. I'm so consumed with Andres that I can barely see straight in his presence.

Each time we have been together this week, it has been impossible for me to keep my hands and mouth off him. Thankfully, he feels the same way. When he drops me off at my door, we have another intense, electrifying make-out session that leaves me breathless, frustrated, and wanting more. I need more.

On Friday, Nolan and I take our usual coffee break in between classes.

"Do you have plans tonight?"

"Yeah, we're going to this new club, La Esquina. Do you want to come? It'll be fun."

"Sure. You know I'm always game for a good time," he says.

"Great! Hey, have you heard from Abby? When is she coming to visit?"

"Two weeks from today."

"Perfect. That's when Cara is coming, too! We'll have to take them out to all our favorite places."

Nolan smiles at me as we walk back to class. Part of my heart hurts when we walk back, and I don't know why. There is an awkwardness between Nolan and me. It's nothing that I have ever experienced with him before. Our friendship has always been so flawless. I sense that Nolan is sad although he's trying very hard to make everything seem normal. I know he misses me. He's definitely seeing less of me now than he did at home, but I know he understands. I know he wants me to be happy, and it is rare that I'm so interested in someone new.

"Are you okay, Nolan? I'm so sorry that I haven't been able to spend as much time with you this week."

"No need to apologize, Liv. You're happy, so I'm happy. That's all I want for my best friend. I'll take you when I can get you and be thrilled," he says, giving me an Oscar-worthy smile and squeezing my hand.

His eyes show a conflicting emotion, and it brings me a feeling of unease. I hold his hand tightly and lean my head on his arm.

La Esquina is another impressive club. It's a tall building, and inside there are five levels. Standing on the ground floor, one can peer up through the center of the room and see the floors above. Each level is open to the center and has a metal railing spanning the level to allow people to look up or down toward other floors. There is not a set dance floor, so bodies are dancing everywhere among the rustic metal tables scattered throughout. The club is huge.

We get a table in the corner of the fourth floor. We order two bottles of Grey Goose with sodas. Nolan seems happy as he talks to the group we're here with. He occasionally glances my way and smiles. There are a few people that I remember from the first night we went out to a club. I'm sitting between Nadia and Andres. Nadia chatters away, giving me details about different people passing by our table. She loves to gossip, and it always surprises me that she seems to know everything about everyone, especially in such a large city.

I find it impossible to focus on a word she says as all my senses are consumed with Andres. I'm keenly aware of the way he smells, and I fight the urge to lean in and inhale him. The combination of soap, fabric softener, and a faint musky scent invades my brain. It's clean, manly, and sexy all at once. It's intoxicating.

Andres leans over and whispers in my ear, "Have I told you that you are stunning tonight? It is making it difficult for me to think about anything other than getting you out of that dress."

I catch my breath, and my skin stands at attention. I'm wearing my favorite short black dress with a low swooping back paired with red heels. Andres is rubbing his thumb along the small of my back at the base of my dress, and he has moved my hair to the side, so he can kiss my neck. My body is on fire, and I'm solely focusing on breathing.

I can feel Nolan's stare on me, but I don't direct my attention toward him. I want to stay lost in this erotic connection with Andres—or maybe I don't want to see what Nolan's face will disclose. I keep my eyes closed and lean into Andres's shoulder, relishing the feeling of his hand on my back.

I'm elated and up on my feet within a second when Andres asks me to dance. I spot an empty space at the far end of the room, and I start to beeline toward it before Andres grabs my arm and pulls me against him. We're closer to our group than I want to be, but that thought is completely lost when his mouth meets mine. In that moment, we are again two bodies moving together without thought or inhibition. I am tuned in only to the feelings of his tongue in my mouth and the warmth of his body against mine. Tingling sensations linger where his hands are touching me. *Oh my God, he is such a great dancer.* It is quite possibly the sexiest thing about him. It doesn't feel like dancing. It is something so much more intimate. I'm unsure of how long we've been dancing because the rest of the world has fallen away.

He whispers, "Let's get out of here."

I get immediate chills. All I can offer in response is a nod. I try to regain my equilibrium from our raw, sexual, overpowering dance, and I motion to the restrooms.

Andres nods, and I take off in the direction of the restroom. I take a few minutes to compose myself, noticing my flushed skin. My chest and cheeks are a deep red from my anticipation. My hair is slightly damp with sweat at the nape of my neck. Taking the hair tie from my wrist, I whip my hair into a ponytail. I reapply my lip gloss before returning to the packed club.

I stop abruptly, bracing myself against a wooden pillar, when I see him. He is standing exactly where I left him, where moments ago we were dancing with heated passion. He is still dancing while his hands grasp firmly to moving hips, his lips grazing an ear as he speaks into it. The hips belong to a girl who is throwing her head back in exaggerated laughter to whatever Andres just said. I watch while she recovers from the forced laugh and brings her lips to his ear. I see her lips moving in conversation while her hands work over his back. I'm unaware I am crying until I taste the saltiness of the tears streaming down my face.

I am not familiar with who this girl is—not that it matters anyway. His hands are on her, and she isn't me. I didn't expect a serious commitment. I'd told him as much, but shit, we came here together tonight. I expected to leave with him. This week had been beyond incredible in so many ways, and the majority of it could be attributed to Andres. In my haze of hormones and giddiness, I forgot that both he and Nadia had told me that he is someone who doesn't do commitment. I wanted to believe that I was different. I'm not special though, and I feel foolish.

It's only been a week, and I shouldn't care as much as I do, but I fell, and I fell fast. Andres made it easy to do. I thought I felt something more than casual, something great. *How could I have been so wrong?* My wish for what Andres and I could have been shatters. I bring my fingers to my temples, rubbing circles, as my humiliation sets in. Then, my humiliation makes way for anger, so much anger. *At myself? At Andres? Both. Definitely both.*

Raising my stare to Andres again, I see the girl's hand running up and down his bicep. I have to get out of here as my panic increases. I scan the room until I see our table. Nolan is talking with Nadia, and as if he can feel my stare, he raises his eyes to meet mine from across the room. His smile fades as he looks at me with concern. I watch as he says something to Nadia, and then he makes his way over to me. I'm still bracing myself against the pillar, my knees locked and holding me upright.

"Oh my God. What is it, Liv?" Nolan asks with sincere worry in his voice.

"I just want to go," I choke out in a raspy voice that's heavy with tears.

Nolan motions toward the others. "Okay, let me go—"

"Now, Nolan. Right now." I don't want anyone else to see me. I want to go immediately.

"Okay, babe, we'll go." He swoops me up into his arms and heads toward the stairway to our right.

I bury my face in his shoulder, wishing for this night to be over. We exit the building, and the air is noticeably cooler than inside.

"Where do you want to go?" Nolan asks.

"Not to my house."

"Mine?"

"Sure," I answer as Nolan hails a cab.

Once we are situated in the back of the cab, Nolan says, "You really should let Nadia know that you left. She will be worried."

I think about it for a minute as I stare out the window. I know Nolan is right, so I grab my cell phone out of my purse and type a text to her.

*Me: Wasn't feeling well. Heading to Nolan's. Be back tomorrow.*

I shut off my cell before throwing it back into my purse. Nolan is silently observing me, giving me the time I need to process all the thoughts running through my head.

We arrive at Nolan's and enter the dark apartment. His roommate, Pedro, must still be out when we arrive to the small two-bedroom space they share. Nolan leads me to the bathroom. Once alone, I opt for a hot shower, scalding my skin. I brace my hands against the shower wall, letting the water hit my skin. I need to wash away the smells of the night—the sweat and lingering scent of Andres where his body and lips touched me. I can still sense his lips on me, the side of my neck and lips burning from the memory of his touch. *What was I thinking? Did I really think that involving myself with Andres was a good idea?*

I wrap the towel around my body and make my way down the hall toward Nolan's room. I scan the floor for killer centipedes, and I can't help the smile that graces my face as Nolan's story plays in my head.

When I get into Nolan's room, he hands me one of his T-shirts and a pair of boxers. "I'm going to take a quick shower." He kisses my forehead before leaving the room.

I am lying in Nolan's bed when he comes back. He shuts off the light and climbs in behind me, wrapping his arm around me. My dejection slowly abates with the familiarity of Nolan wrapped around me. He is my sweet Nolan, who I trust, and he has never hurt me.

"Do you want to talk about it?" he asks.

"He was dancing with another girl, and I freaked out."

"Maybe she was a friend?"

"No. The way they were dancing suggested that it was more." I pause. "I feel like an idiot. I don't know why I even started liking him. I knew how he was."

"Has he tried to contact you? Maybe you should talk to him and clear the air?" Nolan suggests with little conviction.

"I turned off my phone, so I don't know. I am going to have to be around him for the rest of the summer, so I'm sure we will talk at some point, but I don't feel like talking to him right now."

"Fair enough. Well, you have me, babe."

"I know. Thanks for loving me, Nolan."

"Always," Nolan says gently.

My gratefulness for that fills my heart as I drift into sleep.

When I enter my house the next morning, a sleepy-eyed Nadia is sitting in the recliner, sipping a steaming cup of coffee. Her eyes perk up when she sees me.

"What happened last night?" she asks with curiosity.

I don't know what to say to her exactly. I feel silly about the way I responded after dating Andres for only a week—if that was what we were even doing. "I wasn't feeling well."

"Yeah, I don't buy that. What really happened?"

I let out a small chuckle. "What makes you think I'm not telling you the truth?"

"I don't know. I can tell. I'm good like that. Spill it."

I plop down on the couch and let out a long sigh. "I kind of freaked out when I saw Andres dancing with another girl, and I asked Nolan to get me out of there."

"Andres was dancing with another girl?"

"Yeah, quite intently. I left to use the restroom, and when I got back, they were dancing and all over each other. I know Andres told me he wasn't good at relationships, but I really liked him, and it hurt."

"Hmm…that's weird. He didn't mention another girl, but he seemed really upset that you had left."

"Whatever. It is best that we don't get involved anyway," I say, trying to convince myself.

"You should talk to him. Maybe it wasn't what you think. I'm not saying Andres hasn't been a slut in the past, but coming with you and doing that while you were there doesn't seem like him. He's not an asshole."

"Maybe. It wasn't going anywhere anyway. I'm fine."

Nadia looks at me skeptically. "Okay. Well, I'm sure you will figure it out. Let me know if you need anything, okay?"

"I will."

Nadia grins. "Okay, well, my parents are back in town. My dad just finished a business trip, and my mom travels with him. They invited us to the country club today. It's not the most exciting place, but it does have great food and an awesome pool. Do you want to come?"

"Sure, that sounds fun." I could use some time to veg out in the sun.

At that moment, Carlos comes bounding down the stairs. "Hey, Livi. What happened to you last night?"

"I told you she didn't feel well," Nadia snaps.

"Yeah, okay. Whatever. You better have left me some coffee." He makes his way to the kitchen.

"He is such a caring soul," Nadia says sarcastically.

My lips curve up into a smile.

The country club appears similar to how I envisioned it. It has intricate stonework atop a stucco exterior. It is very Mediterranean. The exterior is flanked with deep green foliage and palm trees. The main lobby is tiled with a cathedral ceiling. Windows line the end of the atrium, allowing light to filter in.

"Come on. This way." Nadia motions, and we walk through an upscale changing area. "We can leave our stuff in here."

I take off my sundress and hang it in a locker. I use the term *locker* loosely since these are more like closets with dark wooden doors. "We are only going to the pool, right?"

"Yeah," Nadia replies. "You can leave everything in here."

I leave everything but my sunglasses and iPod, and we exit to the pool area.

"There they are," Nadia says as she leads the way toward some lounge chairs.

We come up to a couple sitting side by side under a large sun umbrella.

"Mom! Dad!" Nadia waves.

Her parents stand and greet her with exuberant hugs and kisses on the cheek.

Her Dad steps toward me and extends his hand. "You must be the wonderful Olivia that I have heard so much about."

I place my hand in his, and he kisses the top of it.

"Nice to meet you, Mr. Rubio." My cheeks flush as the embarrassment of meeting Nadia's parents in my tiny red string bikini sets in.

"Oh, please call me Alfonso."

"Alfonso." I smile politely.

"Olivia, this is my mom, Yolanda." Nadia introduces her mom, who looks like she could be Nadia's slightly older sister.

"Pleasure to meet you, Mrs. Rubio."

"Oh, sweetie, Yolanda, please. Call me Yolanda."

I nod.

"So, dear, how are you enjoying Seville so far?"

"It is wonderful. I love it here, and Nadia has been great. I am so lucky to be able to stay with her and Carlos."

"She sure was excited for you to come. She's always wanted a sister. How is Carlos treating you? Is he behaving himself?"

"Oh, yes, he is fine. He's great."

"And the rest of my boys?"

For a moment, I stare at her in confusion before realizing what she is asking. "Oh, yes, they have all been wonderful. Very sweet."

"Okay, well, please tell me if any of them gets out of line. They know better," she says with a stern smile.

Mr. Rubio cuts in, "Well, Olivia, it was lovely to meet you. I am off to play some golf, but I hope to see you again. Good luck with your classes." He then kisses Nadia and Yolanda each on the cheek before heading in the direction of the greens.

The three of us get comfortable on some lounge chairs by the pool. The heat of the sun feels wonderful against my skin. Nadia and her mom chat idly, catching each other up on all the latest gossip. I listen for a while before I put in my earbuds and lay my chair back. I close my eyes beneath my sunglasses and let my body relax while the warm rays comfort my body and the music clears my brain.

I awake with a start, and the momentary fog of my slumber lifts when I feel a familiar pull in my gut. My chest involuntarily begins to throb with anticipation. I cautiously open my eyes, and I am shocked to find Andres standing next to my lounge chair, shadowing the sun from my view.

"Olivia," he says my name in a clipped greeting.

"Andres," I force out, my voice shaky.

I have to concentrate on breathing steadily. The sight of Andres before me in nothing but a pair of board shorts is almost paralyzing. His chest is hard and beautifully defined. Under my glasses, my eyes roam from his chest to his abs to the delicious inverted triangle that ends beneath his shorts.

I look to my side, and I see the two chairs beside me are empty.

"They went inside with the guys to grab some food," he says shortly.

"Oh."

"Come talk to me, Liv."

Andres extends his hand, and I look at it, confused. Everything in me wants to grab it, but my mind tells me not to. I can't transform to putty the second he shows up, looking all hot and half-naked.

"Please," he pleads, his voice softer now.

I reluctantly grab his hand, and he pulls me up. He leads me around the pool to the side of the building where soft manicured grass is under my feet.

When the pool is out of view, he stops and faces me. Grabbing each one of my arms, he gently squeezes and stares into my eyes with intensity. "What happened last night? Why did you leave? Why haven't you answered any of my texts?"

"Just let it go, Andres." *You broke my heart, asshole, and I didn't turn on my phone because I didn't want to deal with it.*

"Liv, seriously, please talk to me."

I take a deep breath, my shoulders sagging in defeat. "Listen, you told me you didn't do commitment. I get it, but I don't work that way. I think it is best if we go back to ignoring each other."

Andres looks at me as if I slapped him. "Why are you saying this?"

His innocent little act is channeling all of the desire and hurt I feel toward him and changing it into anger. *How dare he come here and confront me as if I did something wrong.*

"When I came out of the restroom, I saw you dancing very closely with some girl last night. I know we aren't serious. Regardless, it made me feel like shit. I can't do this with you anymore." I raise my arms, extending them out, so I can push his hands off of me.

I attempt to head back in the direction where we came, and he grabs me once more, pivoting my body until I am facing him again.

"Are you talking about Stella?" he asks with confusion in his eyes. "She is just a friend."

"I don't know what her fucking name is, and I don't care. Whoever you were dancing with, it was more than friendly."

"It was dancing, Liv! Nothing happened! I was there with you."

"Well, it sure didn't look like it! Her hands were all over you, and yours looked pretty comfortable on her ass."

"She is just a friend from school. I promise, it was nothing."

"Well, it looked like something." I take a deep breath. "Listen, I think it is best if we go back to the way we were. You said you would mess this up, and you did. Lesson learned."

"Liv, don't do this."

"Do what? I'm not doing anything," I say in annoyance.

"Don't end this over something so meaningless."

"End it? We didn't have anything to end! Just let it go!" I say in a harsh whisper.

Andres holds my arms tighter and lowers his face to mine, stopping inches from me. Tingles resonate over my body, and my heart beats wildly in my chest. *Damn my body and its reactions to this man.*

His voice is husky as he whispers, "Don't deceive yourself. You know we have something."

"I don't believe that." My voice betrays me as it comes out in a breathy murmur.

Andres pushes me back a few feet so that my back is against the stone wall of the building. He grasps my face, and his impossibly blue eyes shine down on me. I have nowhere to go when he leans in closer. His lips are so close that I can feel his breath on me.

"Yes. You. Do."

His lips collide with mine, and my hands rise to grasp his hair as our tongues unite in a frantic soul-searching kiss. My need intensifies as my inhibitions diminish. Longing radiates off of Andres in waves that are almost tangible. I can feel his desire for me. My tongue licks his greedily, and the need I feel in my core throbs painfully with want.

Here I am, raising the white flag in surrender before I even went in to battle. I concede. I never had a fighting chance. A small voice echoes a warning in my mind, but I barely hear it. The sound of my heart and the fluttering in my belly reverberate through me as my body melds into his. The way his tongue dances with mine, the feeling of his breath on my face, and the quiet groans he makes into my mouth skew my equilibrium, forcing me to hold him tighter.

Andres pulls his lips away and leans his forehead on mine. We gasp for air, our chests rising and falling in unison.

"We have something," he says in a shaky, deep voice.

*Yes, we do.* I don't know what it is or where it will take me, but regardless of the outcome, I am a willing participant on this ride. I just hope I walk away from the inevitable crash at the end.

# chapter 11

Andres peppers my face with soft little kisses as our breathing slows. I place my outstretched hand on his chest and feel the pace of his heartbeat quicken, matching the cadence of my own.

"Andres, I can't handle the girls. If you want to keep going with whatever we are doing here, it has to be just me."

"Okay," he answers automatically.

"I'm serious. I know you aren't used to being with one person, but I can't do it any other way." I take his hand in mine and trace an indistinct pattern on its surface. "This hand, your hands"—I kiss the top of it—"will only be touching me." I hold his stare intently. "If your hands are going to be touching anyone's ass, it will be mine."

One side of his lips contorts up into an adorable smirk.

"I don't care if it is a friend. I don't share. That's nonnegotiable," I say in my best authoritative voice. I'm proud of my firm stance.

"Okay," he answers again.

"All right." I let out a sigh. "We should head back to the pool. I don't want Nadia and her mom to come back and wonder where I am."

A smile tickles his lips as he runs his index finger under the thin piece of fabric holding my suit together at my hip. "I don't know if I can keep my hands off of you when you are dressed like this."

My stomach clenches with excitement. He bends his head down to kiss my cleavage peeking out from beneath the triangles covering my chest. I close my eyes as the sensation of his smooth lips heats my flesh.

Using all of my willpower, I push his face away. "Okay, seriously," I say with a giggle.

We make our way back to the pool, hand in hand.

"Are you hungry? Or we can go for a swim?" Andres suggests.

"A dip in the pool sounds great."

Our lounge chairs are still empty when we get back. There's no sign of Nadia or her family. Sitting on the side of the large pool, I let my body slide into the water. It feels superb against my sensitized skin. Andres follows me in, and I wrap my body around his, our faces inches apart. He strokes the small of my back with his thumb.

Out of the corner of my eye, I see movement, and I turn right as Carlos cannonballs a few feet away from us, sending a wave of water into my face.

I am wiping the water from my eyes when another surge of water smacks into us after Hugo's tucked form plunged into the water.

Laughing, I wipe my soaked hair out of my face. Like civilized people, Nadia and Julio enter the pool via the steps.

Mrs. Rubio bends down at the side of the pool. "Boys, this isn't the place for such shenanigans." The grin on her face tells me she is stating this fact out of obligation, not because she truly cares how they enter the pool.

"Oh, come on, Mom. We are the only ones in here. We are not bothering anyone," Carlos answers.

"Well, try to behave," she states before walking back to her lounge chair and a waiting book.

"I think it is time we reestablish our chicken-fight championship!" Nadia exclaims excitedly.

Julio groans.

"I call Nadia!" Hugo yells.

"Damn it." Carlos appears annoyed.

I look between the guys and see less than amused expressions on Julio's and Carlos's faces.

To me, Nadia says, "Due to Julio's stature, he gets top." She giggles and wades through the water toward Hugo.

Julio turns to me and gives me a shy grin. "She is saying I'm short."

"We call winner," Andres announces. He pulls me in for a chaste kiss.

Nadia is lifted onto Hugo's shoulders with ease, and with some amusement, I watch as Julio awkwardly steps onto Carlos's leg before very ungracefully climbing onto his shoulders.

Julio calls out, "Seriously, I don't care to hold this title. You can take it, Nadia."

"I second that," Carlos states as he positions his hands around the front of Julio's legs.

"Nope. Everyone must try their best. Otherwise, the championship doesn't mean anything. Best two out of three?" she asks in a perky voice.

"Fine," Carlos and Julio say in disgruntled unison.

The moment Andres calls the start of the game, all four faces involved are in serious concentration. Carlos steps forward first, allowing Julio to push Nadia back hard. I watch as she plunges backward toward the water, but Hugo has a tight hold on her legs, and she flings herself back upright. When she does, she lunges toward Julio, jabbing him in the side under his arm. He yelps and wiggles on Carlos's shoulders. Carlos yells at him to stop twisting. Nadia keeps doing this poking action, causing Julio to bend and cover his sides with his hands. The whole sight is hilarious. I am rooting for Julio. I don't want to be on the receiving end of Nadia's painful tickling. Carlos's balance eventually gives way, and the two go down. Nadia raises her hands in victory, and she and Hugo do some sort of winner's chant.

On the second attempt, Julio takes Nadia down by pulling her to the side in a sharp and quick movement. During the third round, Carlos has a more difficult time keeping steady with Julio on his shoulders, and Nadia and Hugo win. Julio might be of a shorter stature, but he is stocky, easily outweighing Nadia by a good thirty pounds.

Andres lifts me out of the water and onto his shoulders.

"Okay," I say, "none of that poking action, Nadia! That is playing dirty."

Nadia laughs. "There are no rules to chicken-fighting, Livi."

I scrunch my face in an attempt to exude total seriousness. "No poking. I bruise easily."

"Fine," she says. "I can take you down regardless."

"Yeah, good luck with that," I say teasingly.

Max and I spent the majority of our summers at our grandma's house on a lake. I am not a chicken-fight virgin.

I bend my body in half, leaning forward, and give Andres an upside-down kiss.

"Seriously?" Carlos asks with annoyance.

"Okay, let's do this," Nadia says.

Carlos indicates the start of the game.

Nadia and I grasp hands, pushing and twisting on fairly equal footing. Each set lasts a while with much back and forth. We each take a match by sheer fact that our bases below lost their balance. As we regroup before the third match, Andres engulfs me in a wet hug and kisses below my ear.

"What do you say we take this and get out of here? I need you to myself."

The husky cadence of his voice sends shivers down my spine.

I kiss him softly on the lips. "I have a couple of tricks up my sleeve."

The third match begins with another even exchange between Nadia and me.

About thirty seconds into the match, in a high-pitched voice, I yelp, "Ow!"

Nadia stops pushing. "Are you o—"

Before she can finish her question, I push her with as much force as I can, taking her by surprise, and she topples backward into the water.

Coming up from the water, she yells, "That is totally not fair, Olivia! You said, no playing dirty!"

I throw my head back in laughter at her outrage. "No, I said, no poking."

The thought of being alone with Andres outweighs the smidge of guilt I feel at Nadia's bruised ego.

"I'm sure you will get us next time."

"Until then, Liv and I are the champs!" Andres taunts with a huge grin.

"Cheaters." Nadia attempts to look angry, but she can't keep her smile from appearing. "Next time, I won't be so easy on you, Miss Olivia."

I laugh.

After saying our good-byes, Andres and I catch a cab to his house. We sit in the rear of the yellow cab with our hands entwined and thighs touching as the driver swerves in and out of traffic, making our bodies slide on the slick faux leather seat. I grasp the door as he takes a sharp turn, and I flinch and gasp when I think a boy on a bike is going to cross our path. Thankfully, the boy stops inches before we plow him over.

Andres chuckles at my reactions, finding obvious joy in my animated facial expressions. I can't get over the driving here. I am sure it is comparable to the driving in any big city, but the speed and frantic recklessness of it sends my anxiety meter to full alert.

Andres leans in and kisses me gently on my neck. He works his way to my ear and pulls gently on the lobe. My eyes close automatically as I take in the pleasure of his smooth lips. My accelerated pulse begins to work its way through my body. His touch, relatively innocent in nature, creates a reaction in my body that I have never experienced before him. I feel a raw, needy, intense longing. Pure desire courses through my entire being. My skin tingles, and my blood is pumping hard. Shivers cause me to quiver though I am the opposite of chilly. There is an intense throbbing, a painful pleasure, where I want him the most.

My breathing is more audible, and I struggle to maintain my composure as I pull my head to the side, breaking his contact with my neck. I squeeze his hand and motion to the driver as I give him my best let's-not-cause-a-scene-in-the-back-of-the-cab face. He flashes me his all-too-sexy smile. Despite the short time I have known him, it already has the power to completely disarm me. He clutches my hand firmly in his and places a sweet kiss on my shoulder before leaning his head back against the seat.

The cab drops us off at his house. Andres leads me straight upstairs to his bedroom. Before the door has closed behind us, his lips are on mine, and his hands are forcefully running through my hair, pulling me closer. I'm powerless to his tongue's delicious assault. Without taking his lips off mine, he picks me up, and my legs wrap around him. He tenderly places me on his bed. My hands begin to unbutton his shirt, and I explore every inch of his delectable hard chest. He pulls off my dress and stops to survey my body.

His steamy blue stare darkens as he scans from my face to my toes with a carnal surveillance. His chest expands vigorously, his breaths mirroring my own. He leans down and gives me a deep kiss on the mouth before he begins planting succulent kisses down my neck.

He whispers, "You"—kiss—"are"—kiss—"so"—kiss—"beautiful."

He makes his way down to my breasts and unfastens my bra from behind. He carefully slides the straps off my arms. He kisses and sucks and pulls at my nipples, and I think I'm going to detonate from the sensations.

He continues south as his lips cherish my belly and move down my legs. He stops when he gets to my feet, and without taking his eyes off mine, he slides off each shoe, one at a time, and delicately kisses my toes. He then reaches for my underwear and pulls it off. He stands, and in one motion, he unbuttons his jeans and drops them and his boxers to the floor. My eyes widen as I stare at this man standing before me. He's a man who is apparently destined to model for Calvin Klein.

*Oh. My. God. This is really happening.* I am completely elated.

Andres leans over me and inserts first one and then another finger into me, making me groan.

"Oh, baby, you're so wet. Damn, Liv." He leans his forehead against my belly as his fingers work inside me.

Pulling his hand out, he reaches over to his side table and produces a foil packet. Making his intent clear, his face searches mine for my response. I nod and give him a subtle smile.

*Oh my God. Yes. Yes, please.*

He slides the condom onto his incredible length, and I inhale deeply as he slides into me. The sensation is momentarily painful.

"Fuck, Liv. You are so tight. You feel amazing." Andres's voice is strained, almost primal.

All of the initial pain fades away, making way for the most incredible sense of fullness, pleasure.

*Why did I wait over three years to do this again? I don't remember it feeling like this before, or I probably* wouldn't have held out all that time. I close my eyes, relishing every sensation running through my body. Complete warmth and uninhibited enjoyment course through every crevice of my being. It's simply indescribable.

He laces his fingers through mine, holding our hands out to the sides of my head.

Through his audible breaths, he says, "Open your eyes, Liv. Look at me."

When I do so, I am caught in his intense stare. Our gazes are locked with one another for a minute, but the intensity of my pleasure is so overwhelming that I have to close my eyes again.

"Please keep them open. I want to see you," he whispers into my ear before bending to gently bite and suck my earlobe.

With our hands entwined together, our eyes again lock in a passionate stare. He continues to work in and out of me in a delicious cadence. Seeing all his emotions written on his face as our bodies connect is a powerful sensation, and it intensifies my feelings. It's almost too much, and I want to close my eyes, but I don't. I watch him fix his midnight-blues on me as he continues the tantalizing movements.

His skin is starting to glisten, and I desperately want to lick every inch of his it. His mouth is open slightly as he inhales and exhales deeply. His lips are so full and inviting. The sight of him moving above me is the most powerful turn-on.

I can feel the buildup rising in my body. I throw my head back, closing my eyes, as my body convulses and shakes in the most magnificent orgasm I've ever experienced. My body trembles as Andres pushes quickly into me two more times, and I can feel his release as he buries his face in my neck, grunting through clenched teeth.

"God, Livi."

His body falls on mine. With our fingers still entwined, we lie there, listening to the sounds of our ragged, heavy breaths.

Andres lets go of my hands and leans on his side, resting on his elbow. He peers at me quizzically for a moment and then kisses me on the forehead. After he disposes of the condom, he lies on his side next to me. He wraps his arms around my waist and nuzzles soft kisses into my hair.

"You are so incredible, Livi. What have you done to me?" He buries his nose into the side of my neck under my ear.

"You are pretty freaking astonishing, too, Andres. God, I've been waiting all week for that," I say matter-of-factly.

He laughs. "Really?"

"Yes, really. I've wanted that since the first time I saw you in the club on my first night here. You got me worked up every time I saw you this week, and you always left me wanting you. That's really not nice, you know," I say in a mocked angry tone. "You're lucky you put out tonight. I don't think I could have waited any longer."

Andres laughs loudly and gives me his sexy grin, sending shivers through my body.

"I'm sorry, baby. Let me make it up to you." He leans in and kisses my neck.

My senses are on fire once more. "Yes, please do," I manage to whisper.

He apologizes to me two more mind-shattering times.

The sky is dark, and the twinkling lights from the city are visible over the rooftop patio outside Andres's room. My body is humming, completely sated. We are silent as I lie on Andres's firm chest, his arm wrapped around me. I fall asleep to the sound of his heartbeat mixing with the content rhythm of my own.

It takes me a second to realize where I am when I awake. The sun is shining through the window. Andres is still sleeping with his arm and leg wrapped around me. His head is leaning on my shoulder. *Dear Lord, he is gorgeous.* He is like a Greek god in sleep, his body tan and firm, his face peaceful and so breathtaking. *How did I get this lucky?*

I sit up and reach for my phone to see it's ten in the morning. "Crap!"

Andres is now peering at me with a questioning grin. "You okay?" he asks, his eyes sleepy.

"It is ten o'clock! Nadia is probably worried. I never called to tell her that I wasn't coming back last night."

He smiles, obviously amused. "I think she is fine. She knows you are with me. Stop worrying and come back here." He pulls lightly on my arm.

I hold up a finger, indicating that I need a second. I see missed texts from Nolan and Nadia.

*2:00 p.m.*

*Nolan: How are you? You okay?*

*4:35 p.m.*

*Nolan: Worried about you. Do you want me to come over?*

*8:00 p.m.*

*Nolan: What are your plans for the night? Do you want to do something?*

*10:02 p.m.*

*Nolan: Respond, Livi. Love ya.*

*9:30 p.m.*

*Nadia: Hey, are you guys coming back?*

*11:00 p.m.*

*Nadia: We are at La Esquina if you want to join us.*

*Crap.* I can't believe I didn't check my phone yesterday. Nolan must be worried, considering I left his house a heartbroken mess. *What a change a day makes.*

I text Nolan back first.

*Me: I didn't check my phone yesterday. Sorry I worried you! I am great. Let me see what the plan is today, and I will get back to you. Muah!*

I text Nadia back.

*Me: Hey, I'm sorry. I stayed with Andres. I didn't check my phone.*

*Nadia: No worries. Good night? ;-)*

*Me: Yes…great night!*

*Nadia: I want details later! See you soon.*

Andres is watching me with an adorable grin on his face. He raises an eyebrow. "Everything okay?"

"Yes."

"Perfect. Do you want to go out and get some breakfast?" He kisses me deeply on the mouth. "Shower first?"

My heart is already racing, and I'm again feeling drunk with longing. I manage to nod, and he grabs my hand, leading me to the shower.

The hot water sprays across my back as he kisses me. He lathers up some soap and massages my skin. His touch feels so good, and I close my eyes to really experience every moment. His hand reaches between my thighs, and my breath leaves me as he inserts his finger into me. He begins a tantalizing rhythm, and I splay my hand against the shower wall to steady my quivering body. He kneels in front of me and pulls one of my legs over his shoulder. Without slowing his pulsating finger, his tongue begins a cadence of its own, flicking against the spot that needs it the most. I whimper from the sweet, torturous sensations as I throw my head back, facing the shower ceiling, while I moan loudly.

"Omigod, omigod, Andres, omigod," I chant as I become acutely aware of every movement he makes.

His finger rubs against the perfect spot within, sending a longing urge to my belly. My inner walls begin to pulse around his finger as my hips involuntary rock to counter the motion of his mouth. I am so close, and I concentrate on his tongue hitting the perfect spot over and over. I pull one of my hands off the shower wall and push his head toward my core. I'm hungry for this release to wreck my body. I am panting now as small quakes ripple through me.

"Omigod. Omigod. Omigod. Don't stop. Don't stop, Andres," I beg in desperation.

The fire building at my core erupts and sends a deep, raw, mind-blowing burn through my body, out to my fingertips, down to my toes, up to my scalp, and everywhere in between, scalding me with fierce pleasure. At the peak of my sensation, my hand on his head grips his hair and pushes his head forcefully against me. I cry out and double over as waves of vibrations shake my body. I gasp as the currents lessen and then cease.

I moan as Andres slowly removes his mouth and finger. I fall to my knees, and my lips attach to his. Our tongues tangled, I kiss him hard as the water falls around us, streaming down my face and over our lips, as I consume him.

I break our kiss. "Let me wash you."

I stand with Andres and lather my hands with soap. My fingers slide over his wet body, and I marvel at his beautiful skin. His body is nothing short of perfection, and I am in awe that I'm here with this exquisite man. While running my hands over his tight body, I think that I am the luckiest girl in the world. I kneel and massage his legs, working my way from his calves to his thighs.

I hear him inhale sharply when I grab his length, working my hands slickly from the tip to the base, over and over again.

"Oh, Livi," he moans, rocking his hips slightly into my hand.

Holding him at the base, I cover him with my mouth, working my tongue in circles around his tip. I begin a delicious rhythm, my mouth and hand greedily taking him in. I remove my hand and grab the backs of his thighs, pushing him as far into my throat as I can take. I suck hard, my cheeks burning, as I work my tongue around him.

"I'm going to come, Liv," Andres says through clenched teeth.

I increase my pace, and my heart races when he empties into my throat. I take in every last drop before licking from base to tip, sliding my lips from him. *Best shower ever.*

After our shower, we catch a cab since Andres left his bike at my house the day prior when he'd met up with the guys to go to the pool. Staring out the window as the houses pass by, I think of the worry that came across in Nolan's text, and I can't help but question the last twenty-four hours.

*It can't be normal for someone to have emotions so far apart on the spectrum in a matter of a day, can it? Did I forgive him too easily? Am I not valuing myself enough? Am I jumping in headfirst, not knowing how deep the water is?*

It seems reckless, and I am anything but. Andres is only the second person that I have ever had sex with, yet I jumped in his bed like I was a seasoned pro. Truthfully, I was almost begging for it. *This isn't me. Or is it?*

Sometimes, I don't even know who I am. I am a junior in college. *Is there an etiquette handbook that I am unaware of that consists of rules and timeframes of appropriate behavior for someone my age? How long does one lust after someone before giving in to temptation? Who decides what is right and wrong? Who is there to judge anyway? And do I care what that judge thinks?*

All I know is that I need Andres like a flower needs sun. His heat radiates into every pore of my body and fills me up with life. It's unlike anything that I have ever felt. I know this can't be love. It's too soon. It might be infatuation or deep-seated lust. Regardless, it is all-consuming, and I can't get enough of it.

I have never done drugs, but I imagine the need is similar. The powerful craving to be near him, touch him, and feel him is on my brain every second that I am not with him. That need was there prior to feeling his touch, before I dreamed that this could be a reality. But now…now that I *know* what it is like to have his hands and lips on me and know what it is like to have him moving inside me, it's so perfect. It's everything.

Screw the voice in my head that is judging me and telling me I am wrong for throwing caution aside so that I can have a taste of him, warning me that he can and probably will break me. I don't care. I was never whole to begin with. For the first time, I feel the pieces coming back together with Andres. He did it without knowing.

I might very well fall hard and shatter somewhere in the near future, but right now, I feel damn good. I'm not giving that up. I wouldn't be able to if I tried. That cautioning voice can think I am weak or stupid all it wants, but as long as Andres wants me, I will be here because feeling, really *feeling*, is so much better than not.

# chapter 12

Hand in hand with Andres, we walk into the house. Carlos is on the couch, watching TV, and he snickers when he sees us. I'm wearing one of Andres's T-shirts and baggy sweats with my sundress from yesterday in my free hand.

"Shut up," Andres says to Carlos. Then, Andres leans in and kisses me. "I'll wait out here."

Once in my room, I hear a knock before I even have time to pick out an outfit. Nadia opens the door and walks in before I can get a word out. I close the door behind her.

Turning to me and eyeing my baggy sweats, she says, "Hey, nice outfit. Details, please!" She giggles.

I give Nadia a rundown of the evening, supplying only vague details.

She smiles at me. "He really likes you, Liv."

"Really?"

"Yes, really. I've never seen him like this with a girl. He definitely isn't one to hang out with a girl the day after he hooks up with her. Believe me, he likes you."

I can hardly contain my happiness. "Good, because I really like him, too—a lot."

"I think you're good for him, Liv."

"I hope so." I can't help the smile that spreads across my face.

It's a beautiful day, and I put on a knee-length halter sundress, only to take it off when I remember I'll be on a motorcycle. Instead, I opt for jean shorts and a fitted V-neck T-shirt. I wear my hair in a ponytail. I text Nolan before heading out to the living room.

*Me: Hey! Nadia says we're going out tonight. You in? ;-) xo*

*Nolan: Will definitely see you tonight. xoxo*

I'm immediately happy and then uncomfortable about Nolan going out with us tonight. I'm confused. I know Nolan will be glad for me when he finds out that everything with Andres has been smoothed over. Nolan wants me to be happy, and I've always been supportive of his relationship with Abby. I don't know why I feel bad, but I do. It must be guilt that is coursing through me because Nolan's summer of fun with his best friend has been interrupted by her new Spanish love. I'll make it up to him when we get back to the States. We'll have lots of best-friend time.

But I don't want to think about going back. The thought is beyond depressing. The notion of being without Andres leaves me empty. I quickly brush it away. I still have the whole summer with him. I make a promise to myself not to think about leaving Andres. I need to be happy that I'm here with him now.

Andres and I are walking, hand in hand, through the city. We've eaten, and I've shopped lots. He is as sweet as can be, feigning interest as I show him one ridiculous souvenir after another.

Shopped out, he leads us to a park. We sit in the shade of a tall tree on freshly cut grass. I sit between his legs and lay my head on his chest while his arms secure around my waist. We chat idly, and it doesn't go unnoticed that most of the conversation is about me. Andres is a master at changing the subject when the conversation starts heading toward him.

"Why don't you like talking about yourself?" I ask.

"I guess there isn't much to tell." His arms tighten around me as he kisses the back of my head, nuzzling his nose in my hair. "You always smell so good. Just smelling you turns me on."

"It's your shampoo you are smelling. Remember this morning?"

"How could I forget?" he says as he snuggles into my neck, kissing below my ear. "It's not the soap though. You always smell like this—so sweet but so spicy. It is hard to keep my mouth off of you."

Soft lips trail down my neck, causing an epidemic of goose bumps to cover my skin.

"How are you feeling about everything?" I am so curious to know how he is processing our situation. "Like, with us?"

He thinks for a moment. "Good. This is new to me. I like it though…with you. I feel happy when we are together. You make me question everything."

"Question what?"

"Just my thoughts on things. It is a good thing."

I am glad that he is opening up a little but not that he's still so closed off. I wish he would trust me more. I get the sense that he is hiding a lot of sadness under his carefree demeanor, and every instinct I have wants to fix him. It is still all so new, but I hope, in time, he'll trust me enough to let me in.

Andres leaves me at my house, so I can get ready for the evening. I type a few quick texts to my parents and Cara, having received messages from them while I was out with Andres.

Nolan arrives first, giving us some time to hang out. He sits on my bed, and we chat as I get ready. I recap what happened at the country club and how I decided to move forward with the relationship with Andres.

Nolan listens attentively, and he is slow to respond. "So, you trust him? Doesn't he have a reputation for being a player?"

Applying my mascara, I answer, "Yeah, apparently, but I think what he feels about me is different."

"And you think he is being truthful about that?"

"Yeah. His actions seem sincere. When I am with him, I feel that he is really into me."

Nolan sighs, leaning his back against the wall. "I sure hope so. I don't want to see you get hurt."

"I know, and I love you for that. This is the first time I have really been interested in a guy in forever, you know? I want to see where it goes."

"Okay. You know I support you—always. I just worry. It killed me to see you so broken on Friday."

"I know, and maybe that is the inevitable end, but I need to see where all this goes. The purpose of coming here was to get out of my comfort zone and experience life. Maybe this is part of it?"

"I thought the reason for coming here was to spend a glorious summer with your amazing best friend?" The sides of his lips curl up, making his eyes even smile.

I chuckle. "Of course that was my number one reason."

Being with Nolan, idly talking, while I pretty myself up for the evening is so comfortable and normal. It's a normalcy that I take pleasure in after my whirlwind first week here in Seville.

*Has it only been a week?* The thought boggles my mind. The events of the past week surprise even me. Perhaps the spiciness of the lifestyle of this country makes everything happen in turbo time. Possibly, the fact that I have limited time here allows my brain to wrap around the quick pace of events. One thing is for certain—the excitement inside of me, knowing that I am going to see Andres again soon, is threatening to explode out into a bursting volcano of giddiness.

Upon arrival at another impressive club, I wonder how many kick-ass clubs are in this city. The music is loud, and we weave our way through the crowd to our table. The usual people are in attendance—Nadia, Carlos, Hugo, Andres, Julio, Nolan, and the random extra new friends who always seem to be out with us. Nolan greets everyone by name, and they all seem genuinely excited to see him. He has obviously had time to get to know them this past week while I've been in my Andres bubble.

Nadia, her friend Marcela, and I are dancing when some familiar hands grab mine and spin me around. I'm met with Nolan's stunning smile.

"Having fun?" he asks.

"Yes, lots! You?"

"Always."

His hands grab my hips, and I steady myself, holding his biceps, as I move with him to the music. He starts dramatically singing to the music, making exaggerated face movements and all, and I throw my head back in laughter.

A fraction of a minute into Nolan's cheesy performance, Andres approaches, putting his hand possessively around my waist.

He says to Nolan, "Mind if I dance with my girl?"

*My girl? Did he call me his girl?* The thought sends a quiver through my body.

"Uh…sure." Nolan gives me a weak smile and lets go. He walks over to dance with Nadia and Marcela.

I hear Marcela squeal and smile, and I know Nolan is working his effortless charm. As I drape my arms around Andres's neck, I peer over his shoulder to see Nolan dancing with Marcela. My stare meets Nolan's. His gaze is locked right on me, and for a brief moment, I see something in his eyes, an emotion that unsettles me. It's hurt or anger perhaps. But then, he breaks our gaze and whispers something to Marcela, sending her into a fit of giggles. I watch him dance with her for a while, but he doesn't meet my stare again.

I lean my head into Andres's chest and inhale. He smells so scrumptious. I could strip him naked and worship his body with my mouth right here on the dance floor. He takes a hand and grabs my chin, tilting my mouth up to meet his. My hands make their way up his hard chest to his face, and I run my fingers through his soft hair as our kiss deepens. His tongue tenderly explores my mouth, and everything south of my waist tightens with desire.

Andres and I are connected for the rest of the night. The hours seem like minutes as we dance, and it feels like we're the only two people in the world. My lips are raw from endless kisses. I'm intoxicated with all that is Andres, and I don't think I've ever been happier in my life.

# chapter 13

I'm on my bed, propped on my elbows, reading the assigned text for one of my classes. Andres is lying on his side next to me, rubbing my back. His touch makes me feel cherished. I'm happy, thinking about our great day yesterday. We spent the entire day walking through the streets of Seville—talking, laughing, and kissing. I'm usually not a fan of PDA, but with Andres, I couldn't care less. When we're together, nothing else seems to matter.

Andres tucks a stray strand of hair behind my ear. "What's that smile for?" he asks.

Turning my head, I peer into his captivating blue eyes. "I was thinking about what an awesome day we had yesterday." I grin weakly, not wanting to sound too mushy. He's still a bit of a mystery to me, and I definitely don't want to scare him away with overdone affection.

"It was awesome, but every day with you has been great," he says.

I blush.

Closing my book, I face him. "I must say that I love having my own personal chauffeur waiting for me every day when I get out of class." I give him a quick kiss. "You know you don't have to though, right? I can get home on my own and meet up with you later. I don't want you to get sick of me."

"I want to, Livi," he says. "Seeing you light up when you notice me is the best part of my day." He leans in and places gentle kisses on my mouth.

"Well, I'm sure there must be other things you want to do with your day. I feel guilty monopolizing your every waking moment," I say sarcastically.

He kisses my forehead. "No, actually, there isn't anything else I would rather do with my days than spend them with you, my beautiful Olivia."

My heart sings.

"The guys are coming over in a few. We haven't gotten a lot of practice time in," he says.

"Oh, cool."

"Yeah, there is a new song that still has some tweaks to iron out before we play it live."

"When are you practicing?"

The look he gives me sets my insides on fire.

"We have time." He leans into me so that I'm now on my back.

He brings his mouth down to mine. His kisses start off gentle, but they quickly become insistent, full of longing. I run my fingers through his hair and pull him as close to me as I can. He groans in my mouth. He has one hand behind my head, pushing me into him with vigor that's equal to my own. His other hand is rubbing my ribs under my shirt. He inches under my bra and pulls it down, freeing my breasts. He's taking turns caressing, pulling, and twisting my nipples, and I feel a painfully sweet sensation. My hands leave his hair and make their way down his firm back.

I push under his shirt and scratch his back, strong enough to sting but not hurt. Being with him brings out a side of me that I never knew existed, but I like it. He groans and swings his leg around me so he is on top. Sitting up he reaches down and pulls off my shirt and bra in one motion. Then, he trails kisses on my earlobe, down my neck, across my collarbone, and to my breasts.

He explores each of my breasts with his expert mouth and then continues to kiss and suck down my stomach until he reaches my jeans. He quickly unbuttons them, and I lift my hips, so he can pull them off, taking my panties as well. He continues his sweet exploration of my body with his lips, moving down my legs and coming back up again. He stops when he reaches my thighs. Spreading my legs apart, he pushes one and then two fingers into me, and my hips jerk momentarily off the bed. I am building as he finds my sweet spot with his tongue, and he relentlessly flicks while continuing to circle his two fingers inside me. The warmth takes over my body, and I grab the pillow, holding it to my face, as I try to block some of my screams while I fall apart around him.

He continues to gently stroke and suck until I stop shaking. He withdraws his fingers and places kisses on my body as he works his way up to my mouth. Eyes closed, I'm still reeling from my orgasm when his tongue enters my mouth, beginning another sweet assault on my senses. I taste myself on him, and although I thought I would be repelled, it actually has the opposite effect, making me desperately want him.

He stops kissing me and whispers, "Are you on birth control, Livi?"

"Yes," I whisper, having been on the pill since high school.

"I really want to feel you. I've never done this without a condom, and I really want to, but I won't if you don't want me to." He kisses my neck.

"It's okay. Yes. Please," I plead.

He removes his pants and tosses them to the floor. When he straddles me again, he slides into me slowly.

"Ah," I gasp. I relish the feeling of us together, skin on skin. The thought alone is so alluring.

He groans against my throat. "You feel so good, baby."

He starts to pick up the pace, and I drag my hands down his back and grab his ass, trying to push him farther into me.

"Fuck, Liv." He groans and starts pounding into me with a feverish pace.

Us together without a barrier is magical and insanely tantalizing. I can feel myself building again, and I throw my head back, shouting his name, as my body lets go. I feel his warm breath against my neck when he repeats my name over and over, as he comes inside me.

We lie there for a moment, breathing deeply. My arms are wrapped around him, hugging him tightly to me. His back is heated, firm, and sweaty. He's so sexy.

He rolls over. We're side-by-side, naked, with our hands firmly entwined. I listen to our breathing, feeling completely happy and sated.

He squeezes my hand. "That was incredible."

"Definitely. Although, I don't know if we should have done that here. What if someone heard us?"

"No worries. I don't think anyone is here, and if they are, I don't really care," he says, grinning. "I want to do that every day after our study sessions."

I laugh. "Our study sessions, huh? I don't see you doing any studying."

"I'm studying you, of course," he says.

"Well, that isn't very intellectually stimulating."

"Olivia, you have no idea how fascinating you are to me. You're a work of art, and I will never tire of studying you—ever."

The way he says *ever* makes a blossom of hope open up deep inside me.

"I'm going to go set up the sound equipment." He kisses me on the forehead. "You could take a nap?"

"Hmm…" I say sleepily, my muscles lazy from the afterglow of the preceding event. "A nap sounds divine."

Andres chuckles. "See you, gorgeous."

I throw my clothes back on before wiggling into my bed, finding the most comfortable spot. I need to rejuvenate. This schedule of staying out late, getting up early, and then hanging with Andres all day is exhausting.

Nadia comes into my room without knocking before I have a chance to fall asleep.

"So, how was your afternoon?" she asks.

I raise my attention up to her, and I can tell that she's trying her hardest not to smile.

I sit up and cover my face with both hands. "You heard us?" I ask sheepishly, peering at her through my fingers covering my face.

"Are you kidding, Livi? I'm sure the neighbors heard you two in here."

I'm mortified. I look awkwardly at her and shrug, biting my lip, not knowing what to say. "Oh my God, I'm so embarrassed."

She fans her hand in the air, blowing off my shame. "Oh, don't be. I mean, he is basically my brother, so that part is gross." She forces out a laugh. "But I'm happy that he seems so happy. It's been so long since I've seen him like this—excited about life. Before, he was on autopilot, just going through the motions for a while." Nadia shrugs. "I've heard many times that he's great in bed, but I've never been so close to the action." She sits down on the other bed. "I guess the rumors are true."

I stop smiling, and I know she didn't mean to, but her comments really bother me. "What does that mean?"

"Liv, I told you before, or maybe I kind of hinted to the fact, that he's slept with a lot of girls, and well…girls talk."

"Yeah, I know. It kind of makes me sick, thinking about it." I hold my stomach as it is in knots while I think about Andres being with lots of other women. "How many girlfriends has he had?"

Nadia raises her eyebrows, and I can tell she's gaging her response.

"Well, I wouldn't necessarily call them girlfriends. To be honest, I don't think he's ever had a girlfriend. What would I call them?" She pauses a moment. "Maybe you would call them fuck-buddies, one-night stands, or um…short as in one- or two-night flings?"

I let out an exasperated sigh. "That makes it so much better." I fall back on the bed, raising my arm over my face.

Nadia continues, "Liv, try not to think about all that. He didn't love those girls. Hell, he probably didn't even like them. I think they were void-fillers for him." Her voice is thoughtful. "He hasn't been truly happy since his mom died. I think he's afraid to get too close to anyone or to let anyone in."

I process everything Nadia is saying. Andres is irresistible, so of course, he has girls throwing themselves at him. He's a guy. *Can I blame him for taking advantage of his good fortune?* Plus, that was before me. I shouldn't let it bother me. I can't judge him on his past.

Then, I realize that the source of my annoyance with this conversation is fear. *Why me? Am I different than those girls? Is he going to get bored with me and move on?* Emotionally, I'm already in so deep that it scares me.

I sit up. "Why me?"

Nadia peers at me with kind but questioning eyes, and I can tell she doesn't understand my question.

I continue, "I don't understand. I don't feel like I'm a quick fling or a fuck-buddy when I'm with him. It feels real. I don't want to be like the other girls. Do you think I'm different?"

"Yes, Livi! Of course you're different," she says with complete confidence. "He isn't the same with you. He seems happy."

"But why me? Why is he better with me?"

"I don't know, but he obviously likes you a lot. You must be doing something right." She winks at me, and then she comes over and grabs my hand. "Don't let this worry you. Just go with it. You two seem so happy together. Don't question everything or worry about things you can't control, like his past. Simply be happy, and see where it takes you."

My urge for a nap evaporates when I hear the first strum of the guitar. My face lights up.

"Do you want to go watch them practice?" Nadia asks.

*Do I ever.* "Yes!"

I sit on the end of the couch with my knees pulled up to my chest. I lay my head on my knees as I watch the guys practice. They are really very talented but none more so than Andres. He is a double threat with his ability to play guitar and sing. His voice is smooth as silk and raspy as sin, and it has the power to melt my soul. It's truly enchanting and so freaking sexy. Their music has a rock edge with an alternative and mainstream sound. It is very Matchbox Twenty meets One Republic in Spanish.

I lean back into the comfy couch, allowing my head to sink into the cushion, as I feel the vibrations of the music.

Full lips are on mine.

"Wake up, baby."

Opening my eyes, I see Andres leaning over me.

I stretch my arms above my head. "Hey." I yawn, still sleepy from my nap.

Andres chuckles and kisses me on the forehead. "Are you hungry?"

The house smells of freshly made cuisine. Maria must have been here.

After a delicious chicken and rice dish, Andres leaves, promising to return soon to pick me up. He has to go home to get ready for the evening.

Following Andres's departure, Nadia bounces over to me with excitement. "Now, get all sexified because we're going out, and you are in for a special treat tonight!"

I laugh at her contagious exuberance. "What does that mean?"

She holds her hands together, steepling them in front of her face, as she grins widely. "The guys are going to play tonight! Eeek! So fun! You're going to love watching them. They are so great on stage!"

"Oh my God! That is awesome. What should I wear?"

"Anything you want. Make sure you exude hotness though. It'll give Andres something to think about when he's up there."

I am giddy as I get ready. I desperately want to text Cara, so I can tell her about my night out and get her opinion on the look I should go for, but

I know she is at work. I channel my inner-Cara as I pick my outfit. *What would Cara wear? Ha. She'd love that.* I can't wait until she is here to share this experience with me.

I can't even imagine the reaction my body will have when I watch the guys on stage. Seeing them play in the living room is overwhelming. I envision Andres on stage, singing, with his voice amplified by the microphone and his body showcased by the lighting. *Yum.* Yeah, I'm in over my head, way deep. I'm drowning in an overpowering hunger for this man, and I don't want a life vest.

I opt to wear black shorts—emphasis on *short*—a fitted silver corset top, and black heels. I apply a little more eye shadow than normal, giving my eyes a dark, smoky appearance. Instead of my girlie light pink lip gloss, I decide to wear a darker shade, which makes my lips appear quite full. I straighten my hair and let it fall, silky and sleek, down my back.

I walk out to the living room when Andres and Carlos come through the door. They are talking and laughing, and then Andres stops mid-sentence when he sees me. His eyes widen, followed by a devilish grin. He walks over, cups my face, and gives me a quick kiss.

"Damn, Livi, you are smokin' hot. How am I supposed to concentrate when I know you look like this?" His stare darkens with desire as he scans my entire body. "Your legs are amazing. God, you are so beautiful." He pulls me into a long kiss.

A cough echoes from behind Andres.

Carlos says, "Jesus, you two, get a fucking room. Come on, man, we have to go."

Andres releases his mouth away from mine, and I stand with my eyes closed for a second, still tasting him. He then grabs my hand and kisses it softly, and we head for the door.

Carlos yells upstairs, "Nadia, we're leaving your ass if you're not down here in ten seconds!"

I hear Nadia before I see her.

"Shut up, Carlos. I'm coming! What crawled up your ass and died?" Nadia walks down the stairs. She looks incredible in a short black dress and heels.

The boys are playing at Demo. I watch them set up their equipment. I can't wait to see them perform. I want to laugh every time I hear their band name. Apparently, they officially formed their band shortly after Andres's mother died. He didn't have any real investment in the name of their band at that time, and the others couldn't agree on one. So, they referred to their band as such until the name stuck somewhere along the line.

Nadia and I are sitting at a table close to the stage.

I take a sip of my water. "Why aren't you dating anyone?" I ask.

"I don't know. I've dated people in the past. There's no one interesting right now."

"When was the last time you were in a serious relationship?"

She laughs. "Well, since you asked…believe it or not, I got out of a year-long relationship with Hugo a few months ago."

"Hugo? Really?" I'm surprised because they seem so comfortable together now. "I can see why you dated him. He's totally adorable and a complete charmer."

She rolls her eyes. "Yeah, that was the problem. He was as bad as Andres, always having girls around him, constantly flirting. He says he was faithful to me, but I really don't believe him. I couldn't go through that emotional roller coaster anymore. We started as friends, and we are able to be friends now, so that's good."

I ignore her comment about Andres. "Yeah, it is. It would be totally awkward if it were weird between you two since the guys are always together." I catch Andres looking my way.

His grin melts me, and my lips curve up, returning his appreciation.

Nadia smirks at me. "Gosh, girl, you've got it bad. You two are like lovesick puppies. It is sickeningly sweet."

"I know. I am pretty pathetic, aren't I?" I laugh.

"So, how about you?" she asks. "When was your last big relationship?"

I turn away from Andres. "Actually, I haven't been in a real relationship since high school. I've dated guys here and there but never for very long. Most of the time, I hang with Cara and Nolan."

"There's never been anything serious between you and Nolan?" she asks.

"No. Andres keeps asking the same thing, but no, I swear, we've always been just friends."

"I might not be spot-on at reading people, but the way that he is with you, it seems like there's more there."

I chuckle. "No, there isn't. Nolan is a constant flirt. He's like that with every girl."

"Okay…if you say so."

The drums start, followed by the guitars, and my heart is beating out of my chest in anticipation for Andres to start singing. He leans into the microphone, and the sound of his voice fills the bar. I am in awe. His voice is clear, sexy, hauntingly beautiful, and simply astounding. I grin like a giddy schoolgirl as I watch him sing.

The small dance floor in front of the stage quickly fills with bodies, and I notice that most of them are female, scantily dressed in clothing that barely covers the parts of their bodies that really shouldn't be flashed in public. My anger and jealousy rise as I wonder how many of them Andres has slept with. *Do I even want to know?* Sighing, I try to push the thought away and enjoy the music.

Julio is playing the drums. Hugo and Carlos are playing guitars, and Andres is singing. They play a lot of classic rock covers and some of their own stuff. They're incredible at both. I sing along to the popular cover songs with lyrics and rhythms that are familiar and comforting, but the songs sound new as if I am listening to them for the first time through Andres's voice. Each of their original songs draws me in as well. I can imagine hearing them on the radio since their songs have catchy beats and melodies. They have pure Top 100 sex appeal with an edge.

With my arm extended, leaning into Nadia, I take some selfies of us with my cell phone. I take a thirty-second clip of Andres singing and send it along with the pictures of Nadia and me to Cara. She works the late dinner shift at the restaurant on Tuesday evenings, so I know she must be getting ready for work about now.

Her response comes a minute later.

*Cara: Holy fuck, Liv! You look gorgeous. \*Swoon\* I can't believe you are dating a hot rock god! Totally jealous! Getting ready to go prepare some ranch cups and prep some salads. Want to trade?*

*Me: You will be here soon enough! Miss you! You do make the best ranch!*

*Cara: LOL. Can't wait for this week to be over! Love you!*

*Me: I can't wait until Friday either! Talk to you later. xo*

Nadia pulls me onto the dance floor. After a couple of songs, unfamiliar hands wrap around my hips. Turning, I see a cute brunet guy smiling at me. I greet him politely and tell him that I can't dance with him. As he protests, I notice Andres's attention is locked on us, and he seems livid. I regard him reassuringly and continue to explain to the zealous guy that I'm not interested. Eventually, he leaves me, and I can see Andres relax. His eyes return to their normal size, and his body loosens up. I can physically see the tension leaving his body.

*Geez, lighten up, hot stuff.*

I blow him a kiss, and his lips twist up into a smoldering smirk.

After the set, Andres quickly makes his way off the stage. The female population eagerly molests him as he makes his way through the crowd. Upon reaching me, he wraps his arms tightly around my middle, picking me up, so we're face-to-face. He plunges his tongue into my mouth in an all-consuming kiss. Our kiss is intense, urgent, and unyieldingly desperate.

"Ugh!" he groans. "I need you, Livi—now. Let's go back to my place," he pleads into my ear. He lightly bites my earlobe.

"Andres, I can't. It's a Monday, and it's already late. I have school tomorrow."

He puts me down, and I run my fingers through his hair. He starts nibbling and sucking on my neck. I am wet with desire.

"Please," he says.

The longing in his voice tears at my heart.

"Please, Liv, I need you."

"Okay," I whisper. "But I need to be back home tonight."

"Or you can stay at my place, and I will take you to school tomorrow." He grabs my hand and heads straight for the exit, not waiting for my response.

I twist around and wave to Nadia and the guys. They're chuckling as they wave back. Carlos shakes his head with a knowing smirk plastered on his face before Andres pulls me out the door.

*Let them have the club. I have Andres.*

# chapter 15

Fingers entwined, I walk out into the night air with Andres. We walk for a block to a busier intersection to hail a cab. His hand squeezes hard around mine, and I start to protest when I sense his body stiffening. My attention focuses on his face, and he almost looks pained or scared. Confusion sets in. Andres shows no indication that he recognizes me standing here while I scrutinize his features. His stare is locked on something in the distance, and I attempt to follow it. He is peering across the street toward what seems to be another bar.

I don't see anything out of the ordinary. At first glance, I think he's looking at a rundown storefront until I notice the lit beer signs in the window. It appears to be a smaller dive bar. Nothing seems out of place for an entrance to a hole-in-the-wall bar at one in the morning. There are two women, who appear to be a good ten years older than me, waiting on the curb, presumably trying to catch a cab. A couple is leaning against one of the windows, kissing. I see an older man leaning against a lamppost, seeming to need it to stand. Then, he stumbles back before catching himself by securing his grip on the post. Andres's body involuntarily recoils back, startling me.

"Andres? Andres?" I say his name twice before he seems to remember me standing here with him.

He says a hushed, "Let's go."

Pulling me to the curb, he throws out his arm, hailing a cab immediately. Once inside the vehicle, he slams the door with a little too much gusto, and in a tattered voice, he tells the driver his address. I release my hand from his stone grasp and flex my fingers, getting the blood circulating again. Andres's stare flicks down to my extended fingers, and he throws his head back into the seat as he exhales an audible breath.

"Are you okay?"

"Fine," he answers shortly.

"What happened back there?"

"It's nothing, Olivia."

*Or nothing you want to talk about,* I think. "It was something."

He lets out an exasperated sigh. "Listen, Olivia, I saw someone that I would rather not see. It is nothing for you to be worried about, and honestly, I don't want to talk about it."

I exhale, leaning my head into the back of the seat. "Okay."

We sit in silence, deep in our own thoughts, as we take the ride to his place.

Once there, Andres grasps my hand carefully in his and leads me into his quiet, dark house. We head up to his bedroom, and he closes the door behind him. His mouth is immediately on mine. Impatient, hard kisses devour my mouth. He runs his fingers through my hair and pulls my head back. It's rough enough to feel uncomfortable, but it's not meant to really hurt. He starts kissing, sucking, and biting up and down my neck fervently.

He unsnaps my corset and lets it drop to the floor. He wastes no time as he tugs off his shirt, and then he places one hand on each of my breasts, pulling and twisting my nipples. He cups them in his hands and kneads them while rubbing me between my legs with his knee. Bending down, he sucks on one of my nipples as he unsnaps my shorts. Without releasing my nipple from its sweet torture, he slides out of his jeans and grabs my tummy with both hands, pressing his fingers firmly into my hips. He starts to pull his mouth off my nipple, but before he releases it, he gently bites down while stretching it. I scream in agonized ecstasy. I never knew pain could be so pleasurable. My whole body is tense with desire.

His stare burns into me with an intense, tortured expression. "I need to be inside you now, baby. I need to feel you," he says as he picks me up, holding me by my ass cheeks.

I circle my legs around him as he leans me against the wall. Without hesitation, he slams into me, gloriously filling me to my center. I scream again, letting my head fall against the wall. Our eyes lock as he regards me with a passion that resonates to my core. He takes me with a fiery need that can only be quenched through this forceful, animalistic connection we have.

I groan and concentrate on the exquisite feeling of him driving into me and the sound of our skin slapping together in heated passion. He continues an onslaught of rough, passionate, and urgent thrusts, and before I know it, I am taken by a powerful orgasm.

"God, Andres!" I scream.

He continues to thrust inside me, and we find our releases together. He yells my name through his jagged, raw breaths, and then he slumps into me, pressing me firmly between him and the wall, not releasing his steady hold. His strong arms are wrapped around me, and I lean my face against his chest, panting. I can hear his heart pounding. I kiss his chest and rub my hands up and down his firm shoulders.

Still holding me, he walks over to his bed and lays me down. He lies next to me and runs his fingers through my hair, removing all the strands from my face. "You are so beautiful, Olivia." He leans in and kisses me gently and lovingly.

We curl together, and he runs his hands up and down my back, caressing every inch of my exposed skin. I run my fingers across his lean, tight muscles and up into his hair. I know he's not ready to hear it, so I express my love through gentle, passionate kisses. I want him to feel all the desire I have for him.

We kiss for a long time, and without releasing my lips from his, I swing my leg around him so that I'm straddling him. I guide him into me and slide down, taking in every inch, as I feel him moan into my mouth. With our tongues entangled in a staggering dance, I make love to him with all the passion I have. We find our releases together again. I groan as I fall around him.

I collapse against his chest with my legs wrapped around his sides. His hands caress my skin. We're both breathing heavily. A tear rolls down my cheek as I'm overcome with emotion for this man. Luckily, I'm able to discreetly wipe my tear away before it falls onto his chest. I'm afraid I'll scare him with the depth of my feelings.

I know there's still so much he hasn't shared with me, and I want to give him time. My heart is full with the knowledge that Andres Cruz, the sexiest man I've ever met, has changed my life forever. I don't know exactly what the future holds, but I do know that I will never be the same.

We continue to lie chest-to-chest, still connected to one another, melded into one.

He breaks the silence. "I can't even tell you how angry I was when that guy was trying to dance with you tonight. I guess you'd call that jealousy. It's a new emotion for me."

I prop my elbows on his chest, so I can capture his eyes. "Are you telling me you've never felt jealous before?"

"No, not about a girl. I guess I've never let myself care enough about a girl to feel jealous."

I grin. "Well, I wasn't going to dance with him. I was trying to let him down kindly though, and I have to say, it was kind of hard to focus when you were shooting daggers at us."

"He's lucky he took the hint when he did because I was about to jump off that stage and bash his face in."

I laugh, shaking my head. "That would not have been necessary!" In complete seriousness, I add, "You don't have to worry, Andres. I only want you."

He leans up and gives me a chaste kiss on the lips. "Good, because I only want you, too."

I smile and rest my head on his chest. He locks his arms around my waist and hugs me tightly.

"Livi, now that we're talking about jealousy, I want to talk to you about Nolan."

I glance up at him. *Oh no, not this again.*

"I know you and Nolan have been friends for a long time, and I respect that. I understand that you don't see him any other way." He pauses and takes a deep breath. "But, babe, I see how he looks at you, and I know what emotions reside behind those eyes. I know because I look at you the same way. All I'm asking is that you tone down all the touchy-feely stuff. It makes me uncomfortable when his hands are on you. Can you please do that for me?"

I see the sincerity in his expression. "I'm sorry for making you feel that way. I don't have romantic feelings toward Nolan, and he has never led me to believe that he does either."

I think about Nolan and what Andres is saying. Nolan and I hug a lot, but I do that with everyone. It is who I am. I can let the holding-hands thing go. If I am honest, I wouldn't be too thrilled if Andres held hands with his female best friend, regardless of the friend status. Other than that though, I'm not sure what else Andres wants me to give up. Looking at his lost expression, I can only agree. Whatever is going on in his head doesn't need to be confounded with his perceived insecurities about my friendship with Nolan.

"But, of course, I'll try. I don't want you to worry." I lean in and kiss his beautiful soft lips.

He pulls away and kisses me firmly on the forehead. "Thank you. Now, do you want me to take you back? Or do you want to stay here?"

"You know if I stay here, you are going to have to get up early and take me back for my stuff."

"I don't mind. It will be worth it to have your warm body wrapped around mine all night. I would actually sleep better if you stayed. So, you see, if you are worried about my quality of sleep, then you should stay."

I hug him closer, giggling, "Well, when you put it that way, what choice do I have?"

"Exactly."

"I'll sleep better here with you, too."

And I do.

# chapter 16

The rest of the week goes by in a blur, studying with Nolan and spending most of the afternoons and evenings with Andres.

Friday afternoon, Nolan and I sit outside our classroom before class, discussing our plans for when Abby and Cara come to visit this weekend. We're meeting them at the airport this evening. I'm keeping my hands busy, searching for my ChapStick in my backpack.

I've managed to keep from holding hands or walking arm in arm with Nolan all week by always keeping my hands busy—going through my backpack, flipping through my notes, fiddling with my hair, or fussing with my outfit. I've gotten really good at avoiding contact. Either Nolan knows what I'm doing, or he thinks I've recently developed a severe case of ADD. If he knows, he doesn't address it, and I'm grateful. I should tell him, but apparently, I am a coward because I can't. Avoiding has always been so much easier for me than confronting a situation.

We decide that we're going to take them to our favorite clubs this weekend. We will discuss it with them when they get here, but for the next weekend, Nolan and I think that it will be fun to explore Spain by going away to another city.

I'm so excited to see Cara. I have so much to tell her, and I can't wait for her to meet Andres.

I see Cara immediately as she exits the customs area. My chest tightens with emotion, and I realize how much I have missed her. I half run until I close the gap between us, and I beam at her while I bring her into a huge hug.

"I missed you!"

"You missed me? Seriously? While you are here, having the time of your life? I missed you! I have been stuck at home in a summer vacation without you! I've had to resort to recycling through some of my old Delta Sig standbys."

Cara has a bad habit of turning to some of her ex-boyfriends, who all happen to be a part of the same fraternity, when she is bored or lonely. They all still worship her and drop everything when she calls. It is quite pathetic really. Cara always feels bad when she cuts them loose yet again, and she promises herself that she won't stoop to such measures again. It has been a while since she called one of them to keep her company.

"No, you haven't, Cara!" I throw my head back in laughter.

"Yes. Yes, I have," Cara says with resignation. "So, who do you think misses whom more?"

I give her a reassuring grin. "I'm sorry." I grab her hands and bounce with excitement. "But now, you are here, and we are going to enjoy every second!"

"I really can't wait. My summer has been so dull."

I giggle. "It isn't even that far into summer. Stop being so dramatic."

She waves her hand in a *whatever* motion, and we make our way to baggage claim.

"So, when am I going to meet Mr. Hotness who has your panties all in a wad?"

"Tonight, of course! And he usually just takes them off and drops them without wadding them up." I giggle.

"Ha-ha," Cara enunciates. "Well, I'm glad you are finally getting some. I still can't believe you finally threw out your college V-card. I'm proud of you, Olivia!"

"I wouldn't say I owned a V-card, considering I wasn't a virgin," I say dryly.

"Practically!" Cara snorts. "A few fumbling times in high school with your inexperienced boyfriend hardly counts! Speaking of awful, I had Brandon over a couple of days ago, and it was as horrible as always."

"Not Brandon, Cara!"

Brandon is the most pitiful one of them all. He's always following Cara around, ready to do her bidding. Every time she throws him a bone, it extends his stalking window.

"I know! It has been horrible without you!"

I can't help but snicker. Between the two of us, I am usually the mess. My downer of a best friend is quite amusing.

"But Brandon?"

"I know, I know. Let's drop it, okay? Hey, where is Nolan? Wasn't he supposed to be here, too?"

"Yeah, but Abby's plane was delayed, so he is going to pick her up later and meet us out at the club."

"Okay. So, tell me about the guys I am going to have access to here?" she says with a mischievous smile.

We've grabbed enough luggage to keep Cara well dressed for months, and then we start to head toward the area with awaiting cabs.

"Well, the three guys that I see every day—besides Andres and Nolan, of course—are Carlos, Hugo, and Julio. Carlos is Nadia's twin brother. I live with him, too. He is cute in a lanky sort of way. He is extremely sarcastic and low drama. He says it like it is."

We throw her luggage into the trunk of a cab and slide in the backseat. "Julio is adorable. He is short, so I know you won't be all about him." Cara nods her head in agreement.

"But he is so sweet. He is, like, the kind soul of the group. He has always made me feel so comfortable. Then, there is Hugo. He is very attractive with his sandy-blond hair and deep brown eyes. He is definitely charismatic, but he is quite the player."

"Hmm…" Cara contemplates my descriptions. "I guess we will see. You can't force chemistry, but if I had to wager based on your assessment, I would go with Hugo."

"The player? Why?"

"Oh, sweet Livi. Let me tell you a secret. If someone has the reputation of being a player, it usually means two very important things. Number one, he is hot and desirable. If women flock to him, there must be a reason. Number two, he is fantastic in bed. How could he not be with all that practice?" She notices my expression that I am sure is communicating my confusion to her logic. "Livi, I'm here for two weeks. I don't expect to find the love of my life. I just want to have fun. Why wouldn't I go for the one who is a guaranteed good time?"

"Yeah, I guess."

"Um…wait a minute. Didn't you tell me that Andres was quite the player? Is he not gorgeous and good in bed?"

"Fine. Go with your logic!" I grin, feeling my cheeks flush.

Cara smirks with satisfaction.

Cara and I are getting ready for the evening. We've spent every second since leaving the airport talking about my last two weeks here. Cara has met Nadia, and of course, they seem to get along well. Carlos is out with the guys, and they should all be back shortly.

"I can't believe you come to Spain and fall completely in love in a matter of weeks. That is crazy!" Cara giggles.

"Believe me, I know!" I grin as I pack my money, lipstick, and ID into my purse. "I can't explain it. I know it sounds crazy, but I love him, Cara. I know I do. I mean, it might be the fact that he's hotter than all hell. I am drinking mojitos like they're a necessary food group, which makes my inhibition disappear when I'm around him. But it happened fast." I sigh happily. "He is so much more than just a pretty face though. He is a really great person, and I don't even think he knows it. He acts like he isn't worthy of happiness, and I don't understand it. Despite all his attributes, what I love about him most is the way he makes me feel. I am so happy when we are together, and I feel whole, loved. I can't describe it. I can't wait for you to meet him."

Cara listens to me with a warm expression. "I can't wait to meet him either. Maybe it's because you're in a romantic country." She gives me a thoughtful glance.

"Yeah, it must be the geography." I laugh. "I don't know. He could live in a box in the slums of Detroit, and I think I'd still wet my panties over him. He's so freaking awesome. Just wait." I can't wipe the huge grin off my face.

Cara turns to the mirror and applies her lipstick before looking back at me. "What do you think?" She is stunning in a strapless navy jumper shorts with a chunky gold belt. She's wearing very high strappy gold heels, and her long brown hair is shining as it falls down her bare back.

"You are gorgeous—as always," I say. I've opted for a short silver sequined dress. It is strapless and fitted, except for where it poufs out some from my waist. I'm borrowing Cara's silver heels. I dress up my makeup a little more today, using shades of gray to brighten my blue eyes. My hair hangs in messy waves. Despite it appearing very natural, it took me an hour to complete.

"You are seriously hot, Livi. I like how Spain is bringing out this little sex-kitten in you."

I laugh.

"Your makeup is amazing. It's so sultry. The smoky eyes are great on you."

"Thanks," I respond, feeling seriously flattered. "I'm so glad you're here. I'm having the time of my life, and I'm so happy that you get to experience it, too."

"Me, too. And I can't wait to meet your hot sex god!"

I don't know why, but I have the tiniest twinge of nervousness about Andres meeting Cara. I know I shouldn't, but I guess old habits die hard. As secure as I am about Andres and his feelings, I can't silence the voice in my head that tells me he'll eventually tire and leave me for greener pastures. God, I hope that Little Miss Negativity in my head is wrong.

The three of us girls are having a glass of wine in the living room as we wait for the guys to get back. Andres is the first to enter the house, and his eyes immediately lock on me. He smiles and walks straight over to where I'm sitting. I stand and he wraps his arms tightly around me and pulls me into a fiery kiss. I'm breathless when I pull away.

"You are stunning, baby," he whispers in my ear.

"Babe, I want you to meet my best friend, Cara."

Andres turns to Cara without releasing his strong grip around my waist.

He shakes her hand. Thanks to the fact that he studied English in school nonstop since he was four, he speaks to her in perfect English, "Hi, Cara. Livi has told me so much about you. It is nice to meet you."

I watch his eyes as they focus on hers. He's wearing a sincere smile as he regards her. His gaze never wanders, and his expression doesn't emit any emotion other than sincerity. I exhale, realizing that I've been holding my breath. He lets go of her hand and wraps it back around me, pulling me into him.

"So nice to meet you!" Cara beams. "And Livi was right—you are hot!"

My eyes practically burst out of their sockets, and my face burns. I bite my bottom lip and manage to turn to Andres, who is grinning widely.

"Did she now? Well, I'm glad she thinks so. Otherwise, I wouldn't stand a chance with someone as beautiful as her." He kisses my cheek. "You ready to go dance with your hot boyfriend?"

*Boyfriend?* I guess we established our relationship status on Monday when we told each other we didn't want anyone else, but this is the first time I've heard him say it aloud. I'm bursting with glee. "Yes."

The rest of the guys loudly enter the house. Their conversation halts when they see Cara.

"Well, what do we have here?" Hugo asks as he throws one of his flirty stares toward Cara.

I answer him in English, "Hey, guys, this is my best friend and roommate from home, Cara. She doesn't speak Spanish, so if you could put your education to use and practice our language around her, that would be awesome." I scan the room, catching each of their attention before continuing. "And, do know that if you say anything dirty around her, I will translate." I turn to Hugo and point. "That especially goes for you," I say with a smirk.

"Hey!" Hugo pretends to be hurt, and I laugh.

I introduce everyone. "Cara, this is Julio and Carlos, and this obnoxious one is Hugo."

Carlos and Julio chuckle at my introduction while it doesn't seem to faze Hugo.

Hugo advances toward Cara and grabs her hand before bringing it to his lips. "Nice to meet you, *hermosa.*"

I can see the wheels turning in Cara's head. I watch Nadia to see if she is having any sort of reaction to Hugo flirting with my friend, but she doesn't seem to notice or care as she chats with Andres.

Julio and Carlos introduce themselves to Cara. It's somewhat awkward as Hugo dominates the space around her.

"Geez, Hugo, give her room," I say.

Cara half giggles at his attentiveness. She apparently likes the admiration.

*Oh, whatever.* I can see where this night is going to go. It's not like she doesn't know what she is getting herself into.

Carlos, Nadia, Cara, Andres, and I squeeze into one car while Hugo and Julio drive Julio's car behind us. We head to the same club that we went to on my first night here. Due to Abby's late arrival, Nolan and Abby are going to meet us there.

Cara finds the club, El Q, as amazing as I did. We get a large table by the main floor dance area. It's close to the stage and the vast windows overlooking the city. Nolan and Abby arrive shortly after we do. He introduces Abby to everyone. She comes off, in appearance, as the quintessential girl next door, which matches Nolan's charm perfectly. She's quiet, but I don't blame her. She's met a lot of people, and she is sitting in an expansive, loud club. I'm sure it's overwhelming. Nolan's normal exuberant charm is minimized. He sits in the booth with his arm around Abby as he talks politely with everyone. I'm not used to seeing him so subdued, especially in a social situation.

I want to leave a better impression on Abby than I have in the past. I have always felt that she doesn't particularly like me. "So, Abby, how was your flight?" *Lame opener, I admit.*

"Fine, thanks."

"Are you excited to spend a couple of weeks in Spain?"

"Yeah, I guess."

"Nolan talks about you all the time. I'm so happy you could come."

"Yeah, me, too, I guess. Although, he really never talks about you."

*Um…okay?* "Do you have anything fun planned for your summer in Miami when you get back?" I ask, a smile plastered on my face.

"No." Her voice is tainted with annoyance.

*Okay, maybe she is shy, but I think I'm done trying to make conversation.* The awkwardness in the air could be cut with a knife.

"Okay, then…well, I hope you have a good time tonight. This place is one of my favorites," I say.

I turn my attention to Andres, and I'm met with his striking stare. I melt, forgetting the mousy bitch across from me. My hand is already in his grasp under the table, and Andres pulls me up and out a few feet onto the dance floor. I forget about my uncomfortable conversation with Abby and get lost in the music with Andres.

It doesn't take long before Hugo has Cara behaving like a giggly schoolgirl. His flirt meter is off the charts tonight. I'm momentarily nervous for her again, but she knows what she's doing. I gave her a rundown of everyone, giving her extra details on him, so she was forewarned. She said she only wants something fun, so I need to trust that she knows what she wants.

My feet hurt from dancing, but my heart is happy. I love having Cara here to experience this with me. I spot her a few feet away while she's dancing with Hugo. They're sucking face, and they are sharing more than their fair share of spit tonight. I laugh. I wonder if Andres and I come off like that every time we make out in public, and I admit, that is often.

Nadia is dancing with some guy she met at school. Nolan and Abby have danced to a few songs, but they are currently sitting in the corner of the booth. His arm is around her as they both stare off toward the dance floor. Julio and Carlos are sitting at our table, talking with a group of their friends.

Andres leans his face down to mine. "You seem deep in thought. What's on that pretty mind of yours?"

"I was just thinking about how much fun I'm having and how happy I am that Cara gets to experience some of this with me. She and Hugo seem to be getting along."

Andres laughs. "Yes, they certainly are." He gives me a delicious kiss. "You're coming to my house tonight, right? I want you to stay with me."

I hesitate. "I can't leave Cara, Andres. I'm sorry."

"She can come, too. I have plenty of extra rooms."

His mouth finds mine again, and I'm lost to the world. I can only focus on the sensations of my body. Andres's tongue runs against the inside of my mouth in the most seductive rhythm, and I have to focus on standing. He can completely disarm me with his kisses. I don't know how long we've been kissing when I hear Cara.

"Earth to Olivia!" she says, laughing. "You think you guys can take a quick break from"—she points between our faces—"that. Everyone is leaving."

Andres, Cara, Hugo, and I make our way back to Andres's house. Hugo and Cara quickly disappear once we arrive. I'm sure Hugo is familiar with the house, and he has found a perfect spot for Cara and him to hang out. I hope she doesn't sleep with him already. *Then again, who am I to judge?* Everything moves so fast here. If I had to bet, I would say that she won't give in tonight. She isn't one to throw all of her cards on the table the first night. She is going to make him work a little for her.

I lie naked in Andres's bed, blissfully well fucked and sated. We are facing each other, and he's running his finger up and down my arm.

His face is serious. "Do you remember the first night we talked, and I told you that I don't do relationships?"

"Yes," I say, wondering where this is going.

"I've never allowed myself to love anyone since my mom died. I've been so afraid to open my heart. I know how it feels to lose someone you love, and it's a pain that I'd do anything to avoid feeling again." He pauses.

"The pain of losing my mom destroyed my father. I realize now that he's never going to get over it."

He kisses me on the forehead. "I was never planning on finding love in this lifetime. It was not anything I desired. I was content with living my life on my own, but you changed all that. With you, I didn't even have a choice. From the moment I saw you, I knew my life would never be the same. I am destined to love you."

He takes a deep breath. "Believe me, I'm scared shitless of losing you, but my need for you outweighs my fear. I never thought I would have that with anyone." He kisses me softly on the lips.

Tears stream down my face, and my body instantly feels lighter with the knowledge that Andres reciprocates my feelings. "I've never loved anyone like this either. You are my first love, the love of my life." I know it seems soon to make such a proclamation, but it's how I feel. I don't have the capacity to love anyone else as much as I already love Andres.

"You are my first love, too, Livi, and I know you'll be my only love in this life. I was put on this earth to love you. I know it."

The adoration I see in his eyes at this moment is overwhelming, causing my tears to fall harder.

"You mesmerize me, Livi. You are so smart, funny, and caring. When I see you for the first time every day, whether it is when we are waking up or when I am picking you up at school, my heart starts beating faster in anticipation to spend another day with you. You stir up feelings in me that I didn't know existed. You have everything I never knew I wanted, but now that I have you, I need you, and I know I always will."

He places his mouth on mine, kissing me with deep passion. We make slow, sweet, and unrestrained love until we can't stay awake any longer. We fall asleep naked and entwined in one another's embrace.

If there is a heaven on earth, I know that I've found it.

I wake with a start to the sound of loud voices coming from somewhere in the house. *What is going on?*

I stretch and kiss Andres on the cheek. I run my hand down his handsome face that is covered with a manly short stubble. The soft roughness of his face is making me want him badly.

His lips turn up into a slight smile, and he mumbles, "Good morning."

Waking up to a sleepy Andres next to me is quite possibly the biggest turn-on.

My desire quickly hits a wall when I hear the yelling again. "What the hell is going on out there? Maybe we should go check?"

"I'm sure it is Hugo and Cara fighting over something stupid. Let them figure it out." Andres nuzzles his face into the crevice of my neck, sending jolts of need through me.

The yelling continues.

"I really should go check on Cara to make sure she is all right."

"If you insist." Andres doesn't seem the least bit worried.

I rummage through Andres's dresser and throw on a pair of his boxers and a T-shirt. I open the bedroom door and make my way toward the commotion. As I enter the main living room, I see Hugo standing in only his boxers while Cara is in her outfit from the night before. They both appear a little rough around the edges, tired, and slightly frantic.

"Fuck you!" Cara yells. "I don't owe you anything. You have no say in what I do. I will fuck the whole city of Seville if I want!"

"Oh, I'm sure you would try. Stop being such a whore!" Hugo yells.

She throws herself toward him, bringing both of her fists down on his chest. "Whatever! At least I didn't fuck you!"

He grabs her wrists and pushes her off of him. "Only because I didn't want to!"

"Yeah, right! You were dying to get inside me last night, and you're just sorry that you will never get that chance now! I don't fuck assholes!"

Hugo forces out a cynical laugh. "I highly doubt that. I'm sure you fuck anyone who is willing."

Cara advances toward him again and pushes him. "Apparently, not you!"

"Stop!" I yell. "Stop this!"

Both Hugo and Cara turn toward me, and for a moment, puzzled expressions grace their faces, registering that they have an audience, before turning back to each other to continue their argument.

I walk over to Cara and grab her arm. In a calm voice, I request, "Please come with me?"

Cara squints her eyes and twists her lips into a scowl as she glares at Hugo. "Gladly," she states in a firm voice.

Holding her hand in mine, she lets me lead her out of the room and into an extra bedroom. I close the door.

"What was that all about?" I ask.

Her eyes fill with tears. "He is such a jerk!"

"Just calm down, and tell me what happened."

I rub her forearms gently as she takes a deep breath.

"We had a great night. We messed around and cuddled, you know? This morning, my phone kept going off, and I heard it, but I was too tired to get it out of my purse. I knew it was nothing important. Well, at some point, Hugo grabbed it. He was probably sick of the buzzing, and he read my text messages. I had missed texts from Brandon and a couple of the other guys, but they were harmless. Brandon told me he missed me, and a couple of the other guys wanted to get together, obviously not knowing that I am here. One of the texts was from a guy who I haven't spoken to in a year. It was totally not a big deal. Well, Hugo goes all apeshit and territorial, and he starts insinuating things. How dare he! He doesn't even know me, and I don't owe him an explanation!"

I listen attentively. "No, you don't owe him anything."

I can see how their fight escalated. They are both very similar even though they probably would never admit it. I'm sure the situation could have been handled differently, more calmly, but that's not Cara, and apparently, it's not Hugo either. If Cara feels offended, she becomes extremely defensive. I pointed this out once, and it led to a huge fight between us, so now, I simply listen, and I agree. She eventually figures everything out in her own way.

"Let's go back to Nadia's. I will tell Andres that we are calling a cab."

"Okay," she agrees.

Andres insists on driving us in his dad's car that has been left at the house. I don't see Hugo when we leave, so he is either hiding out in the house somewhere, or he already left.

Andres drops us off, and we make plans to meet up later.

"What do you want to do today? Do you want to see some of the city? We could do some touristy stuff?" I suggest.

"Sure, that sounds fun," Cara agrees.

Cara and I basically re-create the exploring adventure that I had with Andres a couple of weeks ago. I take her to the shops that I enjoyed, and we eat at the same restaurant.

Over lunch, I can tell that she is still upset about her earlier altercation with Hugo.

"Don't let this morning bother you. We are still going to have a great time. Forget Hugo. He is trouble," I say.

"He was so mean. I don't get it. He has known me for a day. He almost acted like a wounded boyfriend, but he doesn't have that right. I barely know him."

"I don't know. Who really does with these Latin men? Andres is pretty chill, but overall, Latin men have a reputation for being quite emotional."

Cara laughs. "Yeah, I would say so." She plops a shrimp her in mouth. "I guess I was pretty mean to him, too."

"Your defenses were up as were his. I am sure you both said stuff you didn't mean."

"Yeah, I guess. I wonder if it will be weird the next time I see him."

"I don't know," I answer truthfully.

Knowing Hugo for the short time I have, I am guessing that he will either be his usually carefree self tonight and not address this morning, or he will be a pouty jerk with a wounded ego all night.

Well, I was correct with my first guess. Hugo doesn't address this morning at all. We are sitting in Carlos and Nadia's living room, having a beer. We are going to a bar to play some pool tonight.

Hugo is talking and joking with everyone as usual—well, everyone except for Cara. He is pretending that she isn't in the room, but to be fair, she is acting the same way—talking with everyone, except for him. It is comical actually and very middle school. Two people who are used to being the center of attention are talking over each other, but they are completely ignoring the other.

I am having fun, watching the back and forth of the power struggle, as Hugo and Cara try to maintain the attention of the group. Andres squeezes my hand, and I notice the smirk on his face. He obviously thinks it is pretty funny, too. I don't miss the manner in which Cara's conversations usually involve Julio or Carlos. She is trying to get under Hugo's skin by flirting with the only two accessible guys here. She must really want to get Hugo's attention. I hope it doesn't get ugly.

The bar we go to is small, sitting among houses and apartment buildings on a quiet street. Poorly lit, yellow globe lanterns hang above wooden booths surrounding the perimeter inside. The walls are covered in wooden panels. In the center of the room are a handful of pool tables.

The whole group of us occupies one of the larger corner booths. After giving the waitress our drink orders, we pair off for games of pool and start another makeshift competition. This group is very competitive.

"Okay, so what is the winning team going to get?" Julio asks the group.

"The losers can all buy a round of drinks for the winners," Hugo suggests.

"No. We always do drinks. Let's be original this time," Nadia says.

"I have an idea!" I think back to how much fun Max and I had playing Truth or Dare and how much trouble we got into as well when we were growing up. I think this night could get even more entertaining than the Hugo-and-Cara battle. "How about the winning pair gets to each pick a person and give them a dare and those people have to do the dare tonight?"

"Oh, that sounds fun!" Nadia responds.

Julio chuckles. "Depending on who wins, that could be very risky."

"I think it sounds fun." Andres kisses me on the head and wraps his arm around me.

"Okay, it's settled," Carlos adds.

With the addition of Cara, we have an odd number, so Julio volunteers to be the judge. Andres and I pair off against Cara and Carlos first. Hugo and Nadia will take the winners of the first game.

Andres is really good at pool. It's not surprising, considering he is good at everything. I, on the other hand, suck. Carlos is really good as well, and Cara is better than me.

The white ball I hit doesn't even go in the vicinity of the striped red ball I had been trying to hit into the corner pocket. "I'm sorry, babe," I mutter.

Carlos mumbles something about an easy win as Cara lines up her shot.

Andres stands behind me, wrapping me in his arms. Bending his head, he kisses the side of my neck at the base of my shoulder. "You are adorable."

"Sucking at something is adorable?" I ask with a pout.

"Everything you do is adorable, trust me."

My attention is drawn to Cara, who is asking Carlos for advice on her position. She is leaning over the table, and Carlos is behind her, helping her with the angle of her stick. I know darn well that this is all an act, and it isn't for Carlos's benefit. I watch Hugo as he is glaring toward the scene unfolding. Throwing back her long, shiny hair, Cara laughs loudly at something Carlos said. Carlos puts his hand on the small of Cara's back, guiding her for the shot.

Cara and Carlos win the game. I am happy to be a spectator for the second game. I lean back into Andres's chest as he sits on a stool, his arms securing me close. We watch as Hugo and Nadia set off to play against Cara and Carlos. Andres kisses my hair and inhales deeply, and I melt in his arms.

Cara continues her charade, requesting Carlos's assistance, at every possible opportunity. I stare in fascination as the tension rolls off of Hugo. Something is going to come to a head tonight, and I wonder how it is going to play out. Either Hugo is always an exceptional player, or he plays better when he is frustrated. He dominates the game, and he and Nadia easily beat Cara and Carlos.

Nadia jumps up and down, clapping her hands. "Who should we pick?"

I give Nadia a high five. "Great game, guys. So, you can each pick one of us and dare us to do something. Don't get too crazy." I eye Hugo when I say that last line.

Some of Hugo's jovial humor comes back as he smiles at me. "Are you nervous, Liv?"

"Of what you could dare someone to do? Absolutely—especially if that someone is me."

He laughs. "Well, you are off the hook tonight because I am going to dare Carlos."

We all turn to Carlos. He is mildly amused while he's waiting for the dare.

Hugo faces Carlos. "I dare you to…" He pauses for effect. "Get a kiss, a real kiss, from one of the ladies in here tonight, but it can't be from anyone in our group."

I roll my eyes in amusement because that translates to, *Kiss anyone but Cara.*

Carlos scans the room. "Uh…man, there are not really a lot of women to choose from."

"Well, a dare is a dare," Hugo responds.

"Fine, but give me a few minutes to figure out my game plan."

"Agreed." Hugo nods.

"Okay!" Nadia exclaims. "I think I am going to choose Cara. I will stick to the theme my partner laid out and have Cara find a guy to give her a kiss."

Nadia knows exactly what she is doing. She has obviously felt the tension between Hugo and Cara today.

"Like that will be difficult." Julio winks at Cara.

She giggles. She actually giggles. *Yep, she is laying it on thick.*

I watch Hugo, and I think his eyes are going to pop out of his head. This intense, jealous side of him is such a change from his normal, cheerful, womanizing one. The whole dynamic is fascinating. It's like my own

111

personal telenovela. I look back at Andres, and I can see him smirking at Hugo. Andres is watching the same drama unfold, and I think we are enjoying the train wreck that has been set in motion.

We all take our seats in the booth and order another round of drinks. Cara makes a big show as to whom the lucky man should be even though no more than thirty people are in this bar.

"Oh, that guy in the tight gray shirt is hot. I could get a kiss from him." She puts a finger on her lips, contemplating. "Or that guy with the black button-up at the far pool table is pretty cute, too. Hmm…"

Hugo picks the label off of his beer bottle as if it personally insulted him. I notice his knee bouncing under the table.

Carlos stands. "Well, I am going to talk to that one over there. She is really the only one in here who I would want a kiss from."

We watch him approach the woman, and she instantly laughs at something he said. It seems that Carlos does have some finesse with women. I have never seen him in action. He is always content to simply hang out with the group when we are out.

Hugo lets out an audible breath as he scoots out of the booth. With clenched lips and a hard determination in his eyes, he captures Cara's hand from the tabletop and yanks her until she is standing. She starts to protest as he tugs her hand behind him. Her long chestnut hair fans out from her back momentarily as she is hastily pulled forward. She whines his name, but she walks behind him as he leads her away from the booth where we are all watching this event unfold with curiosity.

"I knew it!" Nadia exclaims when they are out of hearing distance. "He has been all alpha-male over her tonight. I knew that dare would put him over the edge." She chuckles to herself.

"Does he really like her then?" I ask.

Andres absentmindedly twirls his beer by the neck of the glass bottle. "He feels something for her. I don't know if he likes her or if he is pissed because she is playing hard to get."

"It's hard to say, but normally, Hugo isn't one to go all protective over a girl. She might just be a conquest for him. I'm not sure, but maybe you should talk to her, so she doesn't get hurt," Julio says to me.

"Oh, believe me, she knows exactly what she is doing. She will be fine," I reassure Julio.

"You should let Cara know that he isn't the settling-down type in case she thinks he is going to care about their relationship beyond these two weeks that she is here," Nadia says to me.

"She knows. Cara isn't one to immediately get all mushy over a guy anyway." I watch the corner where the two disappeared down the hallway, and I smile to myself. *What is it about these Latin men that makes them so irresistible?* Cara isn't following her usual pattern of behavior either.

Carlos ends up getting a kiss and a number from the girl he pursued. Cara and Hugo come walking back to the table, hand in hand, about thirty minutes after their departure. Cara's already full lips are even more plump and red. I am sure she got that kiss that she was after and then some. Smiles grace both of their faces, and their bodies are visibly less tense.

Hugo is back to his usual cheerful self. "Hey, guys. We are going to get going. See you around."

My eyes dart up to Cara's, and she reassures me that she is great.

She leans in to hug me good-bye. Quietly in my ear, she says, "I might not be back tonight. Don't wait up."

As she pulls away, I shoot her another searching stare, and she smiles big in response. *Yes, she is good.* Curiosity is racing through me, and I am dying to know what was said or done in that hallway to transform Cara's and Hugo's reactions toward one another. I do know that she understands what she is doing, and I'm sure I will hear every juicy detail about it tomorrow.

# chapter 18

"So, Hugo apologized for being a dick and kissed you? That's all that was said?" I ask Cara the next day.

I am sitting in the living room with Cara with my legs pulled up as I slouch into the comfortable couch. I was ready for a juicy story, and I got a one-sentence explanation.

"Pretty much." She shrugs.

"Seriously, Cara? You guys wanted to kill each other yesterday morning, and now, everything is peachy?"

"Well, like I told you, he apologized. He said he was being an asshole. I agreed, and then he kissed me. It was over after that. He is a damn good kisser, Liv—like, totally fantastic."

She sighs almost dreamily, and I have to stop myself from laughing.

"Okay, so what else happened last night?"

"We went back to his apartment. Yes, we did it, and he is damn skilled in that department as well, if you were curious."

"I wasn't."

She smirks. "Yeah, right. Who wouldn't be a little curious? Anyway, we had a great night. It was hot...and tiring."

"So, now, what?"

"Well, neither of us wants anything serious, but we really want to have fun while I am here. So, that is what we are going to do. Fun. Carefree. Sex." She lets out another audible sigh. "Perfect."

I laugh out loud. "Well, I am glad you two worked everything out, and it sounds like we are going to have a fun two weeks ahead of us."

"I agree."

"I'm so glad because it would have been a long two weeks if every day was filled with as much tension as last night was—prior to the making up, of course. Did he say why he'd gotten so upset when your guy friends contacted you? It's not like he wants anything long-term."

"No, to be honest, we didn't really talk about the fight. We'd both said some mean things to each other, so I didn't feel the need to bring it up. He probably has a crazy jealous streak or something. I can be pretty hotheaded myself."

"Yes, yes, you can."

"Hey!" Cara exclaims in mock offense, throwing one of the couch pillows at me.

I catch it. "I'm just saying you are both apparently very spicy. It could make for an interesting time. Just try not to get into any more screaming matches."

Cara and Hugo are two of the most fun, outgoing, and emotional people I know. That could be a recipe for something wonderful, or it could be the perfect storm.

Carlos comes bounding down the stairs and greets us both.

Cara asks, "So, are you going to call the girl from last night?"

"Nope," he responds bluntly.

"Why?" I ask.

"Not worth my time. She's cute and all, but I'm just not that into her. So, let's stop analyzing my love life. Tell me, Cara…what the hell is up with you and Hugo?"

"Nothing," she answers coyly.

"Right," he says, drawing out the word sarcastically. "Whatever. See you ladies tonight."

"Where are you going?" Cara asks.

I say, "The band is practicing at Julio's today."

"When am I going to get to see you guys play?" Cara asks enthusiastically.

"Soon," Carlos responds before he shuts the front door behind him.

My weekly routine remains the same, only varying with the addition of Cara and Hugo. While I'm in class, Cara is at my house napping. *Lucky bitch.* After school, I do my homework in the company of Cara, Hugo, and Andres. The two lovebirds are usually sucking face on the other twin bed in my room while Andres studies me. When the guys aren't practicing, the four of us hang around the house until the evening when we go out with Nadia and the rest of the guys. It is an entertaining and exhausting routine, and I love it.

Cara and Hugo have had a few heated arguments over inconsequential things, but most of the arguments blow over quickly—or as soon as Hugo can get his mouth on Cara's. Those two are so hot and cold that it is thoroughly comical.

On Thursday, we decide to take a break from the bar scene to hang out with Nolan and Abby. Nolan expressed that Abby doesn't enjoy going out to the clubs, so we go bowling. Andres, Cara, Hugo, Nadia, Julio, Carlos, and I are already at the lanes, inputting our names into the scoring machine, when Nolan and Abby walk in, hand in hand. I peer up at Nolan, and he seems different.

His face doesn't light up when he sees us. "Hey, guys," he says, his greeting lacking its usual exuberance.

"So glad you two could make it," I say with forced excitement.

I don't know what it is about Abby, but I don't feel comfortable in her presence. I try to push aside these feelings and give her the benefit of the doubt. She's my best friend's girlfriend, and I want us to get along.

I finish tying my hideous shoes and turn to Abby. "How has your first week in Spain been?"

"Fine," she answers curtly.

"What have you two done so far?"

"Not much."

*Okay...* "Do you like bowling?"

She sneers at me like I have two heads. "Uh...yeah, I guess."

I peer up to meet Nolan's gaze. His face doesn't give anything away, and I find this very unsettling. I've always been able to tell how he's feeling from his expressions. I can't get a read on his take of this very uncomfortable conversation.

Andres moves in behind me and wraps his strong arms around me, relaxing my tense body. He directs his attention to Nolan. "Hey, man, what do you say to a wager? Make this game interesting?"

Carlos joins the conversation. "Hell yeah, let's make a bet. We need something to make this game remotely entertaining."

"Bowling is fun. Stop being such an ass," Nadia says.

"A bet sounds fun, man," Nolan says cheerfully to Andres. "What do you have in mind?"

Hugo cuts in, "How about all the losers have to buy the winner a drink every time we go out for the next month?"

"Uh...no," Nadia says. "That's a little extreme, don't you think? How about everyone buys the winner a drink the next time we go out—like, one night out?"

"Boring, but okay," Hugo answers.

We agree on the terms and start the game. I don't know why Hugo proposed such an extensive wager because he sucks at bowling. It's actually quite funny to watch.

"Ah, damn!" Hugo yells as another ball falls into the gutter.

Everyone laughs.

None of us exactly excels at bowling, but we have a good time trying. I love watching the guys take it so seriously. They'll do anything to be competitive. Julio seems to have the best bowling skills—or he's just getting really lucky.

My vision circles around, taking in this group of people who I've grown to love so much. Everyone has smiles on their faces. They are all joking and clowning around and having a good time.

My stare stops at Abby. She doesn't seem to be having any fun, judging by the scowl on her face, as she solemnly watches Nolan bowl. *God, what a buzzkill. What does Nolan see in her?*

Julio wins by twenty points, and Andres comes in second. I pretty much sucked, coming in second to last. Hugo is the only one who sucked more than me, and the guys tease him relentlessly.

"Whatever. Bowling sucks. Next time, let's play a real game," Hugo says.

Cara pulls him into an embrace. "At least you were hot while you sucked," she says before kissing him.

Abby is talking to Nolan, but the only word I catch is *now* before Abby gives me the death glare.

At which point, Nolan turns to the group. "Yeah, we have to go."

"Um…okay. Well, glad you guys could come out. See you at school tomorrow." I decide not to give Nolan a hug good-bye, which doesn't sit right with me, but I can't get a good read on Abby, and I don't want to make anything worse for Nolan.

After they leave, we decide to call it an early night and head home as well.

Cara and I collapse into bed.

I lie on my side to face her across the space. "That was fun, yeah?"

"Yeah, it totally was. It was a nice change to hang out somewhere other than a bar."

"Cara Lee! Did I hear you correctly?" I ask with exaggerated shock.

Cara answers dryly, "I said, I had fun. That doesn't mean I'm going to trade in my hooker heels for bowling shoes. You know a night of clubbing will always rank top on my list."

I laugh. "Okay, thanks for clarifying." Changing the subject, I ask, "What do you think of Abby?"

Cara snorts. "Besides the fact that she is cuckoo for Cocoa Puffs?"

"She is, right? So, I'm not imagining things. She's weird, yeah?"

"Totally weird. I don't get what Nolan sees in her. She's like a depressed doormat. It wouldn't kill the girl to smile every now and then. Seriously, she is nothing like Nolan."

"I know. I feel bad for him. He isn't the same person when he's around her. It makes me sad," I say.

"Who knows? Maybe she's really jealous and possessive. Maybe she's nicer when she isn't around other girls," Cara suggests.

"Hmm…maybe. But Nolan deserves better."

"He'll figure it out. There has to be something to Abby that we don't see. He's been with the girl since high school."

I think about my interactions with Abby. I really tried to make her feel welcome, and she's been a bitch the whole time. "I hope he figures it out soon. I don't like her."

Cara laughs. "Yeah, me either."

The next day, Nolan is more like himself at school. He apologizes for Abby's attitude, explaining that she was tired. He also says that she doesn't feel comfortable in crowds and that they'll probably just do their own thing the rest of the time she's here. To be honest, I'm thrilled I won't have to hang out with Abby again, but I will miss Nolan.

Andres and Hugo decide to take Cara and me to Barcelona for the weekend. The Primavera Sound Festival, which features alternative rock bands, is going on. Andres tries to go to Barcelona every May for the festival. He says that it is one of his favorite cities, so I'm excited to be able to experience it with him.

We stay at a beautiful brownstone hotel adjacent to the Mediterranean. We have a small two-bedroom, one-bath suite with a connected living space and a balcony overlooking the water.

I stand on the balcony and watch the waves come in. They are the exact color of what I imagined the ocean would be like, a perfect combination of greens and blues. The sun dances off the peaks of the waves as they come into shore. It's breathtaking.

We walk around the city and decide to stop at a bar with outdoor seating for dinner. We share many orders of tapas, which appear to be smaller portions of meals. I compare them to appetizers, but Andres tells me they're different because they eat multiple plates of tapas for the meal and not solely for a starter. My favorites are the seafood tapas. We're on our second pitcher of sangria. It's so good that it puts the sangria in the States to shame. It has a delicious rich taste with the sweetness of the fruit and just the right amount of bite.

Andres is holding my hand and rubbing his thumb against my skin as we eat. He seems to always touch me in some way, and I love it. He has a way of making me feel cherished and beautiful despite my insecurities.

"So, Andres, what do you do with your days? Do you work or go to school?" Cara inquires.

"Right now, I don't do either," Andres says as if that's a good enough answer.

He still doesn't know Cara very well, so he doesn't realize that his answer isn't sufficient.

"Okay, so what do you do?" she asks again.

"I spend my days with Livi." He takes a large gulp of his drink.

"So, when Livi leaves, what will you do with your days?" she pushes.

I cringe. I told Cara that Andres is a private person. Apparently, she's choosing to ignore that fact since she's not taking the hint. His short responses are obviously an indication that he doesn't feel like talking about himself.

He exhales, peering at Cara. I can see the realization on his face that he knows this conversation won't be over until he gives her some answers.

"I don't know. I might go back to school."

"Were you in school before?"

"Yes, for art and design, but I needed a break," he answers dryly. As if realizing he needs to pull off the Band-Aid until she stops her interrogation, he continues, "I'm not sure what I want to do with my life at the moment. I like art. I paint sometimes. I like music as I'm sure Livi has told you, but I don't know if I will be able to make a living with music. So, I don't know. I inherited a little money from my mom's life insurance policy when she passed away. I'm living on that until I figure my life out." He takes another sip, his stern expression silently imploring her to halt her questioning.

Cara nods and redirects her focus to Hugo. I guess bringing up a deceased mother will end a conversation quickly.

I address Andres, "I didn't know you were into art. Do you have any completed work?" There is still so much I don't know about Andres, and I am determined to find out everything I can.

"Yeah, there's a room in the house with my paintings. I can show you if you want to see them."

"Of course I do."

I lean my head on his shoulder, and he kisses my hair. My attention directs toward Cara when I hear her teasing Hugo.

"What kind of a degree is general studies, Hugo? Seriously?"

"It's offered at the university, so it's obviously a real degree." Hugo shrugs with a cocky smirk on his face.

"Really? Okay, tell me one job that requires a degree in general studies." She puts emphasis on the words *general studies* as she finger quotes. "You can't because it's a pointless degree. Seriously, why even go to college if you're going to get a fluff degree that can't get you a job?"

Andres speaks up, "So, he can say that he went to college. He has a job in his father's business anytime he wants it. So, why would he actually take any challenging classes when he doesn't have to? Right, Hugo?"

"Whatever, man. At least I'm going to college," Hugo responds.

Andres grins. "Hey, I know I'm fucked-up. I've admitted that. I was just giving the lovely Cara here a little explanation for your education choices." He winks at Cara and takes another drink of sangria.

"Why go to college at all if you already have a job lined up?" Cara asks.

"I will give you three reasons," Hugo says. "Number one, the hot college chicks. Number two, it'll show my old man that I have some drive. And number three, did I mention the easy hot college babes?"

We all laugh.

Cara hits Hugo on the arm, laughing. "God, you are such a pervert."

"Please, babe, call me Hugo."

We all let out an exaggerated groan at Hugo's cockiness.

"I don't think you could be more full of yourself if you tried," I say with a smile.

Hugo gives me his best smoldering glance. "Oh, Livi, baby…I'm sure I could turn it up a notch if I needed to."

I laugh despite Hugo's arrogance. He's so cute even with his inflated ego. He's the only guy I've ever met who can be an arrogant ass and still be so likable.

"Um…no. Please don't. I think we're good," I say.

Andres gets the waiter's attention and motions for the check.

The Primavera Sound Festival is unlike anything I've ever seen. Walking in the gates, we're met with a sea of people standing around on the blacktop. A band is playing on an outdoor stage. To my left is nothing but the Mediterranean.

Andres grabs my hand, and I grasp Cara's. We weave our way through the crowd to get closer to the stage. I've never heard of the band currently playing, but they're good. Hugo leaves us temporarily and returns with a large bucket of beer bottles on ice. While I'm facing the band, Andres stands behind me with his arms wrapped firmly around my waist. The energy is electrifying within this large crowd. I close my eyes and lean my head back onto Andres's chest. He gently kisses my neck as we sway to the music. My body feels warm from the beer and his touch. I'm intoxicated with the smell of Andres, beer, and salt water.

As the sun sinks into the ocean, a new band sets up on stage. We've had a long day of listening to music, dancing, drinking, and laughing. We're all pleasantly buzzed. The new band starts to play, and from the roar of the masses, I can tell the band is quite popular. I'm facing Andres with my arms draped around his neck. He's leaning down toward me, and our tongues intertwine with amplified infatuation. He is a drug I can't resist. We're slowly dancing and kissing while the mob around us exuberantly jumps up and down with their arms raised.

As our kiss deepens, I withdraw one of my arms from around his neck and run my fingers back and forth under the button of his jeans, tickling the skin of his tight abdomen. My fingers venture farther down, and I can feel the base of his shaft. He groans and grabs my hand out of his pants. He slips his hand up my tank top and pulls on my bra, releasing my breasts. He begins to pull at my nipple, elongating it, leaving me in an almost painful ecstasy. I close my eyes in pleasure as his hand hungrily explores my skin from my breasts to my stomach and then around my back.

My breathing is harsh, and I revel in the sensation. His kisses are fierce as he consumes my mouth with lustful abandonment. My tongue wraps around his as if its hunger will never be satisfied. The crowd of people and the music surrounding us are a dull white noise in the far consciousness of my mind. All I can hear are the soft moans coming from Andres as our tongues dance to our own beat and the pounding of my blood as it rushes through my body.

He removes one hand from under my shirt and slides it beneath my short ruffled jean skirt. Pulling my thong to the side, he plunges his finger into me, and my breath catches as I bask in the feeling. After inserting a second finger, he begins to circle the two inside me, putting pressure on my front inner wall. I'm jostled toward him as the person behind me collides with us while she jumps up and down to the beat of the music. I open my eyes and take notice of the tight cluster of people around us. They're oblivious to our activity due to distractions of their own.

Noticing my glances to those around us, Andres whispers in my ear, "Don't worry about them, baby. No one cares what we're doing. No one will even notice. Just feel it."

He thrusts his fingers deeper into me, causing me to whimper with carnal gratification . He kisses my neck as he continues to circle his fingers inside me while rubbing my throbbing spot with his thumb. The intense pleasure shatters me, and I begin to spasm around him. I bury my head in his chest as I cry out.

He removes his fingers, and I immediately feel vacant, needing to be filled by him once more. His blue stare is filled with desire as he inserts his fingers into his mouth. He sucks them from the base to the tip as if they tasted like his favorite flavor of Popsicle. My eyes bulge as a painful desire courses between my legs.

"You taste so good, baby," he says as his lips twists into a devilish grin. "Do you want to get out of here?"

*Do I ever.* I nod.

Turning around, I spot Hugo and Cara. They appear to have been driven away from us with all the dancing bodies. They're ten or so people away with their arms wrapped around each other as they dance to the music. Lacing our fingers together, Andres leads me to them.

"Hey!" I yell to Cara over the music. "We're going to get out of here! Do you want to come with us?"

"No, I want to stay a little longer! We'll meet you at the hotel!" she shouts.

Entwining his fingers through mine, Andres pulls me toward the back of the amphitheater and through the exit. We follow the sidewalk leading to the water and stop at a street vendor for sandwiches and bottled waters. We walk along the boardwalk, eating and talking about the show.

After we throw our garbage away, Andres kicks off his shoes and grabs them with one hand. "Let's go walk by the water."

I slip out of my shoes as well and pick them up. My free hand is intertwined with Andres's as we move to the water's edge. It's dark now, but the lights from the city illuminate where the water meets the sand as small waves lap up onto our feet. We stroll down the beach for a long time, stopping intermittently to kiss like lovesick teenagers.

He turns to me, grasps my face between his hands, and stares into my eyes. I feel his love deep in my chest.

"We come from two different worlds, literally an ocean apart, and I don't know how we were brought together, but we were. I thank my lucky stars that you came into my life. You have quickly become my everything. You're my everything, baby."

My cheeks flush, and a smile tickles my lips. My heart is full. In this moment, I feel nothing but gratitude, and I can sum up every life-altering feeling of happiness into one word—Andres.

# chapter 19

On Tuesday, the boys invite us to their weekly basketball game. We pack into Nadia's Maxima. I have to laugh when a vision of circus clowns piling into a tiny car comes to life as the seven of us stuff into her car. I sit on Andres's lap in the front seat, and Cara sits across Hugo, Julio, and Carlos in the back. I ignore the fact that if we got into an accident, I'd be toast.

We make our way to a local high school where the guys play on an outside court. They're met by their fifth teammate, another friend named Jose. I can see why Jose is an advantage to the team. He must be at least six-five. I notice Nadia's immediate change in demeanor when we see Jose. She transforms from one of the guys into a giggly and flirty girl as she talks to Jose. When the guys make their way to the court, we girls take a seat on the first row of bench seats.

"So, what's up with you and Jose?" I ask Nadia.

"Unfortunately, nothing. He's hot though, right?" Her eyes light up.

I watch Jose. I guess he's cute enough, but to be honest, standing next to Andres, he's pretty unremarkable. "Yeah, he's cute…and tall," I say. "Does he know you're interested?"

"He has to," Nadia answers. "I couldn't make it any more obvious. He doesn't seem interested in me like that though. I wish he hung out with us more, but he's not really into the bar scene. We really only see him at these basketball games."

"You know, come to think of it, you guys do go out a lot," I say.

Cara nods in agreement. "Yeah, you go out more than we do back home, and believe me, that is a feat."

"Well, I think it is different here than in the States. Forgive me if I am wrong because I've never been there, but from the movies I've seen, it seems like people our age in America go out to get drunk."

Cara and I nod in agreement.

"It's not like that here. Alcohol is accessible at a much younger age for us, so we've grown up around it. Therefore, we don't feel the need to get wasted when we are of age to drink it. It's not taboo. It's simply part of our culture. Going out is more of a way to spend time with our friends. Sure, we have drinks but not to get drunk—usually, that is."

"Yeah, that makes sense. Going out with you guys is definitely different than hanging out with frat guys back home," Cara states.

The conversation with Nadia falls off when the game starts. I'm mesmerized while watching Andres run up and down the court—dribbling, passing, and shooting. *Does he really have to be stunning at everything he does?* The degree of his perfection is intimidating. I switch my gaze to Cara, who has a silly grin on her face, as she watches Hugo. When I turn to my other side and see Nadia's attention focused on Jose, I laugh out loud, thinking about what big saps we are.

The next day, the boys are playing at Demo again.

Cara is giddy at the thought of watching Hugo. "I can't even imagine how hot Hugo is going to be while playing a guitar on stage!" she states. "I mean, really, is there anything hotter than a musician?"

"Definitely not! Andres doesn't usually play guitar on stage, but his voice is so sexy. I almost can't take it." I grin. "However, you're right. I don't think I've ever been more turned-on than when I'm watching Andres sing and play guitar on the living room couch."

"Hey, can you help me with the zipper?" Cara asks.

I reach over to zip up her very tight and very short red pleather dress. Seriously, only Cara could pull off cherry-red pleather.

"Totally hot, Cara. You're going to have Hugo eating out of your hand tonight."

"Thanks!" Cara admires herself in the full-length mirror. "Then again, when don't I?"

We laugh.

"Andres is going to salivate over that sexy number you have on!"

"Thanks!" I'm wearing a strapless, short black dress with a bubble skirt and strappy black heels. The heels and poufy skirt make my legs appear very long and slender.

I put on my chunky turquoise necklace, and then we make our way to meet Nadia in the living room. The guys left earlier to set up, so we're meeting them there.

When we walk through the doors of the bar, I see Andres on stage, and my heart skips a beat. It doesn't seem like I just saw him earlier today. He is so gorgeous in his jeans and tight T-shirt. His hair is styled in sexy chunky pieces, making me want to run my fingers through it and mess it up even more. Every time I see him, my chest starts racing, and desire courses through my veins. I don't think I will ever tire of him. I am addicted to him.

*Hello, my name is Olivia, and I am addicted to Andres. I am unquestionably and unequivocally an Andres addict.*

Andres raises his attention from the wire he's fastening and gives me his drop-your-panties smile. I feel heat on my cheeks as I smile and wave.

"Oh, I'm so excited!" exclaims Cara.

She grabs my hand and pulls us through the bar, following Nadia to our usual table. We get a round of mojitos, which have quickly become my new go-to drink here in Spain. The guys start their set, and I watch as Cara's face gleams while inspecting the guys on stage.

I lean in toward Cara. "What do you think?"

She faces me. "Oh my God, they're amazing! Hugo is like a god up there. No wonder girls salivate for him," she states matter-of-factly.

I laugh.

"I really like the music, too! Let's dance!" she calls.

We head to the small wooden dance floor in front of the stage. We're forced to dance off to the side because the floor is already packed with screaming girls. I watch as Andres works the crowd. I know this band is a fun pastime for him, but man, he is good. He peers down at the giggling gaggle of girls at the front of the stage and gives them a smile. I can almost see them melt, their bodies dissolving into a pool of desire. When I return my attention back to the stage, I'm met with Andres's intense gaze. He winks with his heart-stopping smile that he only gives me, and all is well in the world.

I bring my hand to my mouth and blow him a kiss. His smile widens, and then he turns to face the front of the stage once more. I grin, feeling happy, as I raise my hands with my eyes closed. I dance with my girls, letting his voice soothe my entire body.

With a tap on my shoulder, Cara gets my attention. She mouths, *Restroom,* and points toward the hallway.

I nod, taking her hand. We're giggling like schoolgirls as we enter the restroom, both on a high from seeing our guys on stage.

As I'm washing my hands, a local girl stands next to me. She has sharp facial features, and she's wearing too dark lip liner and clashing lipstick.

"So, I've seen you here a few times," she says in English with a thick accent.

Her English sounds the opposite of the way Andres speaks. Out of her mouth, it sounds ugly.

"Yeah, I've come here a few times with my friends," I answer.

"I've seen you with Andres Cruz. Do you know him well?"

"Yeah, he's my boyfriend," I say.

As I say the last word, she lets out a sound between a grunt and a laugh. I study her through squinted, annoyed eyes.

"Uh-huh," she says in almost a snarl. "Well, I see he went with a sure thing."

"What's that supposed to mean?"

She fakes a concerned tone. "Oh, nothing much—only that it was a sure thing he'd get in your pants. Because you're American, no?" A cruel, patronizing tone drips from her words. "And it's a fact that you're going to leave soon. You're probably only here for the summer, right?" She rolls her eyes. "So, he can continue on with his fuck-fest, guilt-free, after you leave. He knows a win-win when he sees it."

I'm staring at her, mouth agape, unable to speak when Cara flies from the restroom stall. She pushes the girl into the sink, and when the girl turns to face her, Cara slaps her face.

"Listen up, bitch. I don't know who you think you are, but you need to keep your fucking mouth shut. You don't know anything about what my friend and Andres have together, and jealousy is ugly on you. So, take your cheap-ass, someone-please-fuck-me dress and your two-bit-whore clown face—your makeup looks like shit by the way—and don't fucking come near us again."

I watch the girl's wide-eyed expression as she drops her hand from her cheek where Cara slapped her. Her expression morphs from shock to fury as she storms toward the restroom door.

She swings the door open, but before she leaves, she turns back toward us and spits, "Whatever…just wait. You're going to be forgotten like yesterday's trash before your plane even lifts off, and Andres is going to be in another girl's pants. Once a slut, always a slut, and Andres Cruz is a fucking slut! You are nothing but a hole to stick it in! Enjoy!" Her straight brown hair whips around as she exits, the door closing behind her.

Cara lunges toward the door, but I grab her arm.

"Let her go. She isn't worth it."

"She can't talk to you like that!" Cara exclaims.

I smile and pull Cara into a hug. "I love you. Thank you for always having my back."

I thank the powers that be for letting me resemble Cara's cousin, so we could start this crazy journey together three years ago. She has been my best friend, always standing up for me, and she is fiercely loyal. I am so fortunate to have her.

"I love you, too." Cara hugs me back. "Seriously, I want to go beat that bitch's face in."

"Exactly—she's a bitch. Once a bitch, always a bitch," I mock. "She's so not worth our time. Like you said, she's jealous."

"Okay, but promise me that you won't take anything she said to heart. I know you." Cara puts her hands on my shoulders and stares at me with intensity. "I know that you're going to second-guess yourself and your relationship with Andres. You're going to end up sabotaging your own happiness because of insecurities. Please don't." Her eyes are full of sincerity and love. "You are amazing, Olivia. Who cares what Andres did before you? I've seen how he is with you, and I know that he loves you. A guy doesn't fake that. If he solely wanted to get laid, believe me, he could. But he wants you. He loves you. You know that, right?"

I smile weakly, my vision blurred from threatening tears. "I do." I hug her again. "Thank you, Cara. You are seriously the best. Have I told you lately that I love you?"

"Yes, you have—like, thirty seconds ago. What are best friends for? Now, let's go dance, and have fun! I think we need some shots!"

We exit the restroom, and I feel slightly better, but I'm still so shaken up by that bitch. Why do people have to be so mean? I hate confrontation. I'm so glad that Cara was there, or I'm sure I would be a basket case.

We head to the bar and order shots. Nadia peers up quizzically when the waitress drops off six shots at our table.

Cara answers her unasked question, "Two shots each! It's just one of those nights, don't you think?"

I make a mental note to tell Nadia all about the bitch from the restroom later. I've had enough drama for one night.

Nadia shrugs and puckers her lips as if to say, *Why not?*

We laugh and hoist our first shots to the center of the table.

Cara says, "To good friends, fun times, and great memories. Cheers!"

Our group piles out of Demo.

"Are you sure?" a very intoxicated Cara asks.

"Yes, I'm fine. I promise. I'll see you tomorrow."

"I'm serious, Livi. Don't read into anything. Don't let that bitch taint anything that you have going. I want to make sure you're okay. You know you come first. I'll hang with you tonight if you want me to. Hugo can go home alone. You are way more important than him," Cara reassures me, her voice loud.

I laugh at the exaggerated look of shock on Hugo's face.

"Cara, I'm fine. I promise. I'm not that fragile. I'm going to go hang out with Andres. Go with Hugo. Have fun. I'll see you tomorrow."

Hugo hails a cab as I pull Cara in for a hug.

I watch Cara amble toward the cab with Hugo's arm around her. I release a small chuckle when his hand spends a prolonged amount of time on Cara's ass as she climbs into the cab.

"What was that all about?" Andres asks as he takes my hand and leads me toward our own waiting cab.

"Oh, nothing," I say flippantly.

In Andres's bed, legs entwined, I run my hand on his warm skin over his chest muscles, feeling his beating heart slow from our preceding activity.

Andres runs his hand through my hair. "Can you please tell me what got Cara all protective over you tonight?"

I sigh. "I ran into some bitch in the restroom tonight. She didn't have a lot of nice things to say about me or you."

"What did she say?"

"Well, in summary, she said that you are a whore, and you are only using me for sex. She made sure to tell me that the minute I leave, you will be sleeping with someone else. Like I said, she was a bitch. I'm sure you slept with her at some point, and she is just bitter."

I hold my breath in anticipation of Andres's response.

"You know that's not true, right?" Andres asks, concerned.

"Which part?"

Andres's voice rises in frustration. "Obviously, the part about me using you and the part about me sleeping with someone else when you leave. Are you worried about that?"

"Well, sometimes," I say quietly. "You do have quite the reputation, and I am afraid that once I leave, you might tire of waiting for when we can be together again."

"Jesus, Olivia. Does nothing that we've shared so far mean anything to you? Christ, I've told you that I love you. Don't you think that means something? I have never said that to another girl." Andres's voice is tainted with hurt and anger.

"I'm sorry. I know. I'm afraid of losing you. It is hard not to worry when I hear from everyone how you were with girls before me, Andres, especially when we are going to have to go so long without seeing each other."

"Baby, listen, you are the first girl I have ever loved. I know we haven't been together long, and I've never done relationships—let alone, long-distance ones—but I think that what we have is special and worth waiting for. I know what I was before you, and I can't change that. Those girls didn't mean anything to me, and I know that makes me sound like an ass, but it is true. They were my way of filling up the void in my life. You make me feel more whole than I have felt since losing my mom. I don't need my old lifestyle now that I have you. Okay?"

"Okay." I lean in and give Andres a chaste kiss. "I'm sorry."

"Don't apologize, baby, but you have to talk to me when something is bothering you. We need to be honest with one another to make this work."

I take that response as an appropriate prelude to my question. "Do you want to tell me about the issues with your dad and why you feel such a void in your life?"

Andres sighs. "My dad is fucked-up. When my mom died, he lost it, and he left me to figure out how to go on living without any parents at the age of fourteen. That's the story. I know you want to meet him, but you have to understand that I don't want someone as beautiful as you being a part of that ugliness in my life. You make me happier than I have been in years. Can't I just have that for now?"

"Of course you can. I simply thought it might help you to talk about it with someone."

"It won't."

"Okay. I won't bring it up again. I'm sorry."

He pulls me in and hugs me tightly. We entwine our bodies, both deep in thought.

Andres loves me, and that thought sends my spirit soaring, yet in the same breath, I feel myself plummet with fear of losing him. Why can't I feel secure with all of this? I believe the words he said, but my mind won't let me trust them. I simply want to be in love without the fear of loss. That deep-seated worry is tainting everything, and I know it is irrational. I know I should feel secure with our relationship.

Real love, like what I have with Andres, won't break my heart. It can't.

But how can I be sure that it won't?

I'm already in so deep. I don't know how I would recover if our love didn't last.

It's a good thing I will never have to find out because true love lasts forever. *Right?*

# chapter 20

Another two days of uncompromised bliss pass, and it is already time to take Cara back to the airport.

I hug her tightly in front of the security line. "God, I don't want you to go. It is so fun with you here. I love our little group of four." I grin.

"Me, too! I know Hugo and I don't have anything serious, but, man, that was some great sex. Just promise me that you'll wait a few weeks before letting me know that he's already in other girls' panties."

I can tell that the thought bothers her.

"I will," I say.

"Okay, I better go. Make sure to keep me informed of all your juicy details. I will live vicariously through you as I spend my summer waiting tables. Love you, doll."

I release her from my hug. "I will. Have a safe flight."

Cara gives Andres a quick hug and then heads through security. I wave at her until I can't see her anymore.

Andres and I head back to his house.

"I have something I want to show you."

"Really? What is it?" I ask, very interested.

"You will see," he says, giving me his charming smile.

Andres leads me to the second floor and down the hall to a part of the house where I have never been. He opens what appears to be a bedroom door and pulls me in. A table covered in paint and brushes is in the center of the room. The floor is concealed with several white tarps. A few easels with painted canvases are placed around the room. Completed paintings are leaning against the walls of the room.

I gasp at the first painting that really catches my attention. It is a silhouette of a naked woman, all done with shades of black, tan, and white. The woman is kneeling with her hands in her lap, and her gaze is focused on an unknown point in the distance. I can only see her profile. Her long light hair falls in wavy locks down her back. She is flawless, gorgeous, and very peaceful. She is silhouetted against a bright sunlit backlight, making her features all the more stunning, almost as if she is an angel. My fingers reach up to touch the canvas in awe.

"Do you like it?" Andres asks.

"Yes, it is absolutely beautiful, Andres. She is stunning. You are very talented. When did you paint her?" I ask, still gazing at the mesmerizing painting.

"Last week."

I lift my head, so I am locked into his stare.

"That is you." His hand raises and tucks my hair behind my ears. "You are my beautiful angel."

Surprised, I grab his hand and squeeze it. "Andres, it is absolutely lovely."

"You are utterly exquisite. I haven't picked up my paintbrush in a long time. You are my inspiration."

He wraps his arms around my waist and kisses my head. I hug him for a moment before turning to see the other paintings. They are all astonishing. There are some scenic paintings of a snowcapped mountain, the ocean, a grassy meadow, and an old tree in a field. Some paintings are of ordinary objects—an abandoned shoe on the side of the road, a motorcycle propped up by its kickstand, and a wooden door to a barn. Others are of people—a father and son playing ball, two lovers walking, hand in hand, and a lone girl sitting still in the moonlight—but none of them are like the angel. Then, some abstract paintings that are painted with dark and bold colors. I am not too knowledgeable in art, but they symbolize pain and sadness to me.

I complete my circle around the room. "Andres, you are truly talented. These are all incredible. You have a gift." The realm of his talents still amazes me.

"Thanks. I'm glad you like them. I haven't felt like painting in so long," he says, his eyes thoughtful. "Until you." He reaches out for my hand. "Come, my love."

We leave his art studio, and he closes the door behind us.

I wake up to Andres's naked body wrapped around mine. What time is it? We must have dozed off after our afternoon lovemaking. It is dark outside. I reach for my cell phone and see that it's nine o'clock. I carefully slip out from Andres's grasp and start putting on my clothes. I decide to venture down to the kitchen to get a glass of water.

I am filling up my glass when I hear shuffled footsteps behind me. Smiling, I turn. "Hey, ba—" I startle, stopping mid-word.

I am face-to-face with a thin, scruffy man with very hollow, sad eyes. His mouth is set in a grimace. His disheveled black hair has streaks of gray. His skin is especially wrinkled, and it gives the impression that one could lift it off of him, revealing only bone below. The man has little muscle tone to speak of. He is oddly familiar and extremely terrifying.

"Who the fuck are you?" he yells in my face.

His words are slurred to the point that it takes me a moment to translate the garbled language into meaning. He smells of liquor and sweat, unclean and rotten.

Fear courses through my veins. I jump back and lean as far as I can against the kitchen counter. Before I can gather my thoughts to speak, I see his hand rise, and I catch a glimpse of a bottle flying toward me. I cower, turning my face instantly, and the beer bottle misses the side of my head and shatters on the wall behind me, sending glass fragments raining down over me.

I scream, and he grabs my arm above the elbow and painfully squeezes it.

"I asked you a fucking question!" he roars inches from my face.

Before I can open my mouth, I see him raise his other hand, and I instinctually close my eyes, turning my face to brace for the blow. *I cannot believe this is happening.*

I hear the sound of a fist against skin, followed by a loud grunt. Opening my eyes, I watch the man crash down to the floor, blood seeping from his nose.

"Goddamn it!" Andres yells.

He bends down, grabs the man under each arm, and lifts his upper body off the ground. Andres locks his arms around the man's chest and starts to pull him out of the kitchen. I am in complete shock as I watch the man's feet drag on the floor while blood is dripping from his nose onto his soiled white T-shirt. They disappear around the corner, and I don't move. The front door slams shut.

I realize that I am shaking, and I pick up my trembling hands to study them. I see little lines of blood coming out of small cuts made from shreds of the glass bottle. Tears are involuntarily running down my face as the adrenaline coursing through my veins slows. I hear a gasp, and I look up to see Andres's face full of complete shock and sorrow.

He grabs my hands. "Oh my God. Olivia, are you okay?"

Without waiting for me to answer, he picks me up in his arms. Walking me to his bedroom, he kisses my head and repeats, "I'm so sorry. I'm so sorry. I'm so sorry."

He carries me into his bathroom and sets me down on the counter. He turns the shower on. "Let's get you cleaned up and make sure there are no more pieces of glass anywhere."

I am silent as he carefully undresses me. Then, he undresses himself, and picking me up in his arms, he steps into the shower. The cuts on my hands and arms sting momentarily when they first meet the hot stream. Andres allows my feet to fall, so I am standing, facing him, with my back against the water.

"This is all my fault, Liv. I am so sorry." The sadness in his eyes breaks me.

"It's okay," I finally say.

"No, it is not okay! I should have told you. It is my fault. I should have never put you in a position where you could get hurt. I just never thought he…"

Tears trickle from his eyes. I reach up and kiss his soft lips. They are warm and salty from our collective tears.

"It's okay, babe. I'm fine."

"Now, you have met my father." The melancholy in his voice is palpable. "I'm sorry I didn't tell you about him before, but honestly, I didn't want to. The man that you saw down there is not my dad. The dad I know died years ago along with my mom." He sighs and lowers his eyes.

"He is an alcoholic. He's probably on other drugs, too. I don't really know. He is always wasted and usually passed out. He lives in an apartment a little ways from here. He doesn't come here often. I never thought…" Andres closes his eyes. "He rarely comes here. I only know that he's alive because I check on him. I clean up his apartment and bring him food. I'm sorry, Liv. I never thought you would have to see him. If I would have known…" His voice drops into a sad whisper.

"He must have needed money for alcohol. It is the only time he acknowledges my existence. He shouldn't have a key to the house. I should have taken his key away a long time ago. I'm sorry."

He opens his eyes, and I see so much pain on his face.

"It's okay. I understand. I am not hurt. It's just a couple of scratches."

I wrap my wet arms around his strong back and lean into his chest. Closing my eyes, I am lost in sadness for this beautiful man. My core breaks for the pain he has gone through and the sorrow he lives with every day. I wonder if the ache in his heart is more intense for the loss of his mother who loved him but couldn't stay or for his father who is physically present but lost to him by his own choice because he has surrendered to his grief instead of fighting it for his son. I can't imagine how it makes Andres feel to be basically abandoned by his own father after losing his mother. It's heartbreaking.

Andres pulls my hand to his mouth and gently kisses my scratches. "Thank God you aren't hurt more than this. I am terrified to think about what would have happened if I hadn't gotten there when I did. I'm so sorry."

Repeatedly, he trails soft kisses from my lips to my jaw and over my cheeks. He continues to pepper my face with sad pecks. I take his face in my hands and lean my forehead against his.

"Please don't apologize anymore, Andres. I am fine. It is not your fault. Okay? This doesn't change anything. If anything, I love you more…enough to make up for your mom and your dad. I will give you enough love for a lifetime." I hold his face between my hands, and I kiss him deeply, hoping the depth of my love will be evident to him through my touch.

Andres pulls me close and buries his face in my neck. I wrap my arms tightly around him as his body trembles, releasing tears that he has been holding in for years. For so long, he has been alone in his pain.

I silently promise to love Andres forever, giving him all the love he deserves.

I cannot comprehend how his dad could give up on his child, to leave Andres when he needed his parent the most. The unresolved sorrow and feelings of neglect that Andres has locked away for so long come out in a torrent of tears. I communicate my love and solace through our embrace as I stroke his firm back. He continues to cry into my neck, and I just hold him. Arms firmly wrapped around him, I kiss his head, telling him that I love him over and over again, until he doesn't have any tears left to cry.

chapter 21

Nolan is his usual fun, cheerful, flirty self on Monday morning. He said good-bye to Abby over the weekend. I didn't see her after we had gone bowling, and I'm grateful for it. Cara and I were connected at the hip with Hugo and Andres, so it all worked out for the best.

"How was your time with Abby? Did she have fun?" I ask.

"Yeah, I think so. How was your weekend?"

"It was great. Thanks."

I push back the thought of meeting Andres's dad, and I think about the wonderful time I got to spend with Andres the rest of the weekend. Saturday afternoon, the group of us went to watch a Real Madrid game. All the guys are crazy fans. It was an experience. They do not mess around with their soccer here.

"We went to a Real Madrid game on Saturday, and then last night, I got to watch Andres's band. You should come watch them sometime. They are really good."

"Cool. Yeah, I will do that sometime. How was the game?"

"It was intense, crazy fun, and energetic. I never knew a soccer game could be so much fun."

"Yeah, they are really into soccer here. Pedro talks about it all the time."

"So, what did you and Abby do the whole time? It seems like I have barely spoken to you for two weeks."

"Not much really. We just hung out, walked around the city, went to a couple of movies—you know, typical date kind of stuff."

"I'm sorry I didn't get to hang out with her more while she was here. We only hung out twice. I feel bad about that," I say because I think that is what a best friend should say. I am not remotely sorry that my time with Abby was brief.

Nolan flashes me a grin. "Don't worry your pretty little self. She was fine with that. She isn't much into hanging out with lots of people. She is more low-key."

I laugh. "Well, I guess that opposites really do attract. She does know she is dating the life of every party, right?"

He simply smiles at me and squeezes my hand softly. I stiffen up slightly, and I pray he doesn't notice my reaction to his touch. I hate that I feel guilty for being this way with him, but I can't risk hurting Andres. He has enough hurt in his life.

I continue to ask Nolan questions about his time with Abby, and although he answers all my questions, he doesn't seem too eager to give me details. He is probably feeling blue with the departure of his girlfriend.

He asks about Andres, and I beam. Loads of details pour from my mouth. I tell him about our time in Barcelona. I laugh as I describe some of Hugo's escapades. I end by telling him that I couldn't be happier.

He gives me a warm smile. "Who knew you needed to come to Spain to find such a love? I'm happy for you, honey."

I can't help but notice that his smile doesn't reach his eyes. The knowledge that Nolan isn't completely happy here hurts my heart.

Nadia and I are laughing as she twirls me around on the dance floor. The guys have another show tonight. I marvel at the spectacle up onstage. The mouthwatering man is singing as his stare passes over the crowd of adoring women until he is focusing solely on me. I blow him a kiss, and I see the sides of his mouth curl up into a slight smile as he refocuses his attention on the screaming girls in front of the stage. He really is a great performer, his enthralling voice pulling everyone in.

Andres grabs a guitar and sits on a stool behind the microphone stand. The rest of the band is still as Andres starts playing. The music coming from his guitar has an alluringly sensual sound and draws my complete attention. The jumping crowd stills and concentrates on Andres. He starts to sing, and it is just him and his guitar.

The song is new, I think. I have never heard him sing it before. The lyrics talk of love, happiness, wholeness, and light. I watch Andres as he sings the chorus for a second time, and with every word he sings, I search inside myself for any semblance of composure, trying to rein in the uncontrollable sobbing that is on the verge of spilling out.

*You saved me. You made me whole.*

*You brought me from the darkness to the light, and I want to live in your warmth forever.*

*I need to feel your soft touch and sweet kisses. You alone have the key to my soul.*

*If we are strengthened by those who love us, then, baby, you are going to move mountains.*

*There is no one on this earth who is loved more than you.*

*I couldn't love you more if I tried.*

*You are my forever, baby. Forever, baby.*

My eyes well up as Andres's gaze locks with mine. His voice is haunting, beautiful, and so sexy. At that moment, it feels like we are the only two people in the room. All the love coming from him resonates deep within me, and my body aches to touch him. I want him so much in this instant that my need for him is physically painful.

The song ends, and I wipe a tear from my cheek.

"Wow," Nadia says. I face her as she speaks, "If that wasn't a confession of love, then I don't know what is. I almost feel like I was intruding on your moment!"

Still speechless, I smile at her.

Without thinking, I start winding my way through the packed crowd of adoring woman on the dance floor. I need to touch Andres and feel his lips on mine. His song, the lyrics, and the emotion in his voice as he sang to me has filled me with so much love.

A slow smile forms on his lips, lighting up his eyes, as he watches me get closer to the stage. The band is quiet as I approach. The crowd murmurs in confusion, waiting for the next song to start, before they notice Andres's stare on me. They start parting, allowing me through, more so to get a better view than to clear a path for me.

Before I get to the stage, Andres jumps down and takes wide steps toward me. When we meet, he runs his hands along the sides of my face, entwining his fingers in my hair, and then he pulls my mouth to his. He kisses me hard, licking greedily, as our lips tangle in the perfect dance. The kiss isn't long, but it is everything. My blood rushes, pounding so forcefully that it rattles my core with intense sensations of adoration for this man here before me.

As he pulls his lips off of mine, I stand there limply, drunk on his kiss. He moves his face away enough to look into my eyes, and he runs the back of his hand over my cheek, causing the breath to rush out of me. His breath is warm against my skin.

"So, you liked the song, baby?" His voice is low and husky.

Words fleeing my consciousness, I press my lips together and nod. His grin widens before he presses his lips to mine in a chaste kiss.

Pulling back, he whispers against my lips, "I mean every word."

I nod again, overwhelmed.

He kisses me softly once more. "Later," he whispers in my ear, causing my skin to prickle.

He turns and heads back to the stage. The crowd envelops me, and I become aware of the chaos around me. Catcalls come from screaming fans who are ready to get back to the music.

The guys start playing the intro, and Andres holds on to the microphone stand. He gives me a knowing grin before he starts singing. I stand there, still not trusting my weak muscles to move, and I stare in amazement at the view before me. No doubt, it is a beautiful view, inside and out, and he's all mine.

After the set, we all sit at a table, drinking and chatting. A group of girls come up to the table, and with their best seductive expressions, they start talking to the band, but most of their attention is focused on Andres. I understand he wants to be polite to the fans and humor them a little, but I have shared his attention enough for one night, I think.

I subtly place my hand under the table and rub it up Andres's thigh. Stopping it between his legs, I apply pressure. He coughs and continues talking, but he has become immediately hard. I smile and begin to stroke the outline of his cock with my hand. I'm careful to move my hand slowly, so I won't attract attention. Continuing to stroke him, I lean into his ear as if to tell him something, and I plunge my tongue into his ear before biting the lobe and pulling down with my teeth. Andres's hand hits the table, and he coughs again before he takes a drink of his beer.

"Excuse me," Andres says to the girls. "I need to talk to my girl." He grabs my hand from under the table, taking it in his, and he pulls me up in one swift motion as he stands.

Pulling me through the bar, he takes us through a far exit door. We are outside at the rear of the bar in an alley. On the other side of the alley is the back of another building. The alley is wide enough for a single car to fit through. It is dark and dingy, and my stomach tightens with excitement. My cheeks flush, and my pulse quickens as Andres pulls me around a metal storage container standing to the side of the exit door. He pushes me against the brick wall of the bar.

"I'm going to fuck you, baby. I need to feel you—now," he says breathlessly against my neck.

His lips crash on mine, and our mouths meet in a frenzy of desire. His tongue assaults my mouth, giving me a rhythmic preview of what is to come. Andres pulls away, leaving me breathless, and he kneels on the ground. With fiery intent, he pulls one of my legs over his shoulder and shimmies my tight black skirt up, so it is around my waist. He rips off my panties, letting them fall to the ground. My breath comes out in a moan as he inserts two fingers inside me, sending ravishing tingles through my body. His pupils darken as he spreads me open, exposing me to the temperate night air.

"Oh fuck, baby," he groans.

His mouth surrounds my sweet spot, and he licks vehemently, pausing to suck, before continuing the relentless attack with his tongue.

I groan with pleasure. "Ugh, Andres…please!"

I feel myself building with the acute pleasure of his sweet attack. I groan as I surrender myself to a mind-shattering orgasm that racks me with intense sensations. Andres holds me against the wall with his arms, and he continues to lick until my body ceases to shake. I am gasping for air in this alley that suddenly feels private and intimate. *Holy shit.*

He guides my leg from his shoulder to the ground, and I steady myself as my senses begin to return. I quickly unbutton his jeans and slide them with his boxers to the ground. He pushes me back against the brick wall as he glides his hands down around my thighs. He lifts me, and I circle my legs around him as he holds me up against the building. Without pause, he enters me with vigor and begins a delightful ambush of drives in and out. His mouth is meshed with mine, and we are kissing hard and rough as he pounds me into the brick.

The fire in my belly is imploding within, causing quivers to surge through every cell in my body, triggering delicious sensations that rush from my scalp, down my spine, and out to my limbs. He pulls my lip between his, biting it, and the sensation shatters me. I explode around him in another staggering release. He comes with me, growling, repeating my name against my mouth.

His arm is wrapped around my back, gripping my hair, as he leans us into the wall. We are silent, except for our labored breaths, as we try to calm our lungs. He pulls out of me, and I let my legs fall to the ground.

Pulling me tightly against him, he declares, "I love you so fucking much."

I bring my hand up to rub his face. "Me, too, babe."

We stand in the dirty alley among the trash in the darkness, entwined together. I listen to his heartbeat as I rest against his chest. I feel beautiful, loved, and happy. This is complete happiness.

# chapter 22

Per usual, Andres is waiting for me as I exit class the next day. He is leaning up against a tall tree in the garden, appearing downright edible, and I melt. I give Nolan a hug good-bye, and he extends a friendly wave to Andres before walking off. Andres walks up to me and kisses me, pulling me up into a hug, my feet leaving the ground. His lips explore mine, like he hasn't seen me in weeks, and it lifts my soul. He places my feet back on the ground, and I catch my breath.

He says, "I want to do something today…something neither of us has done before." His boyish smile is wide, giddy with excitement.

"What?" I ask excitedly.

He gives me his trademark grin. "You'll see."

He grabs my hand, lacing our fingers together, and we walk toward the street.

We end up at his house, and I give him a questioning glance as I step off of the motorcycle.

"You'll see!" His striking blues gleam down on me as he laughs.

We head inside and go upstairs to the rooftop balcony.

He says, "So, I thought that I could paint you today."

I peer around and see an easel holding a blank canvas next to a table with paints and different-sized brushes.

Confused, I say, "You have painted me."

"I know, but that was from memory. I am sure I could do much better with the real thing in front of me."

He gives me an inquiring glance and grabs my hand. He trails kisses from my fingers to up my arm, and he ends at the base of my ear, skewing my equilibrium.

I shiver. "Sure. Why not? No one is going to see this, are they?" My voice trembles.

"Awesome. It will be for my eyes only, I promise." Andres steps back and slides my backpack off of me before placing it against the back wall.

He takes me in his arms and kisses me. Our tongues start off gently exploring each other's mouths, and then the kiss heightens, becoming deep and intense. I suck on his tongue and then lightly bite his bottom lip, and he pulls away, breathing heavily.

"Okay, stop that…or I will never get to the painting part." He smiles and kisses my forehead. "Let me help you take off your clothes, so I can start painting that perfect body of yours."

I lift my arms as he pulls off my T-shirt. He runs light kisses down my shoulder as he unbuttons my pants, letting them fall to the floor. His kisses make their way up to my neck, and he unfastens my bra. He cups my breasts with his strong hands and starts kneading them before pulling at the nipples.

He grunts, "God, you are so fucking sexy." He steps back and takes a few deep breaths. He sighs, "Okay. Do you want to go and lie on that couch?" He points to the outdoor sofa.

"Sure. Do you want me to take off my underwear, too?" I ask.

"No, go ahead and leave them on. They are hot," he says as he admires my lacy black thong.

I walk over to the sofa. "How should I lie?"

"However you are comfortable."

I lie on the sofa on my side, letting my arms fall to the soft cushions below me. Andres has seen me naked many times, so I don't know why, but lying here has me feeling so exposed. I watch as he takes his paintbrush in his hand and starts working on the canvas. The blue of his irises is piercing as he concentrates on painting, his stare flickering between my body and the canvas. He is so deliciously attractive as he works. My face flushes as I watch his tight forearm flex while he makes strokes against the canvas. I am hopeless.

I can feel my breath quicken, and my blood pressure increase as I lie on the padded cushions. Closing my eyes, I try to relax. Lying here, bare, and having Andres study me with that steamy stare is such a turn-on. I can feel my desire deepen, the wetness increasing between my legs. It is so erotic, here in the open like this, while being examined and painted. Keeping my eyelids shut, I attempt to relax, focusing on my breathing. I don't know how long this will take. It is a real possibility that I am going to incinerate right here from this burning need that I have for Andres to be inside me, now.

The sun heats my skin, and the sofa is very comfortable. My mind wanders to calming thoughts, and I concentrate on my breathing. Relaxing, I can feel myself starting to drift off.

Smooth lips on mine awaken me. I can taste his minty breath on my mouth, and I open my tired lids.

He grins at me. "I'm done, baby."

"Mmm," I manage as I wrap my arms around his neck.

"I'm done," he says again in a hushed voice.

"I want to see it," I whisper through my sleepy fog.

Andres takes my hand and leads me over to the painting. The girl on the canvas is breathtaking. The work of art is sexy but beautiful and classy at the same time.

I don't think it resembles me. "It is stunning, Andres. I love it. But is this how you see me?" I ask, confused.

Andres stares at me, perplexed. "Yes. This is what you look like, Liv."

I stare at the painting. "Hmm…I don't see it."

He wraps his arms around me from behind as I continue to observe the girl on the canvas in front of me.

"Trust me, baby. Believe me when I tell you, this is you—simply gorgeous."

His inviting breath on my neck tickles. He turns me around to face him, and his mouth is on mine, igniting the pull in my belly. He kisses me so tenderly, and my lips shiver against his. He trails his kisses down my neck to my breast, slowly sliding his tongue across my erect nipple. He pulls my nipple into his mouth with more intensity, and I grasp at his hair with both hands as I gasp with pleasure.

I push Andres back. "I think you have me at a disadvantage here, babe," I say as I pull his shirt off over his head. "It is only fair that I get to see your fine body, too. Don't you think?"

I suck on Andres's neck, tasting the salty sweetness of his skin, as I unbuckle his pants and guide them to the ground. I can feel his desire pressing into my skin as I run my fingers through his hair, pulling him into a deep kiss. He kisses me senseless as he smooths his hands over my back, branding me with his touch, drawing me in.

I pull away, panting at the loss of connection. Through audible breaths, I say, "You know what else, babe?"

Andres peers up through hooded eyes as his hands continue their exploration of my sensitive skin.

"I only think it is fair that I get to paint you, too."

He lifts an eyebrow. "You want to paint me?"

"Mmhmm…"

His hands find my butt cheeks, and he squeezes. "Whatever you want, baby."

I lead us to where the table with paint stands.

"First, I think I will start out with a little red." I dip two fingers into the red paint.

A cute, puzzled grin graces Andres's face, and I find myself smiling back at him. I take my two fingers and run them down his chest. Giving extra attention to his nipples, I rub my fingers in a circular motion across each taut peak, moving from one to the other. His cheerful expression goes dark, and his lips part as he inhales.

I dip my hands in the green paint and trace loopy designs up his arms, admiring the curvature of his lean muscles. When I get to his shoulders, I massage them while I lean in and give Andres a delicate, sweet kiss. I insert my tongue into his mouth for a moment, but I withdraw it before he can entwine it with his. Andres groans.

I rub yellow paint on my hands and use them to trace the outlines of his defined abdomen muscles. I outline the inverted V at the base of his torso, and it almost does me in. Andres takes my arms in his.

"Uh-uh. Not yet, mister. I am not done with my masterpiece yet."

"Baby, you're killing me here." His low, gruff voice sends riveting pulses to my stomach, causing me to tremble.

"Just a little more, babe. Your back needs some color."

Dipping my hands into purple and blue, I work my colored palms over Andres's back muscles. I trace paint from his shoulders, down his back, and up to the sides where I rub his lat muscles. I trace my hands around to his front again, admiring the myriad of colors blended on his chest. Andres's face is resonating pure lust, and it's a color that is so erotically inviting on him. I drop to my knees and take his length into my mouth.

"Fuck!" Andres moans, throwing his head back, as I work him in and out of my mouth, holding his hips with my painted hands. "Oh God, Liv. Yes," he says through gritted teeth.

He tangles his fingers through my hair as his hips start a tantalizing cadence of thrusts toward my mouth, letting me take him as far back into my throat as I can. I trace his smooth head with my tongue while I work his base with my hand, and then I take him fully in my mouth again. His breathing becomes ragged, and I can feel his quad muscles tighten as he lets out an unrestrained moan toward the ceiling. I pull my mouth off of him.

"Shit, Livi." He is struggling to find his breath.

"I want to come together, babe. Sit down."

Andres sits on the ground of the patio with his legs straight out in front of him. He locks his arms behind him, leaning on his hands, and peers up at me. I straddle his thighs and position myself at his tip. I crash onto him, covering him completely with my heat. We both moan from the powerfully staggering feeling of our connection. I grab on to his multicolored chest and begin an intense onslaught of rhythmic thrusts. I rise so that only his tip is still inserted, and then I plunge down again, taking his entire length. My legs burn from the intensity of my movements, but I don't slow. The fire in my belly is beginning to take over my body, and I can hear in Andres's breath that he is close.

Andres leans forward, taking his weight off of his arms, and he wraps them around my back. He buries his face in my breasts as I continue to ride him senseless. His strong arms hold me tight as my body explodes in a numbing sensation and heat, and I scream in release. He tilts his hips, entering me one more time, before I hear him shatter, his steamy breath on my chest.

We sit on the floor of the outdoor patio with our arms wrapped around one another, panting with rough, raw breaths. We are still connected and sticky with color, sweat, and sex.

As he holds me tight, Andres speaks into my skin, "Damn, baby, that was fucking extraordinary."

"I am here for your pleasure, Señor Cruz."

"Well, I give you an A-plus on your first art lesson. You have a way with color."

I laugh. "Shower?"

"Yes, shower," Andres says as he releases one arm from my back to steady himself as he stands.

My legs remain wrapped around him, and he carries us into the shower, still connected.

As the balmy water from the shower propels over our bodies, color cascades down in multihued rivers. His mouth meshes with mine, and his tongue takes over, rendering me senseless once more.

Andres drops me off at my house before going to practice with the guys at Hugo's. I open the thick wooden door, and I am met with laughter echoing through the house. Nolan and Nadia are sitting at the kitchen table with their textbooks open. Nadia's head is thrown back in a fit of giggles, and Nolan carries a quirky grin across his face.

I take everything in, and I am overcome with gratitude. Walking into this house feels like home. This country, these people, this life feels right. This is the first time I have truly known that I am right where I am supposed to be. I spent the day with the love of my life, and then I get to come home to tangible happiness among two of my favorite people.

Nolan's face lights up when he notices me. "Hey, Livi!"

"Hi, guys," I answer. "What are you up to?"

"We are trying to study, but Nolan here is very good at distractions. His comedic timing is priceless."

I laugh. "For sure. One has to have a lot of concentration to actually get any studying done with him." I drop my backpack by the table and sit. "I have some serious studying to do, too."

Nolan stands. "I'm going to grab a drink. Can I get you two anything?"

"I'm good. Thanks," Nadia answers.

"I'll take a water if you don't mind. Thank you," I say.

Nolan places a bottle of water on the table in front of me, and I thank him again.

He bends and kisses the top of my head. "Anytime." Returning to his seat, he asks, "So, what are the plans for this evening?"

Nadia looks up from her book. "The guys are playing at a new bar on the west side if you want to come."

"Sure. That sounds fun," Nolan says, sounding interested.

The bar named Memo's is larger and more modern than the other establishments the guys regularly play in. The interior is covered in varying shades of cream and white, giving it a very New Age feel. The interior designer could have taken the scheme straight from a trendy bar in Los Angeles. The large dance floor is covered in ashen tile and is already packed with eager bodies. The guys are getting quite the group of followers.

Although Andres plays the band off as something just for fun, I know it means so much more to him than that. I have seen the way he expresses himself through music, sending a powerful message. He says it is all simply a pastime, but everything he does—from the way he practices every day to the heart and soul he puts into the lyrics and the energy he uses to put on a fantastic performance, no matter the venue—tells anyone who is paying attention that it is so much more. Perhaps he doesn't want to let on how valuable music is to his life and how much he wants the band to succeed because if for some reason it doesn't, it will be another letdown in his life.

I understand his hesitance and need to seem nonchalant about everything. I know he is tired of people he loves letting him down, and although his music is not a person, it is definitely alive. Its heartbeat thrums through Andres, allowing him to breathe, to let it all go in the soul of the music. All of the pain and disappointment in his life can be released with each note that is played and word that is sang, permitting the pressure on his heart to lessen. Music means more to Andres than I think anyone realizes. Unlike his art, which he took a break from when it all became too much, he has never quit music. I pray that his band continues to succeed, not only for him but also for the people who get to hear him. That is a gift in itself.

Andres peers up from the mic stand and finds me across the room, staring at him, as I think this all through. His mischievous smile lights up his face, and I can't help but grin back. His smile sends the butterflies in my belly into a fluttering frenzy. His eyes darken as his stare intensifies, and I feel him in my soul. I can read every message those eyes are telling me right now, and it fills my body with so much warmth as it sends my heart into overdrive. He loves me and wants me just as much as I want him.

One of the band's more upbeat songs charges through the speakers of the bar, and the dance floor is alive with arms flinging in the air, bodies bouncing to the beat, and smiles on all the faces. I dance, grinning widely, as I watch Nolan repeatedly twirl Nadia in a circle. She laughs and tells him to stop. He does, and she falls into his chest. She closes her eyes, regaining her equilibrium, as I'm sure the room is spinning for her at this point.

She looks up and playfully hits Nolan on the arm. "Were you trying to make me puke?" She giggles and grabs my hand.

We raise our arms in the air together and bounce along to the beat.

My life is so perfect, and I know it is too good to be true. People aren't really this happy—at least, not forever. Spain is my heaven. There are no real expectations here besides having fun. Yes, I have a couple of classes, but they cause little pressure. They aren't too difficult, and not having to work here leaves me with extra time to study. I wish I could be like that guy in the *Groundhog Day* movie and relive this time over and over. I know all good things come to an end eventually, but maybe, just maybe, my life will be the exception to that rule.

# chapter

The next two months go by way too quickly. I guess time does fly when you are having fun. I've been doing great in my classes, partly thanks to Andres and my daily study session. I admit that the study sessions are a highlight of my day, and it isn't because of the studying.

Nolan and I talk and have fun every day at school, and he usually goes out with the group once during the weekend. He fits right in wherever he goes, and all of Nadia's and Carlos's friends love him. He and I are different than we were back home, but we are still great.

Andres and I continue to hang out most weeknights with Nadia and the guys, but we take a couple of nights a week to just spend time alone together. We go clubbing at least one weekend night. Dancing with Andres will never get old. The guys usually play a show once or twice a week, sometimes more. A buzz about the band is growing. More people show up when they play. I am so happy that they are experiencing success. They deserve it. Once people hear the music, how could they not love it?

Nadia and Andres make sure I have lots of memorable Spanish experiences. We take weekend and day trips to different cities, soaking in the inspirational culture of this country. I would say that my Spanish is close to perfect. Andres and I also have days where we only speak in English. He likes to practice, but honestly, he doesn't need it. His English is flawless.

I spend a lot of my time at Andres's house, and thankfully, his dad hasn't visited again nor have we run into him in the city. Andres has opened up more about his mom, sharing moments of her life, her horrible battle with breast cancer, and her death. His face lights up when he talks about her life before cancer. He shares more about his dad as well. Andres has tried to get his dad help, but he won't accept it. Andres thinks his dad is numbing the pain until he passes away and can be with his wife again. It is sad that his dad can't be present for Andres, and it breaks my heart, but I vow to give Andres enough love to fill that hole in his life.

Even when I think it can't get any better or I can't possibly love Andres more, the next day comes, and it is better. I love him more, and my love for him is growing every day. I don't know what I did in this life to deserve so much love, especially from someone so amazing, but I am happy.

Today was the last day of classes. I am glad I thought ahead and booked my flight home for a week after classes finished. At the time, I thought that maybe Nolan and I would spend our last week exploring Spain. Now, my last week is going to be spent with Andres. He has a surprise planned for me and is taking me away for the week. I am excited to find out where we are going. Every time I think about my impending flight home, I feel a little nauseous as sadness and anxiety start to take over. So, I am trying really hard to live in the moment and be thankful for one uninterrupted week alone with the love of my life. I can fall apart later, but right now, I want to completely absorb this gift of unadulterated happiness that I have been given.

"Hey, baby. You ready?" Andres is standing in my bedroom door, smiling broadly.

"Yes, I think so. I wasn't sure what to pack since you wouldn't give me any hints, so I packed a little bit of everything." I smirk at him.

He laughs. "You can give me that look all you want, but it's not a surprise if I tell you where we are going."

He grabs my bag from me, and we make our way out to the car. Andres has been driving his dad's car more often over the past couple of months, and it's definitely a welcome change for me. Although I did grow to appreciate the freeness of riding in the open air on a motorcycle, the feeling of the enclosed safety of a vehicle is more my style.

Nadia waves. "Have fun! See you on Friday for your going-away bash!"

"Please don't remind me," I say dryly. "I will be the one wearing black." I give her a sad smile and get into the car.

Andres and I drive for a little over an hour, and we enter a lovely city with an old-world feel.

"This is Cadiz," Andres says. "It is one of the oldest cities in Spain."

I stare out the window as we drive through the town. It isn't small, but it definitely has a small-town feel. The architecture is stunning. Even my novice eye can tell that these buildings are all very old. Most of the buildings are made of brownstone and are majestic in appearance. Driving through town, Andres points out some important landmarks, churches, and historical sights. I can see the ocean on the horizon, and I smile, inhaling the smell of the air through the opened car windows.

Andres pulls into the driveway of a beautiful brownstone house that backs up to the Atlantic Ocean. He stops the car, and we get out. Taking my hand, he leads me into the house.

The interior of the house is breathtaking. The walls are made of stone, and the floor is tiled with an appealing design that runs throughout the house. It is definitely old, but it has been recently remodeled. It has an old-world meets classic-contemporary feel, and it is a very romantic space. I gasp when I see the wall of floor-to-ceiling windows that open to a deck overlooking the Atlantic Ocean. Walking onto the deck, I see a private beach complete with palm trees just steps below. A couple of straw huts with hammocks hang underneath.

I turn to Andres. "This is so gorgeous, Andres! How did you manage to get this place?"

"I am glad you like it. It is the vacation home of one of my mom's old best friends. I just called her up and asked if we could stay here. She was more than happy to offer it to us for the week." He pulls me into him, and his soft lips meet mine. "We have the whole week to be together with no distractions. We can swim, lie by the beach, lounge around, or do whatever we want…many, many times." He winks at me with his adorable, devious smile.

I wrap my arms around his neck. "Have I told you lately how much you mean to me?"

"You have. But how about you show me now?"

"Gladly."

I grin, and he leads me into the bedroom.

The next day, the sun is streaming into the bedroom from the balcony's glass door. I am wrapped in Andres. Our legs are entwined, and his head is lying on my breast. I can feel the warmth from his sleeping breaths on my chest. When my stomach growls, I recognize my pressing need for food, knowing that my last meal was yesterday morning. Once we made it to the bedroom yesterday, we never left.

I delicately untangle my legs from Andres. I guide his head onto my pillow and slide out of bed. Putting on a pair of my short black yoga shorts and a tank top, I head to the kitchen. Opening the refrigerator, I am surprised to see that it is fully stocked. I take out the eggs and bacon, and after rummaging through the kitchen, I find everything I need to make pancakes.

I am flipping the pancakes when strong arms wrap around me, hugging me tight.

"Hey, babe. I was going to bring you breakfast in bed," I say.

I start to tremble as Andres's lips find my neck, and he begins a sweet assault of kisses down to my shoulder.

"If you keep doing that, I am going to burn your breakfast."

He whispers in my ear, "Maybe I want something else for breakfast…something sweeter." He pulls on my earlobe with his full lips.

I exhale. "Although that is very appealing, if I don't eat something, I won't have the energy for such activity. Will you take a rain check?" Spatula in hand, I turn and give him a lingering kiss on the lips.

"Okay, as long as you don't make me wait too long to redeem my rain check."

# chapter

After breakfast, we put on our swimsuits, fill a cooler with drinks, and make our way down the wooden steps leading from the deck to the beach. The sand is hot and soft, giving way under my feet, as I curl my toes in the sand. I walk over to where the water meets the beach and draw designs with my toes in the slick, wet sand. As the waves roll in, I watch the drawings disappear.

I am lifted by strong arms and thrown over Andres's shoulder. Laughing, I slap his butt cheeks with feeble force. I shriek, "Put me down!"

"Put you down?" Andres asks as he walks into the water. "You want me to put you down? Well, I guess I need to give the lady what she wants!"

"Wait, wait, wait!" I manage before I am airborne and then splashing in the water. Coming up from under the water, I laugh. "You jerk!" I wipe the water from my eyes and taste the saltiness on my lips.

Andres is laughing when I make my way over to him. Grabbing a hold of his neck, I pull up, place my feet on his hips, and hoist myself onto him, pushing him under the water. He, of course, pulls me under with him. After coming up, we continue to splash and push each other into the water. When I lamely attempt some wrestling moves that I learned from my brother, my strength is no match for Andres, and he throws me through the air again.

Coming to the surface, laughing, I hold up my hand. "Truce! I give up! You win!"

Andres is next to me again, but instead of shoving me under the water, his mouth meets mine in a firm and salty kiss. I wrap my arms around his neck and my legs around his middle. His arms are around me, and he is kneading my back, rubbing small circles up and down it.

He breaks the kiss and leans his head into my neck. "I am going to miss you so much."

I sigh. "I know. Me, too. Please, let's not talk about me leaving. I don't want to think about it now. Let's just enjoy this time together."

He kisses me, and as our kiss deepens, he walks us toward the beach. He lays me down on the wet sand, and lowers himself down beside me. He is propped up on one elbow, leaning over me, as he showers my face with kisses. The sand is warm and gives slightly under my body. The water is rising and falling against my legs, gently caressing our bodies. My hands explore his firm back, and I commit every contour of his skin to memory.

His kisses make their way to my ear, down my neck, and across my collarbone before stopping at my breasts. Andres takes his time exploring my breasts with the touch of his mouth and hands. He is not rushed in his journey.

I watch the love and need in his eyes as he explores my body, and I can't help but feel he is memorizing every inch of my body. Lying on the beach in the open with the sun shining down on us, I feel an anomalous sense of solitude. In this moment, it is only the two of us in this beautiful world. We make slow and sweet love on the sand, and I yearn for time to stand still, so I will never have to feel anything other than this time with Andres again.

We spend our day cuddling in the hammock and making love on a thick beach blanket beneath the straw umbrella. Andres grills some shrimp and veggie kabobs for dinner, and then we take a walk, hand in hand, down the beach. The colors of the sky are magnificent in irregular swirls of pink, purple, red, orange, and yellow streams of light. The clouds are lit up as if by an internal lavender light bulb. The sun is setting over the Atlantic, and the sight is simply stunning.

Strolling along in this serene setting with this magnificent man, I decide to ask some questions. I need to know what Andres envisions for us after I leave. My heart cannot take the uncertainty of it all. I know he loves me, but I'm uncertain if he expects us to carry on a long-distance relationship.

"Andres, what do you see for us in the future?" I ask in a meek voice.

He smiles down at me, squeezing my hand, as our bare feet continue to stroll through the sand. "You know, Olivia, before you, I didn't think about or really care about the future. Being with you has opened my eyes to love again. You have taken my shattered life and mended my heart and soul with your love. I don't know what our future holds, but I do know that in my future, all I see is you."

I melt from his statement. "I'm so scared. I might not have closed my heart like you did, but being with you and feeling what I do, I now know that it has never been opened before. So, like you, I am feeling all of this for the first time. I didn't know love like this existed, and I am afraid to lose it. We literally live an ocean away. How can a relationship survive that distance?" I try not to sound whiny, but I can hear the shrill in my voice.

"I don't know, Olivia, but I know it can. We will see each other over holiday breaks, and then when you are done with school, we can figure out the next step." Andres stops walking and faces me, pulling me into his arms. "You are my salvation, my beautiful Olivia. I lived in the shadows of pain and loss for too long. I was so exhausted with my life, tired of being in darkness, but I didn't know how to get out. You are my light in this world, and now that I have found you, I will never let you go. I always want to be with you in this life." He leans in and kisses me passionately. Pulling away, he says, "Being separated by time or distance will not keep me from you. You are my forever, baby."

I hug him tightly and feel at peace. For this brief moment, my insecurities are quiet, and I am basking in absolute serenity. Andres lifts me up, and I circle my legs around his waist. Holding me firmly to him, his loving lips find mine, kissing me slowly. My fingers run through his hair, and I pull his face toward mine, needing to feel closer. His tongue runs carefully across my lips and slips inside my mouth, tenderly exploring and twisting in a delicate dance with my own. Pressure radiates from my chest with the love I have for this man. I am wrapped in his strength as his strong hands hold me tight and travel up my back and into my hair, pushing me closer. His lips leave mine to make a path of kisses down my neck, across my collarbone, and over my shoulder.

"I love you so much," he groans into my ear.

I whimper when his mouth finds my neck again, sucking with abandoned longing. Removing one hand from my hair, he runs it across my ribs and down my side. He stops at the side tie of my bikini bottom. He pulls the string, releasing the bow securing my suit. Reaching his hand around to my other side, he pulls that bow, and the material falls to the sand, leaving me exposed to the cooling night winds dancing across the Atlantic.

I throw my head back, moaning, when his fingers find my center and do what they do so well—exploring, cherishing, loving me. With my legs still wrapped around Andres while one of his strong arms secures me, my senses are on overload. My skin is heated from his arm holding me tight. The sounds of the waves coming into the shore, the feel of the breeze against my sensitized skin, my damp hair swaying against my back in time to the cadence of his fingers entering me, and the adorations of love whispered in his smooth, sexy voice send me reeling. My body explodes with warmth. My heart races, and my nipples harden as the rush of ecstasy resonates from my core. Dropping my arms from around his neck, my hands fall to my breasts. As I pull my nipples, the surges of pleasure roll through me, and I cry out.

I barely feel his fingers leave me before he pushes down his shorts. I secure my arms around his neck once more, and his strong hands grab on to each side of my hips. He lifts me up slightly to bring me down onto his waiting erection. I moan as he fills me to my limit. Andres hisses through his teeth as his arms start a divine rhythm of lifting and dropping me onto him. He controls the movements, and I close my eyes. I relish in the pleasure filling my body and the love filling my soul.

On the beach under the moonlight, we spend hours professing our love through our words and touch. We connect with the gentle fierceness of our passion until our bodies are consumed with sated exhaustion.

# chapter 25

To say that my week with Andres at the beach house was heaven on earth would be an understatement. I loved every second I spent with him in and out of bed. He made me feel completely cherished as we walked on the beach, swam in the ocean, and talked for hours while wrapped in each other's bodies.

Nadia threw Nolan and me a grand good-bye party that started at the house and ended at our favorite club. I tried to enjoy it, but even liquid courage couldn't take the edge off of my melancholy mood over my impending departure.

Nadia and the guys said good-bye to me at the house, allowing Andres to take me to the airport. Nolan made his way through security without me, leaving Andres and me to say our good-byes alone—well, as alone as one can be in a busy airport.

Tears are streaming down my face, and panic is exploding through my every pore. "I love you. Please wait for me."

Andres wipes my tears away and places gentle kisses on my tear-stained face. "Of course I will. Don't cry, baby. This isn't good-bye. Think of it as, see you later."

"Please wait for me, please wait for me, please wait for me," I whisper my mantra over and over, barely keeping my hysteria in check as I rest my forehead against his chest.

Andres holds my face firmly between his strong hands. "Olivia, look at me."

I stare into his captivating eyes.

"I. Am. Not. Going. Anywhere," he says, emphasizing each word. "You own me. Nothing is going to change that. I will see you over Christmas break. It is less than five months away. It will go quickly, I promise. Please don't cry."

I bury my face into his chest, and I sob. Andres wraps his strong arms around me, hugging me to him, as he kisses my hair. I raise my head and find his lips. Our kiss becomes urgent and passionate. I tell him how much I love him and need him through my kiss. I kiss him with all the passion from this summer and with all my hopes for the future. I kiss him as if I will never kiss him again. If I know anything about the future, I know that it is not guaranteed. Nothing is.

Andres pulls away. I can see his lungs expanding through his T-shirt as he struggles to find his breath. My heart is racing, and I, too, am breathing heavily. A choking sob comes to the surface. Andres grasps my hands firmly in his.

Through his raspy breaths, he says, "Baby, you have to go. I don't want you to miss your plane."

"I know." I stare at his face, the face that I have grown to love so much, and I try to commit every tiny detail to my memory. Giving him a feeble smile, I manage to say, "See you soon."

"See you soon, beautiful. Call me when you land, okay? I love you, Olivia."

I step back toward the security line, not releasing my grip on his hand. Our arms are outstretched, and my fingers desperately cling to his, wanting to remain in contact. When my final finger slips from his grasp, I feel the sting on my skin from the loss of his touch. My tearful eyes don't leave his as I walk through the security line. His penetrating stare seers a deeper impression on my soul. The security guard thankfully spares me embarrassment and doesn't acknowledge my current state of despair. On the other side of the metal detectors, I gaze at Andres, and before I can no longer see him anymore, I blow him a kiss. His hands are in his pockets, and as I round the corner toward my terminal, I see his chin fall to his chest.

My legs feel shaky, and I could fall to the floor and weep, but then Nolan's arm wraps around me, securing me on my feet.

He pulls me close to his side and kisses my hair. "I've got you, baby girl."

I lean my head into Nolan's side, and we walk to our gate.

I sit in silence, peering out the window of the plane. I am vaguely aware of Nolan's thumb stroking the top of my hand. As we ascend into the clouds and I see Seville becoming smaller beneath me, I wonder why I am experiencing such despair. Of course I will miss Andres, but I will see him in five months. I will be busy with work and school during that time. I will have Cara and Nolan, and they will keep me busy and happy. *It's not good-bye but see you later.*

Then, why do I feel so dreadfully empty? I experienced the best moments of my life this summer, and I can't quiet the sinking fear that I will never feel that level of love again. I believe that Andres loves me, and I believe that we are meant for each other, but I can't shake this internal doubt I have. I need to silence the nagging voice in my head that keeps reminding me of my flaws, my insecurities, and all the things that could go wrong. I need to push this negativity from my mind. It is not going to help me get through these next five months.

I am going to focus on the amazing memories and stay in the light. Stay positive. I will see Andres again, and we will have our happily ever after. I know it. I just know it.

# chapter 26

Cara throws my favorite little black halter dress at me.

"Ow," I state dryly although I know this is a silly reaction since it didn't hurt at all. I'm lying on my bed in my yoga pants and a T-shirt amid a mess of gossip magazines and granola bar wrappers.

"Enough moping," Cara says as she starts our favorite pre-party song mix on my iPod. Flo Rida's "Club Can't Handle Me" plays from my speakers. "Get off of your bed. Take a shower. Get cute. We are going out."

Flicking my dress to the side, I continue to lie facedown on my bed with my head resting on my hands. "I'm not moping. I just don't feel like going out."

Cara lets out an exaggerated laugh. "Not moping my ass, Livi. You've been home for a week, and you have barely left the house. Despite my begging, you have refused to go out with me. We only have a couple of weeks left before school starts up, so we need to take advantage of the rest of our summer." She sits down next to me on the bed and moves a lock of my hair behind my ear. "Listen, I know you miss Andres. I get it. I do. But lying around, feeling sorry for yourself, isn't going to help anything. I actually think you would feel better if you got back into your regular routine—you know, keep yourself busy?"

I know she has a point, but all I want to do is fall into a coma in my bed and wake up in five months when I can see Andres again after Christmas. I haven't experienced a long-distance relationship or the overwhelming emotions that go along with it before—hell, I haven't experienced being in love like this before.

I miss him terribly. I miss the way his deep blue eyes would sparkle when they looked at me. I miss how I could peer into those midnight blues and see all the love he feels for me. I miss the way he made me laugh. I miss his soft, strong hands touching me, sending shivers through to my core, setting fire to all my senses. I miss his smooth lips. God, I miss his lips. I miss feeling his warmth around me. When I close my eyes, I can almost imagine the way I felt when he would wrap his strong arms around me and pull me close. My body aches for everything about him, body and soul.

I know I am throwing myself a major pity party here, but it simply isn't fair that I finally fell in love—real, deep true love—and it has to be with someone who is literally an ocean away. My heart aches, and my sadness is all-encompassing. I feel like going out with Cara and having something resembling fun would be a slap in the face to my sorrow, not giving my misery the time it deserves.

"I don't know, Cara. I can't."

"Please, Livi. Please? I miss you." She flashes her perfect smile, and her eyes are slanted in warning. "Plus, do you think that Andres really wants you to lie around, feeling sorry for yourself?" She grabs my iPhone and holds it up. "Do I need to FaceTime him and show him that you are refusing to get out of bed while drowning yourself in celebrity gossip and convenience snacks? I think he would side with me on this."

Exasperated, I sigh, "Ugh, fine! I will go!"

I grab my phone from her hand. Cara always gets her way, and she knows it. She is very persuasive when she wants to be.

"Yay! It is the best night of the week—Greek night at Theo's Bar! I will text Nolan and let him know you decided to get out of bed!"

"Fine. I am going to hop in the shower."

After taking a long, hot shower, putting on my favorite going-out dress, and applying my makeup, I do feel marginally better. Nolan arrives as Cara is placing three lemon-drop shots on the counter.

"Sweet. Perfect timing," Nolan says as he enters the kitchen. "Hey, beautiful." He walks over and swoops me up into a hug, lifting me off the floor. "I have missed you this week." He kisses me on the forehead.

I bury my head into Nolan's chest, comforted by his strong arms around me. "I just needed to feel sorry for myself for a while. I missed you, too," I say as I hug him tight.

"Okay, shots!" shouts Cara. As we all pick up a shot glass and clink them together, she says, "To best friends and bar nights!"

"Cheers!" we all say in unison.

We lick the sugar off of our shot glasses and tip our heads back. After taking the vodka down our throats, we finally grab our lemons and suck.

"Yum!" exclaims Cara. "Let's go!"

Greek night at Theo's is the same as always. A crowd of scantily clad sorority girls and beer-in-hand fraternity guys gather in this hole-in-the-wall bar every week. I see the same faces I did before I went away for the summer, minus some of the seniors who have now gone off into the world. I am greeted with hugs and waves from all the people I have gotten to know over the past three years. Coming back to a life that hasn't seemed to change at all in my absence feels surreal, especially considering the experiences I lived over the summer have changed me so profoundly.

Nolan and Cara know the key to abolishing the blues, and they kindly keep me adequately quenched. Consequently, after a few shots, I have embraced the evening, and I am having a great time. I love to dance. It is very freeing, and when I am tipsy, I am the best dancer in the universe. Swaying to the music with my best friends on the dance floor is really great therapy for my aching heart.

The three of us walk, arm in arm, home from the bar, a giggling trio of cheerfulness. After we chow down on some mac and cheese, Nolan heads home, and Cara and I head to bed.

When I get to my room, I decide that it is a great time to drunk FaceTime Andres. There is a six-hour time difference between Michigan and Spain, so it is eight thirty in the morning in Seville.

Andres picks up, and I see that he is still in bed. His bare chest is visible as his head rests on his pillow.

"Hey, baby! Good morning!" I am more than thrilled to talk to him.

He chuckles sleepily, rubbing his eyes. "Good morning, baby. Are you drunk-calling me?" He flashes his tired but beautiful smile.

"Maybe," I say with a wink. "I miss you so much. I can hardly stand it."

"I miss you, too. Tell me about your night."

"I went dancing with Cara and Nolan. I didn't want to go at first, but Cara talked me into it. It was fun after a while. I'm glad I went."

"I'm glad you went, too. I know you miss me, baby, but you don't have to prove it by being miserable, you know?"

Sighing, I say, "I know." Then, a smile creeps onto my face. "I especially miss you now...like, really, really miss you."

Andres smirks. "Oh yeah? Why do you really miss me now? Please explain."

I can tell by the teasing tone in his voice that he knows exactly why I really miss him at the moment. "You know why I miss you," I say sheepishly.

The hue of his eyes gets darker. "Tell me what we would be doing if I were there with you right now."

I suddenly feel shy, not sure how to do this over the phone. "I don't know," I say timidly.

Andres's voice sounds deeper, huskier as he says, "Touch yourself for me, Livi. I want to see you."

I bite my lip, contemplating for a second. *Oh, what the hell?* I hesitantly lift up my dress and pull off my thong. Lying on the bed, I tilt the phone down, so Andres can watch as I stick my fingers between my wet flesh and rub the area throbbing with need. I hear Andres groan.

"Are you touching yourself, too, baby?" I ask between my heavy breaths.

"Yes, baby," Andres answers. "I want to see you stick your fingers inside, like I would do if I were there right now."

I continue to hold the phone down, giving him a clear view, as I insert my finger, feeling my warmth and wetness.

"Oh my God, baby," Andres grunts. "Show me your beautiful tits. I want to see you pull on your nipples."

I moan as I remove my finger from myself and use my hand to slip my dress off over my head. I pull my nipple between my thumb and index finger, achingly stretching it. "Ah…Andres," I moan. "I want to see you."

I peer at my phone as Andres points his toward his hand moving rhythmically over his smooth skin. The sight of him touching himself sends a deep-seated rush of desire and want through my body, and I shiver. I pull my nipple once more, and then I start rubbing my throbbing core between my legs. The desperate need to relieve this aching pressure is almost unbearable.

I whimper, "Andres, I need to come."

His voice is shallow and breathy when he answers, "Come for me, baby. Point the phone toward your face. I want to watch your face when you come."

His words are my unraveling, and I let out a gasp of pleasure as my body convulses with a much-needed orgasm. I hear a carnal groan and watch Andres's face as he comes with me. We both lie there, panting. I watch Andres's chest expand between his labored breaths.

A tear rolls down my cheek. "I miss you so much. I want you to be here with me."

He sighs, "I know, baby. I miss you, too."

We lie there for a few minutes, watching each other breathe.

"Get some sleep, baby. Call me later." Andres blows a kiss toward the phone.

I let out a sad chuckle and blow a kiss back. "Okay, babe. Night."

"Night, baby," he says.

I hang up and hold the phone to my chest before my intoxicated, sated, and sad body falls quickly to sleep.

# chapter 27

Life starts to slowly go back to my pre-Andres college life. I go back to waiting tables at La Fiesta, the Mexican restaurant where I have worked for two years. I pick up as many doubles as I can, anxious to pay off some of my Spain credit card debt.

Nolan, Cara, and I fall back into our old routines with midday study sessions, dinners together— usually consisting of cheap processed pasta— and regular visits to our favorite bars. All is as it was before Spain—that is, except for the constant, sad ache in my heart that I try desperately to ignore while I go about my day.

I text Andres every day. We also message each other, FaceTime, and chat on the phone every couple of days. Andres has gone back to school, and he is taking extra credit hours in an attempt to catch up. It is challenging, given the time difference and our busy schedules, to find the time to actually talk on the phone, but we always have some sort of daily contact.

Classes have started. It is a hot and humid beautiful September day— one of summer's last hurrahs. Nolan meets me at my house, and we leave to walk to Spanish class.

"Hey, babycakes. Did you finish your homework?" I ask.

Nolan grins. "Yes. You know, I am capable of doing my homework without you…on occasion." He winks.

I laugh. "Okay, just checking. I actually wasn't sure." I worked a double the day before, and I wasn't able to get together with Nolan as we normally do. "So, what did you do yesterday during your entire day without me? Did you spend lots of time talking to Abby?" I peer up toward Nolan.

Nolan wears an expression that I can't quite place. "Well…no. Actually, Liv…Abby and I broke up." He looks down at me as he runs a hand through his hair.

"What? When? Why?" I am completely thrown off guard.

"Well, actually"—he takes a deep breath—"we broke up in Spain."

"What?" I stare at him in complete shock, my mouth wide open.

"I ended it with her right before I took her to the airport. I know it was horrible timing, but I couldn't do it anymore."

"What do you mean, you couldn't do it anymore? What happened?"

"I don't know. When she came to visit me in Spain, I realized that we weren't as compatible as I'd thought we were. I no longer saw a future with her, and I didn't want to string her along anymore just because it would be shitty of me to break up with her after she'd flown across an ocean to see me. I wanted to do it in person, so I had to do it then." Nolan shrugs.

"And you are just now telling me this crazy news? That was months ago, Nolan!" I try to hide the hurt in my voice.

"I'm sorry, love. It never came up."

Thinking back, I realize that after Abby and Cara left Spain, I really haven't brought Abby up, which sends a wave of guilt through me. *Am I really that self-absorbed?*

"Nolan, this was a huge change in your life. You should have brought it up! How do you think I feel that you didn't tell me, your best friend, that you'd ended a relationship with the girl you thought you would marry? I know I have been a little preoccupied with my own life drama this summer, but that doesn't mean I don't want to hear about your life." I stop and pull Nolan in for a hug. "I'm sorry."

Looking down at me, Nolan smiles sweetly. "Don't worry, babe. It's fine. I am fine. I am really great actually. I think breaking up with Abby was the best thing for me." He kisses me on the forehead and grabs my hand.

We continue walking to class.

"Any other major life-changing events happen to you this summer that you want to share with me now?" I ask in a sarcastic tone.

Nolan laughs. "Maybe, but I think we can wait to delve deeper into my life another time."

"Nolan, I'm serious!"

"I'm joking, babe. All is good with me. Seriously, I will keep you informed. I promise. Okay?" He flashes me his pearly whites.

"Hmm…now my question is, why didn't you date or at least go out on a date with anyone in Spain? You know the girls were all into you."

"I wasn't into any of them."

"So? You could have just had some fun. You are a twenty-two-year-old guy. What is your deal, Nolan? Cara is more of a guy when it comes to that than you."

My last comment incites a loud laugh from Nolan.

"Maybe she is. I just got out of a long relationship, Liv. My first thought wasn't to jump into bed with someone else."

"Okay, fine, I understand. So, what's your timeline on that? When are you going to start dating again?"

"When the love of my life realizes that she loves me, too."

"Well, you have to find her first."

"Yeah, maybe I do," Nolan answers quietly.

After classes, I enter our house and head straight to our living room. I let my backpack fall to the wood floor with a loud thud. Cara startles and turns her transfixed eyes from a reality TV show.

I walk over to Cara and shove my phone in her face as she is taking a bite of cereal with milk dribbling down her chin.

"Look! He was tagged in another slut's photo!" I shriek.

Cara grabs my cell to study the photo that I have pulled up on Facebook.

"Livi, calm down. He is obviously not into that girl. It looks like she is mauling him into a hug while another half-brained groupie took the photo. You know he is going to have more of those girls all over him."

"A groupie that he is friends with on Facebook?"

"Okay, so he might know her from high school or something. Who knows? You have about a thousand friends on Facebook. Can you name even one thing about all of your friends? You know how it is," she says.

She obviously isn't as remotely concerned over this most recent photo as I am. My freak-outs over Facebook photos of Andres with other girls have become an almost daily affair. Apparently, all the whores in Seville think they should take photos with my boyfriend and then tag him in them so that I can be tortured from afar. None of the photos have been incriminating. They usually consist of a girl wearing a giant cheesy grin with her arms wrapped around Andres. This whole long-distance relationship gig that I have going on here is driving me crazy. It has transformed me into an anxious, obsessed, jealous, moody girl, and I hate myself like this. I have never been this way before in my life, especially about a guy.

"Ugh, I know! I am just so sick of this shit. Stupid whores!" I know I'm completely overreacting as I plop down on the couch next to Cara.

Cara laughs. "Don't worry, Liv. You know Andres loves you. As we have discussed and discussed…and discussed…posing with girls in photos is PR for their band. It's not a big deal. Stop getting your panties in a wad, or you are going to go crazy. Chill already."

Leaning my head against the back of the couch, I close my eyes and sigh. "I know. I just miss him. I still hate those bitches."

"Absolutely! I hate those bitches, too. Just don't let it stress you out so much."

"Okay," I say. "I'm going to go take a nap and do a little reading for my philosophy class. Nolan will be here at eight, so we can start the pre-party."

Tonight is karaoke at the Wooden Nickel, which is always a great time.

Mentioning Nolan's name reminds me of our previous conversation. "Oh, that reminds me. Did you know that Nolan broke up with Abby in Spain?"

"No! When did you find this out?" Cara sounds as surprised as I was.

"Today. I can't believe he didn't tell me when it happened. He tells me everything."

"Well, good for him. I'm not surprised. They had zero chemistry. Good riddance, I say!" Cara waves her hand dramatically.

"Why do you think he didn't tell me?"

"I have my guesses. But who really knows? Did you ask him? The important thing is that she is gone. Nolan deserves so much better."

I nod in agreement. "I did. He said that it never came up. What are your guesses?"

Cara laughs. "Oh, Liv, you can be so clueless sometimes."

"Uh…what does that mean?" I scrunch up my face in exasperation.

"It doesn't surprise me that you held on to your college V-card for so long. You have no skills when it comes to reading guys, and you are always pushing them away."

I groan. "Ugh, not this again. First of all, as I have stated before, I lost my V-card a long time ago. Second, you don't know what you are talking about."

She laughs again at my growing annoyance. "Okay, look, I don't want to pick an argument. I'm just glad Andres broke through, that's all."

"Andres? Weren't we just talking about Nolan? Are you speaking in some sort of code that I'm supposed to understand? Because I don't."

Giggling, she responds, "Love ya, Liv. Go take your nap. I have to run and pick up my paycheck." She stands and half skips to her room before calling back, "Don't worry about it. It will all work out."

I head to my room, trying to translate Cara's comments and innuendos. I have a history of misunderstanding guys and pushing them away before they can get too close, which is partly why I haven't had a serious boyfriend in college. I know that some of my insecurities still dictate the way in which I interact with people, especially guys. However, I don't see how that relates to Nolan's reason for not telling me about Abby. I hope Cara knows that I will revisit that conversation later.

I try to call Andres, but I get sent straight to voice mail. He's probably practicing with the guys, getting ready for tonight's show. *Great. I can just wait in anticipation for more pictures tomorrow.* I let out a long sigh.

I decide to text him instead of leaving a voice mail. I know that my voice would come off as whiny and needy at the moment, and that's never good for keeping a guy. Yes, a text is my best bet.

> *Me: Hey, babe. Just wanted to see how you are doing. I miss you. Hope you have a good night. Talk with you soon. Love you. xoxoxo*

I have less than four months until I see Andres again. I need to keep the crazy in check until then. I am being ridiculous and overly dramatic, and

I know it. I simply can't help it. It is not fair that any random girl in Spain can get all close to Andres and touch him. It doesn't matter that it is for a photo. Girls are feeling his firm arms wrapped around them, and I'm not. Jealousy doesn't begin to explain my feelings. Not only do they get to touch him, but he is also touching them—with a smile on his face.

I know what Andres and I had…but what do we have now? *Is our love strong enough to last through this time apart and all of the insecurities it brings?* I feel myself unraveling, and it has only been a month, but it has been one lonely month. I have four more to go. I am hoping and praying that I can make it.

# chapter 28

I walk out of my last class on Thursday and immediately study my phone. I still have no messages. *Ah!* I haven't heard from Andres in two days, and it is driving me batshit crazy. Two days with no word is nearly an eternity. Every minute without word feels like an hour. I am checking my phone like a manic person, and I've sent him way more messages than a normal person should. I shoot him yet another text.

> *Me: Hey, baby. Done with classes for the week. Heading out with Cara and Nolan tonight. Love you so much. Miss you. xoxo*

The trees are bursting with colorful leaves in shades of green, yellow, orange, and red. Fall in Michigan is truly amazing. It is one of those seventy-degree October days, full of sunshine and warm winds carrying dancing multicolored leaves. Days like today are rare and special, and I look forward to them every year. Every fall, since I was young, I have made it a point to take note of these ideal fall days. Warm weather, sunshine, fresh wind, landscapes full of multiple tints of color create a recipe for heaven. On days like today, growing up, my mom would always let everyone know it was a perfect day. She would remind us to enjoy and be present the entire day, so we didn't miss a minute of it. It's a sentiment that I still carry with me. These days are precious and fleeting, and if one doesn't soak in the astonishment of it, it will be missed. In the blink of an eye, all the leaves will be lying dead and brown on the ground. The tree branches will be bare, appearing lonely against the blue sky. Then, the torturously long and cold winter will set in, and one will wonder where the magnificent fall went.

Normally, days like today would have me giddy with joy. But today, I'm walking through campus under a cloud of sadness, not taking notice of my surroundings. Instead, I keep pulling the screen down with my thumb, refreshing my Facebook feed, hoping that the little red notification circle will appear, letting me know I have a new message.

Freshman year, I learned to design my class schedule to avoid Friday classes. I usually have longer days on Tuesdays and Thursdays, but it is completely worth it for a three-day weekend every week, which is beneficial for both my social and work life. Thursday nights are normally one of my favorite nights with college night at Theo's, but I don't have the slightest desire to go out tonight.

I round the corner, passing the bright green shack-like party store down the block from our house. I refresh my Facebook News Feed and immediately freeze as a photo of Andres pops up. My eyes open wide, staring at the picture. He is kissing some girl on the cheek, and her arms are draped around his neck. They are at a bar, and they both appear very happy, too happy. Andres's posture appears comfortable, familiar. As I stare at the shot, I can't help but get the impression that he knows this girl…well. My heart races as my brain scrambles to make sense of this image. *Why is he at a bar, kissing some girl? Why is he so happy? Is this why I haven't heard from him?*

I run the half block to the house and pound up the stairs, tears falling from my eyes. I shove open the door, causing the doorknob to slam into the wall, and I run down the hall, searching for Cara. I find her lying on her bed, her fingers clicking across her phone screen.

She looks up as if she fully expected her crying roommate to barge into her room. "Let me guess. You saw the picture he was tagged in?"

"You saw it? What the hell, Cara?" I choke out.

"I don't know, Liv. Don't freak until you talk to him. It is probably nothing."

"Nothing? He is kissing another girl, and he looks pretty damn happy about it!" I yell.

"I know, sweetie, but don't jump to conclusions until you talk to him. He is only kissing her on the cheek. He might have a reasonable explanation."

"How can I ask him when he won't even call me?" I lie down next to Cara on the bed. "I freaking hate this!"

I feel like I am on a merry-go-round of emotions. Just when I breathe easy because everything is going well with Andres, something happens to drag me back down. My heart can't take all the ups and downs that go along with this long-distance dating crap. This constant state of uncertainty is driving me mad. I hate feeling like this all the time.

"He is probably fucking cheating on me!" I lay my arm across my eyes, willing myself to calm down.

"I know this situation blows, Liv. It sucks. Just wait until you talk to him. Don't come to any conclusions until you speak to him. You know what is the perfect cure for what you are feeling?" Cara's voice becomes all too cheerful.

"What?" I ask dryly, already knowing the answer.

"Shots! Followed by a fun night out!"

I laugh weakly. Cara's cure for any situation is a night out. It has become a joke between us. Are you stressed about an upcoming test? Then, go drinking! Do you have horrible PMS? Then, go drinking! Are you less than pleased with your new haircut? Then, go drinking! Are you worried that your boyfriend is cheating on you? Then, go drinking!

"Besides, don't think I didn't notice your"—she lifts her hands to do air quotes—"perfect fall day." She smiles at me. "You live for days like today, and look at you. Did you even realize how beautiful it is today? Normally, we would be out, taking a jog or doing our homework while sprawled under an oak tree at the park. Instead, you are inside, crying, and far from happy. Don't let a guy rain on your parade, Livi. We never have before. Why start now? There is nothing you can do about it right at this moment. He's not worth it."

With a voice tainted in stark sadness, I ask, "But what if he is?" The tears pool in my eyes once more.

Sighing heavily, she answers, "He's not! No man is worth this constant cloud of stress and gloom you have found yourself under for the past two months. This isn't you, Liv! Now, go outside! Sit on the deck or take a nap in our backyard. I don't know. Go be one with nature. Soak in the *perfection*, and get happy."

I took Cara's advice and did my homework outside on a blanket in the backyard. After a nap in the sun and a long, hot shower, I feel the same sense of dread as I sit on my bed, glaring at my phone. I'm willing it to buzz with a response. I sent Andres a text, telling him to call me. Then, I texted Nadia and asked her who the girl in the photo was. It doesn't appear that either one is going to respond at the moment.

"Hey, gorgeous."

I raise my head to see Nolan smiling at me from the doorway.

"You know a watched pot never boils."

"Hey," I sigh.

He walks in and gives me a kiss on the forehead. "What's bothering you, babe?"

"Oh, nothing—other than the fact that Andres is probably cheating on me," I snap. "Ah, I can't do this anymore!" I throw my phone on my bed. "Let's go do some shots."

I stand and grab Nolan's hand, and we head to the kitchen.

We are met with Cara's beaming smile as she is pouring vodka in the last shot glass. "Ready to do some shots, and forget you know anyone named Andres for the night?"

"Yes, please," I say, picking up a shot glass.

We head to Theo's, our favorite hole-in-the-wall bar. I am dancing with Cara and Nolan on the wooden dance floor in front of the bar. It is dollar-fifty pitcher night, and we are each drinking from our own pitcher of beer. Although I am not a fan of beer, after a handful of shots, the beer tastes like water anyway.

Cara is pulled away to dance with her new fling, Luke. I put my pitcher on the closest table, and I wrap my arms around Nolan's neck, leaning my head against his chest. I am perfectly buzzed and carefree.

*Mission accomplished.*

Nolan's arms are tightly wrapped around my waist. He pulls me in close and brings his head down, resting it on my shoulder. I feel him placing small kisses on my neck, and it feels good and comforting. He makes me feel loved and cared for, and I fully embrace that feeling after the stressful week that I have had. Our bodies meld into each other, and we continue to move to the music as one until I hear the DJ announcing last call.

"Hey, Livi!"

I pull away from Nolan to face Cara.

She is standing behind us, her fingers entwined with Luke's. "I'm going to go to Luke's tonight. Are you okay?"

"Yeah, I'm fine. Nolan will walk me home. Have fun." I smirk and lean in, giving her a hug.

"Ready, babe?" Nolan asks.

"Yes, let's go." I grin.

We make our way outside into the gorgeous fall night.

"Ugh, I can't wait to get back. My feet are in severe pain. Why do killer heels actually kill your freaking feet? This is the price I pay to look this good." I release a clipped laugh.

Nolan turns his back to me. "Hop on."

I giggle as I jump onto his back. I wrap my arms around his neck, and my legs around his waist. He hikes my butt up, securing me with his hands. I laugh as he jogs the two blocks back to my house, jostling me all over the place, making my head spin slightly. He carries me on his back into my room and falls on his front onto my bed. I giggle as I roll off of him onto my back.

"God, Nolan, I love you." I laugh and poke his side where I know his ticklish spot is.

He positions himself on his side, facing me, and when our eyes meet, he isn't laughing. His gaze is intense, and I stop laughing. Nolan leans over me and places his mouth on mine. My body stiffens, and my heart races. He places several slow, sweet kisses on my mouth, and then he pulls away.

"I love *you*, Livi, more than you know."

I inhale sharply, staring at him. I'm confused, and my head feels fuzzy. He leans in and kisses me gently on the mouth and my cheek. Then, he trails lingering kisses down my neck. I remain very still.

Somewhere in the back of my mind, I know that I should tell him to stop, but I don't. I can't make my mouth say the words. In this moment, I am happy, and his kisses make me feel loved.

He kisses my chest and gently rubs his index finger around the outline of my breast peeking out at the top of my tank top. He trails his kisses back up my neck, and I melt when his mouth begins nibbling my ear.

*I should stop this. I should totally stop this! What am I doing?*

But I can't make my mouth utter the words. I want this too much. This feeling of being wanted, the closeness—I need it.

My hands, finally moving, run through Nolan's hair, relishing in the softness, and I pull lightly. Desire courses through my body. Every cell in me is starving to feel sensation—the kind that fills me up, makes me warm, calms my nerves, and brings me happiness. I need that release—so much. I am aching to feel him. It is a dull, painful ache, and I need him.

Anything and everything that isn't Nolan leaves my mind. My brain is solely focusing on him. My hands grip his hair, and I pull his mouth to mine, kissing him fiercely. Our tongues are exploring—licking, tasting, entwining around one another in a sultry dance of longing. All his love and passion and the unspoken words that he wants me to hear are evident through this kiss.

He sucks on my lips and bites slightly. I moan into his mouth as every nerve ending in my body burns, lighting on fire, aching for more. He groans in response and pulls away, leaving my lips burning from his absence. He pulls my tank top off over my head and unbuttons my skinny jeans. I lift my hips as he pulls them down, taking them off along with my heels. His green eyes sear into me, only leaving me for a second when he pulls his shirt off. Dropping his jeans, he stands there in his tight boxers, and I grab the sheets as I squirm with anticipation. His hungry stare slowly takes in my body. I can see his chest expanding as he takes in deep breaths.

He leans over me once more. He slides my bra straps down my shoulders, following the path with sweet kisses. He reaches around my back with one hand and unsnaps my bra. He slowly pulls it off and drops it to the floor. He starts a slow crusade to suck, lick, and taste every inch of my breasts. I arch my back and lean my head back against the bed. I close my eyes and whimper. His touch is disarming and so incredible. He continues to pull and twist one of my nipples as his mouth pursues south down my belly. When he reaches the black lace at the top of my thong, he licks my skin around the perimeter of the fabric. I groan, and my hips move from side to side with eagerness. He pulls my thong down, letting it fall to the floor.

His heated stare traces my naked body as his hands massage my legs and inner thighs. "God, Livi, you don't know how long I have imagined this moment. You are so much more perfect than my wildest dreams."

I gasp as his mouth finds the spot that so desperately needs him. My back bows from the pleasure, and I yell out when his finger enters me. His finger rubs on the exact right spot as his tongue continues its sweet assault.

My toes start to curl, and my body tightens, begging him not to stop. I thrust my head back, screaming out, as a rippling orgasm runs through my body, fueling every nerve ending with pleasure.

My body is still shaking when I feel him enter me, and I moan at the sheer rush of pleasure of having him inside me. He feels so good and right. My body accepts him as if it has been waiting for him all this time. My hands tear at his back, pleading for him to take me harder and faster. Nolan is panting, and his body is glistening with sweat, allowing my hands to glide smoothly over all the muscles in his back and arms. I crush my mouth against his and kiss him violently.

Pulling my mouth away from his, I gasp. "I want you as deep as I can get you." I push him away from me, breaking our connection, and I flip over onto my hands and knees. I lay my chest on the bed, leaving my bottom slanted upward.

Nolan enters me, and I can take all of him like this, every last inch. "Hard, Nolan!" I yell.

He groans loudly as he slams into me. I yell out from the immense feeling each time he pounds into me. The frantic passion in the room is tangible, and I can't get enough of Nolan. He feels so good that it is almost painful. It's overwhelming perfection. My whole body begins tightening, and I can feel the build. I sway my body back and forth, meeting him thrust for thrust, in a frenzy to feel as much of him as I can. I scream as my body convulses and falls apart.

"Fuck, Liv!" Nolan groans, and he slams into me once more, holding my hips as he fills me.

He falls on top of me, his chest to my back, and we are both breathing heavily. Our warm, sweaty bodies are rising and falling together, working to calm our breaths.

Nolan plants a kiss between my shoulder blades, and he rolls off of me. Pulling my back into his front, he wraps his arms around me, snuggling his face into my neck. "I have loved you for three years. I'm sorry it took me this long to tell you. You are the only girl that I will ever want. You have my heart forever, babe.

I squeeze his hands in mine, relishing in the feeling of his body against me. I think about his words, and they make my chest swell. My body is tingly all over. I'm sated and tired. I close my eyes and quickly drift to sleep, wrapped in his strong arms.

# chapter 29

My body feels heavy, comparable to having a hundred pounds added to me while I slept. My head hurts. I need Excedrin and water. *Yes, water sounds perfect.* My exhaustion is too much, and I don't have the energy to open my eyes. Sleep trumps thirst and a pounding headache at the moment. I open my mouth slightly and feel the stickiness of it, and my throat hurts. *Gross, cotton mouth. Yes, I need water. I can get up, get a glass of water and an Excedrin, and go back to sleep. Yes, that is a plan.* Now, I just need to make my body move. *Ugh.*

While giving myself a very sleepy internal pep talk to move my limbs, I lie still for another minute...or ten. I'm not sure.

Then, it happens. I feel him. He moves behind me, letting out a sleepy sigh. I jump out of bed faster than I thought was humanly possible. I stumble to catch my balance as my fuzzy head catches up to my body's actions. I steady myself, recovering my equilibrium, and I turn around to face the bed. There he is.

*No, no, no, no. Fuck! No!*

I quickly throw on a tank top and a pair of shorts, and I stand on the side of my bed. I peer down at Nolan while he is sleeping peacefully, wrapped in my sheets. I watch his toned back muscles slowly moving up and down as he breathes.

I see my phone blinking on the floor next to the bed, and I pick it up to see that I have two missed texts. The first text is from Nadia.

> *Nadia: Hey! Oh, that is his cousin, Isabel. She is visiting this weekend, and we all went out last night. I miss you, Livi! Call me soon!*

The second is from Andres.

> *Andres: Good morning, baby. I know you are still sleeping there. I didn't want to start my day without saying good morning and letting you know that I love you. Sorry, I have been so busy with school and the band lately. I will call you tonight. I miss your voice. xoxo*

The memories of the previous night come back to me, invading my brain like a deadly infection. *No! No, no, no, no!* I bury my face in my hands as tears start pouring from my eyes. Sobs rack my body. I look back to

Nolan, and the feelings of despair resonate down to my soul. Tears are flowing from my eyes in a continuous stream. They fall down to my chest, making a river of sadness pool between my breasts.

I can't even articulate all my emotions into words. Confusion, sadness, hurt, and guilt come to mind, but that doesn't touch the surface of the complexity of my anguish in this moment. I can't believe I let that happen. What have I done? I have sabotaged my happiness again! I cannot fucking believe this! Why do I always do this? Why do I let my insecurities persuade me to make horrible decisions! *Fuck. Fuck. Fuck!* I've sabotaged every situation that could have led to a relationship in the past, but I thought I was different with Andres.

Nolan stretches his arms above his head and rolls over to face me. His sleepy grin fades when he sees me. "Oh my God, Liv. What's wrong?" He sits up in a panic.

I can't find my words as I continue to cry.

"Come here, babe. Please." Nolan holds his arms out to receive me in a hug. He moves to sit on the edge of the bed, his bottom half covered by the sheet.

I take a few steps toward him. Avoiding his embrace, I sit down next to him and turn to face him.

He smooths his hands up and down my arms. "Liv, tell me…what is it?"

"What have we done, Nolan? We have ruined everything," I whisper.

Shock spreads over Nolan's face, his expression conveying the hurt he feels from my words. "Babe, what are you talking about? We didn't ruin anything. We started something, something wonderful. I told you…look at me, Livi."

I am staring at my hands sitting in my lap and watching my tears fall onto them. I raise my head and meet his gaze.

He grabs my hands and holds them in his. "I meant everything I said last night. God, I love you, Liv."

"Why are you doing this now, Nolan? Why now?" I choke out.

Nolan stares at me as if he is unsure of how to answer. I stand up, pulling my hands from his.

When I see his boxer shorts lying on the floor, I pick them up and throw them at him. "Put these on. I need to get a drink."

I walk over to my bathroom and down three glasses of water. I turn back to face Nolan. Feelings of anger are starting to replace my sorrow.

In a raised voice, I ask again, "Why are you doing this now, Nolan? Why fucking now? We have been friends for over three years. Why did you wait until I fell in love with someone to tell me that you love me?"

Nolan stands and faces me, grabbing my hands in his again. "I'm so sorry, Liv. I'm so sorry. I was a coward. I know this! I am sorry that I didn't do something sooner. I just—"

"Just what, Nolan? Just what? Waited until someone else wanted me? Waited until I fell in love with someone else? Just what?"

I was single throughout our entire friendship. I am so angry that he is saying this now. My sobs overtake my body once more, and I fall to my knees.

Nolan follows me to the ground, sitting on his knees in front of me, as he holds my hands in his. "Livi, baby, I am sorry. I was a coward. It was always assumed that I would marry Abby. As you know, our families are very close, and we grew up together. We started dating in high school, and our parents always talked about our future together as if it were a given, as if there was no doubt that we would be married one day. I believed it, too. It was what I knew."

He takes a piece of my hair sticking to my tear-stained face and places it behind my ear. "Because I only saw Abby during holiday breaks, I guess I made myself believe that we were good together, but we weren't. I didn't realize until I lost you in Spain that it has always been you. It has *always* been you, Liv. These past few years, of course, I knew that I loved you, but I thought it was a deep-friendship type of love—at least, I convinced myself that it was. Look back at our time together, Livi. Do you honestly think that there was only friendship between us? Honestly?"

He locks my eyes with his and waits, but I don't respond. I can't.

He continues, "These past three years, I think you and I have had the perfect relationship, the kind of relationship most people aren't lucky enough to find in their lifetime. I've discovered that you are the one person in this world who is meant for me. You are meant for me. I think we were able to pretend what we had was innocent because the idea of Abby was always there. But what I had with Abby wasn't real. What we have is real. You are my forever, babe."

He tilts his head toward mine and kisses my forehead softly. "I knew it in Spain. I knew that I was in love with you. Maybe it was seeing you with someone else that made everything so clear. Maybe it was the fact that you didn't let me touch you, and it was physically painful to be near you and not have some sort of contact. I wanted to tell you after Abby left, but you were happy, and I told myself that if you were truly happy, I wouldn't interfere. But you don't seem as happy with your relationship with Andres anymore, and to be honest…I couldn't keep my feelings to myself one second longer. I love you, Livi."

I am so numb and so confused. God, of course I love Nolan. He is so special to me. Hearing him talk about us in this way sends an ache through my heart because I know he is right. I guess if I am being honest with myself, we have always been more than friends. I don't know why I didn't see it before. Nolan has been the rock in my life. He has supported me these last three years, holding me up when I made horrible decisions, giving me strength when I needed it. He has been my sounding board, my strength, and my best friend through everything. A life without Nolan isn't one I would ever want.

But I love Andres. I know it down to the depths of my soul that I am madly in love with Andres.

I know that I could be happy with Nolan. Of course we would be head over heels happy together. If the past three years have shown me anything, it is that Nolan has the ability to make me so happy.

I can't. I just can't. I can't lose Andres. It would kill me. I love him. Andres is my forever.

*How could I do this to him? How could I do this to Nolan? Why did I do this to myself? I am never drinking again. I obviously can't trust myself to make rational decisions.*

Sitting here, I am drowning. There is no other way to explain it. I am drowning in my own self-inflicted despair. Realization sets in that I might have already lost Andres. I have to tell him about Nolan. I have to, but I am afraid that I will lose Andres. God, I don't want to lose him.

A small voice inside my head is telling me that I would lose him anyway, that he wouldn't stay faithful, that he would get tired of the long-distance relationship and the waiting…and he would leave me. I hate her—the insecure, loud-mouthed, opinionated version of myself that puts doubts in my head and ruins everything. She has always been there to make me doubt myself, urging me to make decisions based on fear and insecurities. I fucking hate that bitch. She has always made me doubt myself, which might be the reason I have never had any serious boyfriends until now. I seem to always sabotage every attempt at a relationship that I have had.

But what if she is right? Can Andres really wait all this time for me? He has beautiful, available girls throwing themselves at him every day. It simply takes the right one to catch his attention, and then I would lose him anyway. I don't know if I could handle the pain of Andres leaving me. That rejection would end me.

Nolan is mine, and he is here. I love him. I do. Nolan has been by my side almost every day for three years. He knows me—the good, the bad, and the ugly—and he still loves me. I know my heart would be safe with him.

*But does my heart want him? Does it even matter at this point?*

My head hurts. I can't make a decision yet. I have to talk to Andres.

"Nolan, I need a little time. I have to think about all this. I am feeling extremely overwhelmed right now."

"I know you love me, Livi. I know it. We are so good together, babe. You know we will be happy."

I study Nolan as he is kneeling before me. Despite the war of regret waging internally, the rhythmic beat in my chest quickens at the sight of him. His hair is disheveled, and his rich green eyes are staring at me with so much love and fear. I see the concern all over his breathtakingly handsome face, a face that I have loved for so long.

Emptiness assaults me from within at what I am doing to him. Regardless of how this all plays out, someone I love is going to be hurt, and I take the burden of the blame. I ache to comfort the man in front me, who is baring his soul to me.

I raise my hand and cup his cheek. "I do love you, Nolan. Of course I do. I just…need…time."

Nolan secures his hand over mine, holding it to his face. "Okay, babe. Listen, I know you love Andres, and I know that you had a great summer with him. But listen to me, that is not real. A summer of fun with a Spanish lover is not real life. I am real. The love that I have for you is real. I am here, and you know that we are great together. We have lived real life together for three years now, and we are amazing at it. We are so good." He places a chaste kiss on my forehead. "You would be taking a huge gamble by staying with Andres, and baby…it would be a gamble that you would lose. Long-distance relationships do not work, especially ones with the foundation being a summer of fun. If he hasn't cheated on you yet, he will soon. I'm not trying to hurt you, but it is the truth."

I gasp, my hand leaving his face. "You don't know that, Nolan. You don't know what he and I have. He loves me."

Nolan grabs each side of my face with his hands, his emerald eyes latching on to mine. "I love you, Livi…so much. I will not cheat on you. I will not leave you. I will not hurt you. If you agree to be mine, I will make you so happy." He leans in and puts his soft lips on mine.

I hesitate before opening my mouth to let him in. His kiss is slow, sweet, and so loving. I relish in his passion for me, and I allow myself to get lost in it, if only for a moment. For one moment, I feel his kiss and nothing more, and it is so sweet.

Nolan pulls away, leaving me breathless. "I will give you time."

He levels me with a gaze, one filled with so much love. Right here, right now, all I see is a boy in love with a girl. A beautiful boy is giving his love with no strings attached to a broken girl. Memories of his devotion over the past few years flood my brain. He is there in every recollection, supporting me always.

I don't know why I didn't see it before. He's always been mine, and I don't deserve him.

Nolan stands and gets dressed. He lifts me off of the floor and places me in bed. He kisses my forehead and whispers, "I love you." Then, he leaves my room and quietly closes my door behind him.

# chapter 30

I hear P!nk singing, and it takes a few seconds before I awake from my sleep to recognize the song as my ringtone. *My phone!* I propel my arm to the side, grab my phone, and swipe the slide button on my screen before the song stops.

"Hello?" I say a little too desperately.

"Hey, baby. How's my beautiful girl today?"

*It's him. Finally.* Hearing his voice in my ear—the one that has become so soothing to me, the one that makes any bad day immediately good, the one sends my heart pounding with love—is too much. I have no words. I only feel a sharp pain in my chest.

"Did I wake you, babe? Rough night?"

"Yeah," I say weakly.

*What do I say? Do I tell him? I can't tell him. I will lose him!*

*I have to tell him!*

*But I can't. I can't lose him. I love him.*

*Nolan. What do I do about Nolan? I'm going to crush Nolan.*

*What the fuck is wrong with me? How have I screwed things up so badly, so quickly?*

There's nothing but silence.

"Are you okay, baby? Talk to me. How are you?"

The genuine concern in his voice feels like a jagged dagger going through my chest.

I'm such a bitch, a total bitch. I can't lie to him. I have always been a horrible liar. I don't think I can even lie over the phone. In fact, I know I can't. When I call into work with a fake illness, I make Cara call in, pretending to be me. That is how much I can't lie. He will know that something is wrong.

*He deserves to know though, right?*

*I don't know.*

"Um…" I say, thinking about what to say.

I have to tell him. It will come out eventually. I know it. I can't keep something this big from him. Plus, I owe it to Nolan to at least be honest with Andres.

*Not to mention,* says the snarky voice in my head, *you are going to lose Andres anyway. It will not work. He will not wait for you. He will cheat on you. He probably already has. Long-distance relationships never work. Nolan is right. They never work, especially when your boyfriend is a hot singer with access to hot girls on a daily basis. It was just a summer fling, and nothing more. Move on already.*

The negative bitch in my head doesn't stop until I officially feel like crap. *Uh...have I mentioned that I hate her?* But she's right. I know she is. *Right?*

"Baby, talk to me. Whatever it is, we can work it out," Andres says so lovingly.

My heart shatters.

Before I can process what I am saying, the words come out of my mouth like vomit, like three-day-flu, sick-on-your-death-bed, rocket-propelled vomit. The words are so revolting that they burn as they uncontrollably spill from my mouth. "I can't do this anymore, Andres. I'm done. I don't want to date you anymore. I am sorry. I love you, but I can't do this. I'm going to date Nolan. I'm sorry."

*What the fuck? Why did I say that? Is that what I want? I don't want to lose Andres! God, my life is a hot mess at the moment.*

"What? What are you talking about, Liv? Where did this come from? Why are you doing this?" The hurt in his voice is palpable.

He might be a great distance away, but I can feel his pain as if he were standing right next to me.

Well, what was said is already said. I can't stop the train wreck once it is in motion.

"I'm sorry, Andres. I can't do this anymore."

"Did something happen between you and Nolan?"

*Do I tell him?* I have already crushed him and broken his heart. I can't stomp on it, too.

Pulling on all my inner strength, I say, "No." The lie is quick, and I'm not sure even I would believe the conviction in my voice, but I hope he believes me. I can't hurt him more than I already have. "It was never going to work, Andres. We are from two different worlds. Long-distance relationships don't work. I'm sorry."

*It's better to hurt than be hurt, I guess. Am I making a mistake?*

What is done is done. "I have to go, Andres."

"What? Wait! Let's talk about this. You can't do this, Livi! What's wrong? We can figure it out. You don't even sound like yourself. Please talk to me!"

I can't stand the pain I hear in his voice. I have to end this call while before I make a bigger mess than I already have. "I can't. I am so sorry. Know that I am so very sorry for everything. Good-bye, Andres."

I hear his protests as I hang up just as the rush of violent, painful sobs wreck my body. I bury my face in my pillow, and I cry for what I had, what I wanted, what I lost, what I ruined, and what I was too weak to fight for. I've lost it all, and it was my fault, my choice. I sabotaged my relationship with the only man I've ever been in love with because I am too scared, too weak, too pathetic, and I don't think I could ever recover if he had ended it with me. So, I had to do it first. I had to.

It was my choice to end it, so that will make it easier to recover from this devastating loss in the long run. I hope. I hate myself for being so weak. *Seriously, isn't Andres worth taking a chance on even if it might end with my broken heart?* But I know there is no going back. My insecurities are too great, and my self-preservation mode has kicked in. I have to put myself first.

Nolan is here, and he loves me. He is all I need. Nolan will fix this. He will fix me.

*Who am I? What kind of a person does this? How could I end something I was so sure of? Why did I destroy a relationship that filled me with so much love?* A rational person doesn't act like this. Perhaps my mother has been right all along. I let my insecurities lead me to make a terrible decision. A stable person doesn't sabotage every happiness.

Andres's gorgeous face pops up on my screen as I hit the Ignore button. I know he wants answers, but I don't have the strength or resolve to talk to him. I don't have answers to his questions. Hell, I don't have the answers to my questions. I know I am being a horrible person by ending it this way, by refusing to talk to him, but I can't do it any other way. I'm emotionally shattered.

I stare at his face on my phone screen for a moment, haunted by those midnight blues that I love so much, before I turn my phone off and toss it on the floor. Wrapping myself tightly in my down comforter, I pull it up to my chin and cry until my body is so exhausted that I fall into a deep, tormented sleep.

I am vaguely aware of a touch on my face and a hand in my hair. I feel the bed dip down next to me, and squinting my eyes open, I see Nolan sitting at my side. I incoherently grumble and turn my face into the pillow. My eyelids feel heavy, and I know that the skin around my eyes is puffy as if I had gone twelve rounds in the ring with some strong fists making repeated contact—well, it's like that minus the bruises. I am not pretty after a violent, ugly cry. My swollen lids are the result, a trait I inherited from my mother.

Nolan's hand runs through my hair as he says with concern, "You haven't returned any of my texts or calls today. I wanted to make sure that you were okay. Cara told me that she checked on you while you've been sleeping in here and that she has received several frantic calls from Andres. Do you want to tell me what happened today?"

I shake my head into my pillow.

"Have you been in bed all day?"

I nod. "What time is it?" I ask into my pillow.

"Eight. Are you hungry? Can I get you anything?"

"A bottle of water," I say.

Nolan comes back a minute later with a bottle of water.

I sit up, blocking my eyes as if shielding them from the bright sun. "I'm ugly. My face is a puffy mess."

"You could never be ugly, Liv." Nolan grabs my hand. "Tell me about today. What happened?"

"I don't want to talk about it." I place the bottle of water on the side table and lie back down.

Nolan climbs into bed behind me and pulls my back tightly to his front, wrapping his arm around me. He kisses the top of my hair.

I only have the strength to utter two more words before I fall back asleep, but the undeniable power that these words have is not lost on either of us. "I'm yours."

For good or bad, I have altered the course of my life in a single day. The perfect dream of my life that I envisioned a mere two days ago will never be now. My new dream could be better. I just haven't dreamed it yet, but I will.

Nolan's warm arms tighten around my belly, and it brings me a fraction of solace. Although my heart, my soul, and every fabric of my body drips with loss as I lie in bed, broken, I know this will pass. Time heals all wounds—at least, I hope so.

# chapter 31

The next month passes in a blur of faux smiles and a shattered heart. I ache to mourn my loss of Andres, but I can't succumb to my sorrow completely. I have fleeting moments of mourning during stolen moments of my days—in the shower, walking to class, at the store, in my car. In these moments, I allow myself to miss him. I cry, praying that my tears will take my pain with them as they fall. These moments, of course, are contingent on whether Nolan is completing these activities with me. I know he would accept my grief, but I can't let him see it. I don't think that would be fair to him to know that I am so lost without Andres in my life.

Andres has finally stopped calling, texting, and emailing me. I have yet to actually speak to him about any of it. I know that if I were to speak to him at this moment and if he still wanted me, I would break, losing all resolve that I have desperately tried to hold on to. Then, I would only have to go through this all again when he leaves me, which I know he eventually would.

I have written him a handful of emails, trying to explain the reasoning behind my choices, only to delete them before I hit Send. I feel like an evil person. I know I am horrible. If the roles were reversed, I know it would have been even more painful for me if he had refused to speak to me about it. I am a cruel, heartless, weak person by not giving Andres closure, but I can't. He deserves it, but I'm not strong enough.

Nadia calls and texts, and although she is trying to keep our friendship separate from my relationship with Andres, she has let me know how crushed he is. This further adds to my guilt because I have Nolan to fill the void in my heart. I wonder who Andres has to help him through this transition.

My thoughts recall Andres crying in the shower after the incident with his father and me. I think about Andres's pain over the loss of his parents and all the promises I made to him. I am a disgusting human being. Not only did I not keep my promises, but I also added to his pain with my self-centered actions. I know I need to own up to my mistakes and talk to Andres. Although I dig deep, I can't find the courage to do so.

In the past, if I had issues in my life where I needed guidance, Nolan would be there to walk me through it. I can't go to him with this. *No way. How selfish and inconsiderate would that be?* I created this awful mess, and I have to deal with it, regardless of how difficult it is for me.

Nolan has been great, of course. He is kind, loving, warm, and funny. At times, I actually do forget the mess I have made, and I am happy. It's not every-cell-in-my-body-bursting-with-ecstasy happy, like I was in Spain, but I'm happy. Our relationship is, in essence, exactly like it has been for the past three years, but now, it's more physical. The chemistry that Nolan and I have is incredible. Maybe the connection is not as heavenly as it was with Andres, but it's definitely close to paradise. If I have to live in near paradise for the rest of my life, then I am a lucky girl. All the comforting familiarity is there with Nolan. It is the effortlessness of it that is so soothing to my soul. I don't need to work to be content around Nolan or work to make him happy. We have always fit so well together, and it simply works. I can simply *be*, and that is my saving grace. If I had to work at anything more in my life at the moment, I would crack. Like always, Nolan is the glue holding me together.

The Wednesday before Thanksgiving—also known as the biggest bar night of the year—rolls around. I shove my laundry into baskets to lug home over the long weekend. It takes so much time and effort to haul a month's worth of laundry to and from my parents' house. In reality, it would probably cost me five dollars to do it at the local Laundromat, but the idea of actually spending my money at the Laundromat when I can use my parents' machines for free doesn't sit well. So, I carry another basketful of clothes to my car, steadying myself down our wobbly wooden staircase leading from our back porch.

Coming back into the house for another load, I stop to sit next to Cara. She is sitting on the couch, legs pulled against her chest, as she watches some stupid reality show about what appears to be—I don't know...rich duck hunters? If she didn't have such a scowl on her face, I would have taken this opportunity to tease her about wasting so much time watching complete crap. *Duck hunters? How is that even a show?* She is the queen of wasting time watching reality shows.

Anyway, since I caused Cara's bad mood, I need to cheer her up before I leave. She is upset that I am heading home early and skipping out on our annual night-before-Thanksgiving party fest. Nolan flew home to Miami last night, and to be honest, the last thing I want to do at the moment is to get all fancied up and go out. I am looking forward to spending time with my parents and brother—all of whom are far removed from the mess I created in my life. I want a few days where I don't have to think about any of it.

"I'm sorry. Please don't be mad." Frankly, I am surprised she wasn't able to sway my decision. I have never been able to say no to her.

"I'm not. I know the past few months have been a whirlwind for you. I thought it would be fun to go out together, but I totally get why you want to go home and chill with your family for a few days. I wish you could leave tomorrow morning, like always."

"I know. I'm sorry to bail. I really don't feel like it tonight. Thanks for understanding."

"Maybe you should call him this weekend to get some closure? You know, you went from super anxious and freaked-out about everything he was doing over there—which I was definitely not a fan of—to being in limbo, not fully committing to anyone or fully letting yourself be happy. I don't know which one is worse. At least when you were freaking out daily, you were showing some emotion. Maybe if you spoke to him, you would feel better." She sighs, leaning her head down to mine.

"I'm not in limbo, Cara. I made my choice. I chose Nolan."

"I know you, Liv. You might be able to convince Nolan of your happiness—and I doubt that because he knows you almost as well as I do—but you are definitely not fooling me. I know that you are still troubled over your disconcerting love triangle. The smile that you plaster on your face every day isn't fooling anyone. You need to let Andres go, and maybe talking to him would help you do that."

"I can't, Cara. I'm sorry. It takes time to get over someone you love. I just need a little more time, and I will be completely back to myself." I don't know who I am trying to convince more—her or me.

I pull up to the country-blue farmhouse with the big red barn, and I see my mom racing out of the house. She's waving her hands with a wide smile that could light up a dark night. She loves when I come home, and considering I go to school an hour and a half away from my parents' home, it's not very often.

"Livi, baby!" she squeals as she pulls me into a bear hug. "I'm so glad you could make it home tonight." She holds my face between her hands, plopping kisses onto each cheek. "Now, you can help me make all the pies for tomorrow while you tell me what is bothering that pretty little head of yours."

My mother has always been able to read me like a book, and apparently, my smile isn't fooling her either.

I walk into my parents' house to see my brother and Dad sitting on the couch, watching ESPN. I honestly don't care to even register what sport they are watching. Despite my three years on the varsity volleyball team, I have never been a fan of sports. I have a natural athletic ability, or so I am told, but I've never enjoyed competing. It has always brought such a state of anxiety to me. The simple act of watching sports brings back the sense of unease that always went hand in hand with competing. I was continually fearful that I would mess up and let others down. It wasn't worth it, and senior year, I finally had enough courage to quit it all, much to my parents' disappointment.

"Hey, Daddy," I say as I bend to give my dad a kiss on the head.

He is a quiet man. We have never had deep conversations, like I do with my mom, but he is a good dad. He works hard, provides for his family, and has always been there when I needed him.

My dad opens his mouth to say some socially required pleasantry that one would say to his daughter who he hasn't seen in a while—like *you look great, great to see you*, or perhaps *welcome home*—but before he can get anything out, Max has me in a bear hug.

Max is lifting me off my feet as I squeal. "Baby sister!"

I giggle as he twirls me in typical Max fashion.

Max is tall and well built with dark skin and dark eyes. I'm told he is insanely gorgeous. Growing up, all my friends always had a big crush on him. I don't know much about Max's biological parents, but it is evident he came from a good gene pool. Max is loud, fun, and confident to the point of being cocky. He had a football scholarship to the University of Notre Dame. He was slightly disappointed at the time since he has always been the biggest University of Michigan fan. Since college, he has been *finding himself*, which has consisted of a lot of traveling, partying with friends, and trying out new and exciting careers. He is currently residing in L.A., where he and a college buddy have been dabbling in producing music.

I'm sure it won't take off, just as none of his other ambitious ideas have, but who am I to judge?

Squeezing me tight once more and setting me down, he asks, "How is that sexy piece of ass doing? Has she come to her senses yet?"

He is referring to Cara, the only friend of mine he has ever been interested in and the only one who won't give him the time of day.

"Maybe if you didn't refer to her as a piece of ass, she might be interested. Seriously, Max, you need to learn how to speak about women. Real women don't want to be referred to as a piece of anything, especially ass." I roll my eyes.

"I don't know. I haven't had any problems with that term of endearment with other hotties."

"Well, I'm not sure what skanky STD-contaminated girls you have been hanging out with, but I can tell you that Cara is not going to be one of them."

"Hey," Max responds in a mock offended tone. "My hotties are STD-free. I'm not down with that dirty shit."

"Language!" Mom calls in a singsong voice from the kitchen.

"Mom, *shit* is not even a real cuss word. Seriously, you should hear the shit people say out there now. It's not 1960 anymore," Max calls back.

I grab my belly and double over in laughter. I love my brother. It is impossible not to be happy in his presence. Regaining my composure, I continue speaking to Max, "You should visit us! You haven't seen us since before I left for Spain. I think that is the longest you have gone without visiting."

"Yeah, I should. I've been busy with Tony in L.A., but maybe I will stick around here until Christmas. I'm sure I could make it up there between now and then. I haven't tried to get in Cara's pants in a while. Maybe I will break her down this time," he says with a wink.

"First of all, you won't." Using my fingers, I air quote as I say, "She's just not that into you." Laughing, I continue, "Second of all, ew…Mom and Dad can hear you talk like that. Have some decency. Gross."

"Not listening!" Mom joyfully calls from the kitchen.

Max and I both break out in laughter.

I have always taken for granted how much work is involved in making a homemade, melt-in-your-mouth Thanksgiving feast. My mom is a great cook and makes most things from scratch—on top of working as a full-time nurse. Holding the metal whisk, I whip the egg whites. I switch hands when I think my other hand is going to fall off from sheer pain and cramping. The egg whites will turn into meringue for the lemon meringue pie, which my mom makes every year because it is my grandma's favorite.

Trying to focus on our conversation instead of my cramping hand, I get my mom up to speed on everything, including the Andres-and-Nolan fiasco. I have largely kept her out of the loop about that because I don't really understand it all myself. It is unlike me to keep things from her, but she doesn't seem hurt or mad as she listens to me ramble on.

She sprinkles seasoning onto the bread that she is going to toast to make the stuffing. "Livi, love, I'm not going to give you an earful of advice. When it comes to matters of the heart, sometimes, you just have to figure it out for yourself. No one can tell you what the right answer is. You know we love Nolan, and we would be delighted if you ended up with him. I don't know Andres, but I am sure he is wonderful as well if he captured your attention. You have to go with your heart on this one, honey. But what I won't accept is you selling yourself short. I don't understand. If you were so in love, why would you break it off solely on the possibility that it might not work out in the end? There are no guarantees in life, Liv, but if it isn't worth fighting for, it isn't worth having. Would Andres have broken up with you at some point in the future? Who knows? Maybe. But would the possibility of losing him be worth the chance to spend forever with him if he never ended it? I don't know. You tell me." She places the pies from the counter into the oven and wipes her hands on her apron before turning to me. "What does your heart tell you, honey?"

"I don't know. I love them both. I know that sounds wrong, but I do. Is that even possible?"

"Sure it is! I think that you can love more than one person at the same time. Which one can't you live without? That is the million-dollar question," she says with a warm smile.

"I don't know, Mom. I honestly don't," I say softly as tears threaten to spill.

Pulling me into a hug, she says, "You will figure it out, honey. Just give it time."

I hug her tightly, relaxing into her warmth. The scent of my mom—a mix of lavender, soap, and sugar—comforts me. The combination takes me back to being a little girl and the love I felt as I snuggled up with my mom while reading a book on the couch.

Pulling back, I ask, "What if I choose Andres, but it is too late, and he doesn't want me anymore? I could lose Nolan forever, and then I will have lost them both."

"Liv, no one ever said love was easy. You need to decide if losing Nolan is worth the risk of having Andres." She lets out a small chuckle. "Goodness, honey, you could end up with someone other than either of them. You are young. You could have several more heartbreaks until you find the one. Follow your heart, love, and enjoy the ride."

"Maybe you were right all along. I am a messed-up person. I can't believe I let it come to this. I should probably go back to therapy," I say with a tone of resignation in my voice.

"Olivia!" my mom exclaims with exasperation in her voice. "I have never, ever said or thought that you were a messed-up person. You are a beautiful person, inside and out, and it saddens me that you don't see that." She lifts her hand and gently twirls a lock of my hair before releasing it.

Sighing, she says, "Honey, maybe I was wrong with the whole therapy thing. I'm sorry that I made you go. You had such an aversion to it that you didn't experience the benefits it could have brought you. At the time, I thought that it would help you. But, I know now that you have to be an active participant in therapy for it to work. There is nothing wrong with talking things out with a professional. It doesn't mean that you are any less because you need help sorting things out. I've been to therapy. I personally think it is a wonderful tool."

I gasp in disbelief. "You've been to therapy? When? Why?"

She chuckles. "You would think I just told you that I have hidden a third arm from you all these years." She shakes her head with a grin. "Your father and I went to therapy on and off during the first ten years of our marriage."

"You did? Why?" I think back to my parents' seemingly perfect marriage, and I don't understand why they would have ever needed therapy.

"Oh, honey, life is not always easy. Your father and I had a lot of stress in our relationship in the beginning. We had the usual struggles, like learning to live with someone new when we were first married, and we had the stress of not being able to get pregnant for so long after trying so hard. Then, we had to go through the pressure of the adoption process with Max, and we almost lost him to the whole bureaucracy of the foster care system."

"But I always thought that you and Dad were happy?"

"Oh, honey, we were. Sometimes, it helps to have an impartial person as a sounding board. It is helpful to voice your problems and concerns to someone who is not involved in those problems, so that person can give you perspective. Therapy isn't a tool only for those who are unhappy. Many people use therapy as a tool to stay happy."

I think about my mother's words, and I wish that she had told me this when I was going to therapy in high school. It would have released some of the shame I felt, and maybe I would have tried a little harder to let the process make me a stronger person. Perhaps if I had figured it out then, I wouldn't be standing here in a pool of despair as I contemplate the mess I have made of my life. Then again, maybe I am the type of person who has to experience rock bottom, so I can learn how to climb to the top again, gaining strength the higher I climb.

# chapter 32

I lie on my childhood bed in my pastel pink room that we never got around to repainting after my tween years. The walls are adorned with framed photos of me with my high school friends, Twilight posters—always Team Edward—and randomly placed quotes about saving the rainforests, all endangered animals, and basically the world. I had high hopes of ending many of the world's environmental calamities.

I stare at one of the framed photos of my high school boyfriend, Ryan, and me. We're standing in front of his dad's red sports car before our junior prom. I have a tight black floor-length gown on with my hair swept into a bun of messy curls. I remember back to that night. It was the night that Ryan and I decided we wanted to take our relationship to the next level, and I lost my virginity. It was so cliché, going to a hotel after prom, but we did it. It was nice enough. Ryan tried to make it special, but neither of us knew what we were doing. I thought maybe I was in love with him, but toward the end of senior year, after dating him for almost four years, I ended it, knowing I was more in *like* with him. I liked him a lot, but it was never love. He was my first and only relationship until Andres.

Love would be what I have now with Nolan and what I had this summer with Andres. Yeah, that was love. *Is* love?

I stare at my phone as I contemplate calling Andres. I think I owe it to him and myself to at least entertain a conversation about us. Whether it leads to closure or something more, at least I will know. My earlier conversation with my mom has given me an ounce more of strength, and perhaps I can be strong enough to make the call and give Andres the conversation he deserves.

I absentmindedly scroll through my Twitter feed, weighing the pros and cons of calling Andres. I see a picture that Nadia tweeted of her and Marcela. Their arms are wrapped around each other as they pose for the camera at a club. Marcela is doing the duck face. *So last year.* Then, what stops my breath isn't Marcela's lack of taste as she pouts her lips. It's the person I see in the background. It is Andres. He is dancing…and kissing…a girl. He is kissing a fucking girl, and it's not like the kiss he gave to his cousin. This is no innocent cheek kiss. I can tell from the photo that he is full-on dancing dirty with this hooker. Call me crazy, but his hands on her ass give me that impression. His mouth is over hers, and I know, I just know, that his tongue is in her mouth.

Someone might as well hit me in the gut with a baseball bat because that would be less painful than what I feel now. I am sitting on my knees, bent over on my bed, with my arms wrapped tightly around my waist, and I am wailing. Thank God my parents are sound asleep in their room downstairs on the opposite end of the house and my brother is in the basement playing Xbox because the last thing I want to do is explain my excessive loss of sanity in this moment.

Seeing Andres with his hands and mouth on another girl that way is the most painful feeling that I have ever experienced. I know I don't have room to talk since I was, after all, the one who broke it off with him, and I was the one who proceeded to ignore him for more than two weeks. Lord knows, I have been doing way more than kissing with Nolan…but the visual, the fucking visual, has made it all so real, so depressingly fucking real. The sight of his hands and mouth on her will forever be seared into my memory, haunting me forever.

*He is moving on.*

*I have lost him, and it is entirely my fault.*

I hold my hand to my chest and sob. The pressure beneath my palm is so painful. I deserve to feel like this because I am an idiot. Thank you, Karma, for taking *closure* and torpedoing it into my fucking soul.

A long month passes. I am surrounded by my two supports, Nolan and Cara, and they love me. I smile every day, but I don't truly mean it, and I should. I ought to mean it. I want to. I walk through my life, seemingly happy, but I can't find my joy.

After returning from my family's Christmas party, I sit in my living room, cross-legged, on the couch, talking to Cara.

"What do you mean you aren't going?" Cara asks in frustration.

I informed her that I would not be going to Spain for New Year's after all even though the plane ticket was purchased in August.

"I'm not going. I am sure I can pay the airline to use my ticket at some other time…to some other place," I answer.

"No," Cara states firmly. "You need to go to see Andres in person."

"No, Cara!" I whine. "Andres has moved on. I have moved on. Nolan and I are really happy. Why would I go there to see him and open up old wounds? I'm not going to do it."

Cara sighs and states with stark disappointment, "Fine. Continue to live your life in fear. I thought you didn't want to be that girl anymore, but whatever, it's your life." She stands and starts walking to her room.

*What?*

I stand and follow her. As she walks away, I yell toward her back, "I am not canceling my trip out of fear! That has nothing to do with it!"

She turns and faces me. "Oh, stop lying to yourself! If you are *so happy* with Nolan, then it wouldn't matter what Andres's reaction to you might be. Whether he runs to your arms, begging for you back, or he's pissed and hates you, it wouldn't matter because everything in your life is rainbows and lollipops, so his actions would not affect your life of bliss. But it does!"

I open my mouth to protest, but Cara continues before I can a word out. Her arms are adamantly waving around as she speaks. "You are afraid to know how he will react because you are terrified of the feelings that you have and the choices you will have to make! You are content with the status quo because you don't have to make any hard decisions. You can just pretend that all is well in the world and go along your merry little way, but it is all bullshit, Livi. I love you, and I want you to be happy. I don't care whom you end up with as long as you are happy. And I know you are not truly happy now. I know that all the little what-ifs are running through your head, making you question everything. The truth might be hard, and you might get hurt, but it will be worth it to put your mind to rest. Then, you could start making decisions based on your best interests instead of what is easiest, most convenient, and safe."

"Are you saying that I chose Nolan because he is the safest choice? Do you not believe that I love him and that he makes me happy?" I yell.

"Do you believe that you chose Nolan for reasons other than because he was the easy, safe choice? Really? To be honest, I think you are unsure of why you chose Nolan, and I don't think you are going to find the answers you need until you talk to Andres and get some real closure. Of course you love Nolan. I totally believe that, but I don't know if he is the one for you, and I don't think you do either. I don't think you will ever know for sure until you talk to Andres."

She turns and walks into her room, leaving me standing in the hallway with my mouth open. My cheeks burn from the proverbial slap in the face I just received. Anxiety courses through my veins because I know deep down that she is right.

# chapter 33

I am gripping Nolan's hand as he pulls up to drop me off at the airport. I cannot believe I have to fly alone. I am two seconds away from calling this whole trip off.

Nolan squeezes my hand gently and uses his free hand to pull me in for a kiss. "Babe, you will be fine. Your plane will land safely. Don't freak out. Remember," he says in a voice fit for a cotton candy commercial, "it's the safest way to travel." He gives me his signature smile as he winks.

I let out a sigh, and using both of my hands, I pull his face into a deep, lingering kiss. I am lost in our kiss until I hear the smack of a hand hitting the car roof.

A gruff voice yells, "Hurry up! This is a drop-off zone only."

Startled, I break away from our kiss and see airport security standing next to the car passenger window, glowering down at me. I give him my sweetest smile while holding up my one-minute finger, imploring him to have a tad bit of patience and decency. *What an asshole.*

I turn back to Nolan and stare into his gorgeous green eyes. I want to stay here and snuggle with him for the rest of the break because I know this is where I will be happy and my heart will be protected. Instead, I have decided to fly off to Spain. Who knows what mess I will encounter there? Cara was right. I am scared. I'm completely terrified.

"I am going to miss you, baby," I say to Nolan as I place my palm on his cheek, rubbing my thumb over his smooth skin.

Leaning into my hand, he says, "Me, too, babe."

I see the love in his eyes, but I also see the fear, and my heart breaks for him. He has every right to feel afraid. God knows I feel the same. I want to comfort him and reassure him that nothing will change between us after I return, but I can't make that promise. I have no idea how this trip is going to change things. I can only hope it changes things for the better.

Nolan helps me with my bag, and we stand outside his car in the freezing, blowing wind. We say our good-byes as my face gets pelted with wet snow. We exchange a lot of I-love-yous and I-will-miss-yous. One would think that we were going to be apart for a significant amount of time, especially with my tears, but no, I will be gone for only a week. It's just one week. If my teary good-bye is any indication of my trip, my homecoming might not be a joyous one. I don't know if the tears are falling because I will miss Nolan or because I'm afraid I won't.

I hope Nolan doesn't sense my apprehension over this trip. I have tried to play it cool since telling him that I was going to go and welcome in the New Year in Spain with my Spanish friends as originally planned. I put emphasis on all the fun activities that Nadia has planned for us. Andres was never brought up. He was like the white elephant in the room. Nolan and I both know that I will see Andres and talk to him, but neither of us wanted to talk about it. So, we didn't. I'm sure Nolan is nervous about me seeing Andres. I know I am.

I don't know where my head will be when I return, but part of me hopes that the world of rainbows and lollipops that Nolan and I have been living in will become brighter and explode with butterflies, gumdrops, and sparkly pink unicorns...for Nolan's sake.

I survive the flight with no terrorist attacks, engine malfunctions, or plummets into the deep blue ocean. *Thank God.* I did a lot of thinking on the plane, and basically, I am more confused than I was. I have no idea what to expect here, and it is terrifying.

Nadia meets me at the airport, and her peppy little smile and warm eyes soothe my nerves. It is so good to see her. As she drives us back to the house, she jabbers away about how everyone is doing, informing me about people I remember and people I don't. I met a lot of people when I was here before, but I really only invested in relationships with a handful of them. Hugo, Julio, and Carlos are the same. All three are busy with school, the band, and their weekly basketball game, and they are still enjoying being single. Apparently, Marcela and Hugo hooked up, which was shady since Marcela is Nadia's best friend. Obviously, Nadia used to date Hugo, but she informs me that she is past it. Hugo and Marcela are over it as well since their hookup ended after a short couple of weeks.

I notice that Nadia is yammering away about every random person I encountered in Spain, except for Andres.

When she stops to take a breath, I say, "How is he?"

Nadia's temperament changes from one of a bubbly cheerleader to one of a depressed librarian. She is hesitant, and her voice is quiet when she answers, "He is good."

"Please tell me about him, Nadia. I'm not going to break. I truly want to know how he is. The past few months have been so confusing for me, and part of that is because I don't know how Andres is doing."

She continues, "Well, he is good—at least I think so. He is not the best at letting people in. He completely fell off the radar for a couple of weeks after the breakup happened, but then he started coming back around. He was closed off before you came because of all that stuff with his mom and deadbeat dad, so I guess it really isn't much different. Um..." She trails off as if figuring out how to proceed.

"Just tell me," I say calmly.

She takes a deep breath. "Well, he is kind of seeing someone—at least I think he is. He hasn't come out and said that he is dating her or anything, but she is around a lot."

"Is it that girl kissing him in the background of your photo?"

"Yes, that's her. Livi, I am so sorry about that! I was totally tipsy when I tweeted that pic, and I honestly didn't even realize they were in the background! Please forgive me," she says, sounding concerned.

"It's okay, Nadia. I'm not mad. I'm kind of glad that I saw it—wait, no, I would give anything to get that image out of my head!" I laugh dryly. "But it was something I needed to see. It put some things into perspective for me. I am nervous to see him though. Does he ever talk about me?"

"No, he doesn't," she says with apologetic eyes. "But he knows you are coming in for this week. He hasn't said anything about it though."

"What about the girl that he hangs out with? Do you like her?"

"Yeah, Ruthie is nice. We aren't super close or anything, but I like her."

*Ruthie? I didn't know anyone under the age of fifty was named Ruth anymore.* Maybe I am pulling at straws to find things not to like about her, but I definitely don't like her name. I actually envisioned her name to be more along the lines of Summer or Candy or Destiny, and I pictured her in hooker heels while working the pole. She's a tramp. I might be biased, but that is my story, and I am sticking to it.

"Huh," I respond noncommittally. "So, what are the plans for tonight?"

"I figured we could go out to a club with my girlfriends."

"Sounds fun," I answer although it doesn't sound fun in the slightest. Nothing is going to sound fun until I see Andres and figure out what it is that I am here to figure out.

# chapter 34

Nadia, Marcela, and I hail a taxi and make our way to a club called Abril. We are meeting a couple of Nadia's other friends at the club.

Abril has a modern chic appeal to it with LED lighting, cream-colored furniture, and glass-tiled walls throughout. Pink and purple ambience lighting makes it come off as cozy and welcoming. It is a very popular club that plays mainly techno music, which is not my favorite but not my least favorite either.

We get a table, and I order a mojito. A few more of Nadia's friends join us, and they are all doing their best to make sure that I'm having a good time. They are sweet. I can't help but feel odd though because the whole night has a different mood than when I was in Spain previously. We never went anywhere without the four guys, and it is oddly lonely not having Carlos making fun of everyone with his dry humor, or Julio shooting me apologetic eyes to Carlos's jokes, or Hugo trying to feel up some girl's skirt, or…Andres with his hand on mine. *Sigh.*

A couple of hours and twice as many mojitos in, I am dancing with the girls, and remarkably, I'm having a decent time.

Then, Nadia says, "Crap! I thought they weren't coming here tonight."

I follow her glare across the room. I see Hugo, Julio, Carlos, and…him. I lose my breath, and I want to fall to my knees from the pain in my chest. I think someone is talking to me, but I don't hear what the person is saying. I stare at him, and I want to cry. He is drop-dead gorgeous, even more so than I remember. His shiny hair is perfectly messy and flawless. He is talking to Hugo, and he is smiling. Oh, how that smile would warm me if I were frozen in a twenty-feet-deep glacier. I watch his lips move as he speaks, and I try to remember what they felt like on mine. He is wearing worn jeans that fall just right at his hip and make his butt irresistibly squeezable. He has on a black T-shirt that gives an idea of the lean muscles underneath, and the way it wraps around his arms shows off his unflawed firmness. I close my eyes and try to imagine the sensation of his arms wrapped around me.

What I wouldn't give to feel him, to smell him, to kiss him again? When I open my eyes, the breath is knocked out of me as a pair of impossibly blue eyes pierce straight into the depths of everything I am. He is so strikingly handsome, and I struggle to find air. Andres's face is frozen and expressionless. I can't tell what he is thinking, but I don't dare to even blink, afraid of losing this connection.

He takes a step toward me, not breaking our eye contact, and I instinctually react as my body starts walking toward him. Our strides don't stop until our bodies collide into each other in the middle of the dance floor. Simultaneously, his hands are in my hair, and he is pulling my head toward him until our mouths are locked in a frenzied, panicked, intensely fierce kiss. His lips are rough against mine, pressing and pulling. He is kissing me with so much passion that my mind is vacant of anything else.

Andres and I are, in this moment, the only two people in existence. We are standing alone, suspended in space. There are only the sounds of our breaths, our pounding hearts, and our frantic lips smacking together. We are on the precipice in front of a black hole, and the only thing keeping us from being sucked into the hole to be ripped apart and trapped forever is this kiss. This kiss is so desperate, so amazing.

His tongue explores my mouth, and his hands grip my hair as if they are struggling to survive. My hands are ravenous as they run up and down his back and into his hair, pulling him closer. My need to be close to him is insatiable, and no matter how hard I draw him toward me, he is not close enough. His lips bruise mine as we sink into this soul-devouring kiss. My chest is shuddering as the tears fall, and I sob into his mouth. I am shaking and gasping as his mouth is yanked away from me.

A woman's voice yells, "Let's go, Andres! Now!"

With a torrent of emotions pulsing through my body, I watch as the blonde girl from the photo pulls Andres away from me and leads him toward the door. He walks backward as she drags his arm behind her, his gaze never leaving mine. The look in his eyes haunts me as he stares at me standing in the middle of the dance floor with tears rolling down my face, heavy breaths heaving my chest, and eyes beseeching him to come back to me. His expression shows—I'm not sure…maybe despair, sadness, hunger, and loss. My heart shatters into a thousand pieces because, although I try to find it, the emotion that I don't see in his eyes is hope. He has given up on us, on me. When the door shuts behind him, I fall to my knees, slapping my hands out in front of me on the dirty floor, and I cry.

Someone grabs my arm and wraps it around his neck before sliding an arm under my knees, and then I am pulled up off the floor. Hugo has picked me up, and he is carrying me like a child out of the club. I wrap my other arm around his neck and lean my face into his chest.

His strong arms around my back and under my legs pull me close. "Let's get you back to the house, Liv."

I hear a gentle knock on my door, and Nadia comes in.

Sitting down on the bed next to me, she rubs my arm soothingly. "Are you okay, Livi?"

Feeling like an idiot from my breakdown at the club the night before, I weakly answer, "Yeah." My body feels like it was in a car accident. My chest aches, my head hurts, and my eyes are squishy puffballs once more. "I bet that was quite the show last night, huh?"

Hesitantly, she answers, "It was…interesting." The pity is palpable in her voice.

"I have to go see him today, Nadia. I have to talk to him."

"Do you really think that is a good idea? Maybe you should give it a day or two," she suggests.

"No! I have to go today. I am only here for a short time. I have to figure this mess out," I plead.

"Okay, I will drop you off at his house when you are ready."

I take a long, hot shower and try to compile my thoughts. However, I honestly have no idea what I am going to say to Andres when I get to his house. I just know that I have to see him. The one thing that is clear to me is that whatever it was that I experienced with Andres last night, I have never experienced with Nolan, not even remotely close. I love Nolan. I totally love him, but what I feel for Andres is so much more than love. It is an emotion that is ten times stronger. It is an unnamed emotion that makes every cell in my body ignite with passion, love, adoration, desire, and painful need. It is such a strong sensation—a desire for someone that is so great that it is agonizing.

I realize now that I will do anything to ease my pain, and the only thing that can do that is Andres. It became crystal clear last night that Andres is the one. I was made to love him, and I am going to fight for him. I was able to hide from these feelings when I was sitting on another continent and being loved and adored by someone as wonderful as Nolan. I know that I was hiding behind my fear and insecurities at the possibility of losing Andres, but now, I know. *I know* that if I can feel a love like I have for Andres…no other love will ever be enough. I might have ruined it all, but I have to try.

# chapter 35

"I will be at my friend's house a few miles away. As soon as you want me to pick you up, text me, and I will be here in minutes. Okay?" Nadia gives me a reassuring smile.

I nod and step out of her car.

As I'm facing Andres's door, the cadence of my heartbeat is pounding a mile a minute. I tentatively knock and wait. Andres opens the door and peers at me with an expression somewhere between bewilderment and anger. He is standing there in only a pair of shorts, and I have to reach out and brace myself against the trim of the doorway because the sight of his bare chest is sending a mad rush to my brain, causing me to feel faint.

In a jaded tone, he asks, "What are you doing here, Olivia?"

It takes me a few seconds to find my voice. "Um…I thought we could talk."

Andres dips his head to his chest, closing his eyes, as he takes a deep breath.

After a few moments of silence, I add, "Please?"

Without saying anything, he opens the door wide and waits as I walk through. He shuts the door behind us, and I follow him up to the roof patio. I take a seat on the outdoor sofa and watch as he puts on a T-shirt.

*Thank God.* That was more sexy distraction than I could take. "I was afraid you might have company," I say tentatively.

"No one has slept over since you, Olivia," he says dryly.

*Oh, that's a good sign.*

He walks over and stands several feet from the sofa with his hands in his pockets. "Talk," he prompts with a thick air of dejection in his voice.

*This is so awkward.* My hands feel sweaty from nerves, and I wipe them on my shorts.

"Can you sit down, please? You are making me nervous," I say.

He sighs and steps forward, sitting on the opposite end of the sofa. He turns toward me and waits.

"Um…I don't really know where to start," I admit.

We sit in silence for a few breaths, staring at one another, and it is taking every ounce of self-control I have not to lunge toward him and wrap myself around his beautiful body. I am dying to kiss him, touch him, and feel him in any way that I can. To be this close to him and not be connected in some way is torture. He waits in silence, and it is obvious that he isn't going to make this easy on me, but then again, I don't deserve that.

I take a deep breath and steady myself. "Andres, I am so sorry for everything. I am a complete and utter idiot, and I know this. I took what we had and ruined it, and I am so sorry. I know it is no excuse, but when we were still together, I would worry that you were going to cheat on me. I was so scared…so very scared. You have no idea. I was so afraid of losing you, Andres, and I thought that it was inevitable that you would leave me. I know now that it had nothing to do with you or what actions you might take. It was all on me. I had so many insecurities, and my mind was convincing me that I wasn't enough for you, that our end was unavoidable.

"It was hard, watching you on Twitter and Facebook while you were out having fun…with all these different girls. I should have had a little bit more confidence in us, but I didn't. The long-distance part was really hard for me. I was afraid that I would break if you left me, and somewhere deep down, I guess I thought it was a better idea if I ended it first. It was stupid and wrong, and I'm sorry.

"I'm really sorry that I refused to talk to you afterward. I have so much guilt over this. I know you were probably upset and angry, and I didn't talk to you about it. That was so selfish of me. I didn't know what to say, and I was so confused. I didn't feel strong enough come to you.

"Seeing you yesterday was the wake-up call that I needed. There has never been anyone in my life like you. I have never felt what I feel about you toward anyone else. I love you, Andres, and I think you love me, too. I guess I need to know where you stand. I need to know where we go from here."

I stop talking and wait for him to respond. He sits there, motionless, staring into the depths of my being. In this moment, I bear the weight of his desolation, the months of anguish that he had to work through without a word from me.

Guilt surrounds me.

I am flooded with a tsunami of remorse for what I put him through. Pain is no stranger to me either. I've felt it every second of every day since the phone call ending it all, but at the very least, I knew the so-called reason. He was left with the weight of my selfish decision and no form of rationalization to aid him in making any sense of it all.

He sits quietly for what seems like a devastating eternity. With his elbows on his knees, he runs his fingers through his hair, his head facing the floor. He sighs deeply. Then, he lifts his head to face me with anger in his eyes. "We don't go anywhere from here, Olivia. You go home, and I go on with my life."

The anguish radiating off of him is so tangible that my skin is tingling with its unwelcome sensation. My whole body tightens, and I grip the sofa cushions. Those words are like a strong tide pulling me under an ocean where I am drowning, unable to breathe. I internally start panicking. I realize that if I cannot get through to him, I am going to drown in this overwhelming love I have for him. Only he can save me and pull me to the surface.

"Listen, Andres, I know you are mad, and you have every right to be. But can't we start over? Please. I'm sorry! I will make it right. I will make it up to you! I am so sorry! I love you so much." I am working to keep my voice even, but my panicky shriek is starting to make its way in.

"I'm sorry, Olivia, but it is over. You should probably go." His expression is blank, cold.

*Wait, what? No!* I am freaking out now. "Wait! Let's talk about this! Is this about that girl you are with? Why are you choosing her? Why are you choosing her over me?" The time for calm conversation has passed, and I am officially yelling. I know my window is closing, and I might never get a chance with him again. I shout again, "Why are you choosing her over me?"

Andres's attitude of tolerance has turned into one of rage, and he stands up, facing me. He yells, "Are you kidding me? I am not choosing her! I am choosing me! I am fucking choosing me!"

He turns from me and runs his fingers through his hair, pulling at it in frustration.

I stand and plead, "What does that even fucking mean, Andres? Is she so much better than me? Do you love her more than you love me? Are you over me? Because that is not what that kiss last night told me!"

Andres turns toward me, and I can see the pain in his eyes.

"She is just a fucking girl. What we have is not serious, and she knows that. She is leaving in a couple of weeks, and I will never see her again." He takes a deep breath. Very slowly and clearly, he says, "She is not you. She never was you. She never could be you. No. Girl. Will. Ever. Be. You! You have ruined me for every girl to come. I will never be over you, Olivia! THERE IS NO GETTING OVER YOU! Ever."

My breath hitches as the tears start to roll down my face. The anguish I see in Andres's face and hear in his words is paralyzing.

He regards me sorrowfully, and in a much softer, sadder voice, he says, "You have ruined me, Liv, and all I have to look forward to for the rest of my life is a bunch of mindless, meaningless encounters."

I long to touch him, to hold him. "I don't understand what the problem is, Andres. I am here. I want you. Why can't you choose me? Choose us? You know we are meant to be together. You know we can be happy. I will not make the same mistakes again. I can't lose you. We are perfect together, Andres. We were made to be together."

With near tangible sadness, he replies, "I thought so once, Olivia, but I was wrong. You had a choice, and you made it. You made the choice, Liv.

YOU made it, and YOU did not choose us. You were it for me, the one. I always chose you. It was always you. But when things got a little difficult, you ran. You were not strong enough to fight for us, and I almost lost everything. I took a chance on us, and I gave you my heart. I gave you EVERYTHING, and you left me with nothing! You left me a completely hollow, empty man. These past two months, I have been barely holding on. I can't give you my heart again. I can't give it to you because you already have it. You have all of it, but you took it and destroyed it. Now, I have nothing left to give you. So, I am choosing me. I am deciding to go with the only option I can—self-preservation."

He stares into my eyes, his own brimming with tears. In a low voice, he says, "I have to choose me."

He appears so broken, and my heart shatters into a million pieces because I know that I did this to him. I step forward to hug him, and he steps back before I can reach him.

"I can't do this, Liv. Please go."

I know I have lost him. I don't want to cause him more pain, but because everything is now so clear to me, I say, "You are the one for me. I was so stupid, and I ruined everything. I know sorry isn't enough, but if you ever come back to me, I promise I will spend forever making it up to you. If you ever come back to me, I promise that I will never hurt you again. I know the love that we share is something special, and I don't think everyone gets to experience such a love. Now that I know what it is like to love and be loved by someone like you, I can never settle for anything else. If you don't ever take me back, then I will spend the rest of my life searching for a love like ours, but I know I will never find it. I'm sorry I hurt you. I'm so sorry. I pray that someday you can forgive me and trust me again. I will hold on to your heart and keep it safe, and if you come back to me, I will cherish you with everything that I have and never break you again. If you can't trust me again and don't come back, then know that I will love you always, down to the depths of my soul…forever, baby."

On the last word, my voice cracks, and I walk out of his house as fast as I can. I'm afraid that if I have to be in a room with him for one more second and not be allowed to touch him, then I will surely lose it. I will lose every molecule of strength I have left, and I will crumble into the depths of despair.

# chapter 36

Three days pass, and I don't hear from Andres. I know I shouldn't because he made it clear that he doesn't want to hear from me, but I text him multiple times a day. I write words of apology, love, and my all-consuming desire for him. He never responds, but I pray that he is at least reading my messages. It is a cruel fate that I am in Seville, so demographically close to Andres, but I feel further away from him than ever.

I honestly can't believe he hasn't contacted me yet. I know he still loves me. He made that clear with that kiss. I guess I feel that he would have come around by now. I was hoping that he would internalize everything I said to him, and he would return to me, but he hasn't, and I am starting to fear that he won't.

I have spent the past few days with Nadia, trying to plaster a smile on my face. I would rather lie in bed and wallow in my misery, but I can't do that here. I have a couple of more days, and then I can go home, face Nolan…break his heart, and then fall apart for multiple reasons in the privacy of my own bedroom. I have chosen to run with this numb feeling and empty smile. I can keep it together a little longer.

Tonight is New Year's Eve, and there is an all-night party at our favorite club. I am counting down the minutes until I can leave this country.

The club is teeming with life and exuberant energy as we make our way through the throng of moving bodies. I am pleasantly surprised to see Julio, Hugo, and Carlos sitting at a table when we arrive. Andres's absence does not go unnoticed, and the nervous flutter that I had at the thought of seeing him turns into one of dejection. I am not surprised that he didn't come, but God, how I would love to see him.

Hugo turns his attention from the hot brunette in a short skirt sitting on his lap to me. "Livi! Good to see you, hot stuff!" He takes hold of my hand and pulls me toward him, causing me to land on the leg that the brunette is not occupying.

Giggling, I put my arm around his neck, and I kiss his cheek. "Good to see you, too, Hugo."

Julio and Carlos are sitting across the table, and I greet them with a grin.

Julio extends his arm and hands me a mojito.

"Thanks, Julio. You remembered."

Julio gives me his charming grin. "Of course I remembered your favorite drink, Liv. How are you doing?"

I can't help but notice the sympathetic tone in his voice. I decide to go with honesty. "Well, I've been better…but it is great to see you three. I have honestly missed seeing you this week. It isn't the same here without you guys."

"Yeah, well, bad breakups tend to make things a little messy, don't they?" Carlos responds.

"Carlos!" Nadia yells as she hits him on the arm. "Seriously?"

"What?" he asks. "It's the truth."

I can't stop the smile that spreads across my face. If Carlos is anything, it is truthful. "It's okay. Yes, Carlos, breakups suck. Thanks for the reminder. I totally forgot." I wink.

"That's what I'm here for. Cheers." He smirks as he leans his bottle of beer toward my glass, clinking them together.

"So, is Andres coming tonight?" I ask in as calm of a voice as I can muster.

"I doubt it," Hugo answers. "He says he might show up, but I don't expect him to."

More guilt invades my body, knowing I am keeping Andres from celebrating New Year's with his friends.

The guys keep my hand occupied with a full drink throughout the night, and I am grateful. My head is hazy, and I am thoroughly drunk. I feel warm, fuzzy, talkative, and loving. This becomes evident as I repeatedly tell Nadia and the guys how much I love them and have missed them.

Julio laughs. "You are so cute when you are tipsy, Livi. We have missed having you around, too."

In my blurred mind, I have decided for the sake of my sanity—and so everyone else can enjoy the party without Debbie Downer sucking out their joy—I am convincing myself that it is circa six months ago when all was incredible in my world, when all was irrevocably perfect. Maybe in my warped faux reality, Andres is somewhere within the club, getting us drinks or on an extended restroom break, but wherever he is, he loves me, and we are happy. Just for tonight, with the help of sweet drinks infused with alcohol, I pretend to be in a happy place, and I enjoy my night with these great people whom I might never see again. I don't see another trip to Spain in my future. In a future without Andres, what would be the point?

Nadia and I are dancing, our arms raised in the air. My eyes are closed as I sway to the music. Icona Pop's "I Love It" starts blasting from the speakers, filling the club with positive energy. The chorus of the song resonates with my temporary upbeat vibe of the evening, and I belt out the lyrics.

Uninhibited, I bounce up and down on my stilettos as I scream along, "I don't care! I love it! I don't care! I love it!"

Nadia has joined me, and we sing and bounce together. The song ends, and I grip my stomach as I laugh. It's a full-on belly laugh, and it feels so freeing.

Nadia excuses herself to go get a drink refill, and I contemplate following her when the little hairs on my arms rise, and a chill runs through my body. I wrap my hands across my chest and use them to rub up and down the opposite arm, warming the chill. As I turn, I see him. He is still, halfway between the entrance door and where I'm standing, frozen. I am riveted by this man's exquisite beauty. He is so gorgeous, vulnerable, and simply sad as we stand, transfixed on one another. *God, I love him.*

I lift my hand to my heart and raise it to my lips. Peeling my fingers from my lips, I blow him a kiss, and I hope he sees how much I need him. His eyes go wide in turn, and in a stunned silence, he bows his head and turns. With his hands in his pockets, seeming like the weight of the world is resting on his shoulders, he walks toward the exit and out the door.

I stand, motionless, on the dance floor, watching the entrance, silently imploring him to come back. I don't know how long I am in this prayerful trance when I hear the countdown. It's the goddamn New Year's Eve countdown. *Fucking great.*

Right when I think that my knees are going to give, allowing me to fall to the floor, I feel arms around me. I turn and see Julio, and I couldn't be more grateful as I fling my arms around him and bury my face in his neck.

He squeezes me into a hug and whispers, "Happy New Year's, Livi."

Tears flow freely, falling on his shirt, as confetti descends around us. I faintly register the joyous music, party horns, and cheers exploding around me.

Julio rubs my hair. "It will be okay, Liv. You will see. You won't feel like this forever."

*God, I pray he is right.*

# chapter 37

Seeing Nolan standing by his car—perfectly mouthwateringly gorgeous, eyes full of goodness and love with the face of an angel…a very hunky angel—my heart drops to the pit of my stomach, turning my already depressed mood into one of utter doom and gloom. I plaster on a grin as I walk forward and throw myself into his arms. He squeezes me tight, and I hug him. His arms around me lessen some of the sadness that has taken permanent residence in my soul, if only a little, but it is comforting, and I relish in his warmth until he breaks our contact.

Peering down at me, he kisses my mouth. He pulls his mouth from mine and as I gaze into his stunning green eyes, he says, "I have missed you so much, baby."

I lean my face against his chest and hug him tighter. I swallow the emotion in my throat and prohibit any words to come. I know if I speak, the truth will come, and I can't let it flood out here on the curb.

The ride back to my apartment is quiet, and I am thankful that he doesn't press me for answers. I know he has questions, but I am trying to gauge my feelings now that I am in his presence. I have to admit that I couldn't accurately decipher my feelings for Nolan while I was in Spain, surrounded by my all-consuming Andres addiction.

Holding Nolan's hand, I turn to watch him while he drives. He turns to me and smiles. His grin exudes love and acceptance. It is not questioning or doubting. I know that no matter what I tell him about the trip, about what I did or didn't do, regardless of what I felt, he will love me.

I am relieved to see that Cara is still at work when we arrive back to my apartment. I need to talk to Nolan first and foremost. We take a seat on my bed, and I peer into his eyes.

He rubs my face with one hand and says, "Just say it, baby. I can see the wheels turning a mile a minute in that beautiful head of yours."

Sighing, I say, "I don't know where to start, Nolan."

"Well, let's start with the obvious question. How was it, seeing Andres again?"

"Honestly, it was very uncomfortable. He hates me."

"So, nothing happened between you two?"

"We kissed…once. I'm sorry." I squeeze his hand as I wish that I were anywhere but here, breaking Nolan's heart.

He sighs. "It's okay. I forgive you. I figured something would happen. So, you didn't, like, plan a future with him or anything, right? Your relationship is over…for good?" The hope resonates through his words.

"Yeah, it is definitely over."

"Okay then, let's just get back to us and leave that chapter behind."

A tear rolls down my cheek as I whisper, "I can't."

I can feel Nolan's body tense.

"What do you mean?"

"I don't think I can date you anymore. I want to still be friends, if we can, but we can't be together as more than that."

"Why? I don't understand why you are doing this, Liv. I know you love me, and you know how much I love you. So, why?"

"You're not *the one* for me, Nolan, and you deserve to find the girl who you are meant for."

"I am meant for you, Livi, only you."

He leans in, taking my face between his hands, and he kisses me, hard. I kiss him back, relishing in the feeling that his tongue in my mouth provides. Warm tingles invade my body, and my heart begins to beat at a quicker tempo. The kiss is hungry, needy. Through this kiss, Nolan is urgent to show me how good we are together. I weave my fingers through his hair, pulling him deeper into my mouth.

He pulls away, leaving me gasping. "Tell me you don't feel that, Olivia. We are amazing together. The kind of chemistry that we have can't be faked. It is real. Please, stop overthinking everything, and let yourself be happy. I can make you so happy."

I take a few moments to steady my skewed equilibrium and calm my breathing. Nolan and I have great chemistry for sure, but somehow, my current resolve is solid. I don't want Nolan. I want Andres. I don't know how I am managing to be so strong. Normally, I would crumble and need Nolan to lift me up—but not anymore. One way or another, I have changed. I am not the same person I was seven months ago, let alone last week, and I have strength that I never knew was possible.

"I don't want just happy. I want a can't-breathe, can't-live-without kind of love. Nolan, I love you. I think I have loved you since the moment I walked into that classroom and met your gaze years ago. I know you love me, and I know that we could be great together. You are an amazing person, and any girl would be lucky to have you. I don't want to hurt you, but I want you to understand, so I have to tell you…" I pause.

"When I see Andres, I literally lose my breath. He does something to me that I can't explain. You know that quote—something about life being measured by the moments that take our breath away? I used to think that it was a cheesy saying, invented by some underpaid Hallmark card writer, to make people feel all warm and squishy inside, but it is true. It is so true. He does that to me. What you and I have is wonderful, and I know that you would spend the rest of your life making me so happy. If our relationship had begun seven months ago...I would have felt like the luckiest girl in the world. But now that I know, I can't go back to when I didn't."

"Liv, I understand that you love Andres. I get it, but we can get through this. As you said, we are amazing together. As time goes on, we will grow to be more in love, and our relationship will only get better. I love you so much, Liv, that it hurts. I don't want anyone else. I want you. Please just try?"

"I love you so much, Nolan...too much to let you be my consolation prize. You deserve to be someone's first choice. You deserve to find that kind of love. I know it doesn't make sense now, but someday, when you find her, you will thank me."

"God, Olivia, please don't do this. So, you are going to end this incredible relationship we have to...what? Be alone? Let me love you. Let me make you happy."

"Yeah, I guess I am. I am not afraid to be alone anymore. You have been my rock, my comfort for almost four years, but I can stand on my own two feet now. Being alone is better than settling, Nolan."

"Settling? Fuck, Liv, that's low." The hurt in Nolan's eyes is crushing.

I reach for Nolan to pull him into a hug, and thankfully, he lets me.

"I'm so sorry to hurt you. I never wanted that. I'm sorry that you aren't the one for me. I really wish you were." And as I sit here, hugging this beautiful man, my best friend, I really wish he were.

# chapter 38

*The one constant is time. While one is alive, it will continue to pass, refusing to cease, regardless of whether one is equipped to face the next day.*

I've taken one step in front of the other. At first, there was nothing to do but go through the motions. My heart was a black abyss of remorse. One day at a time, I've worked to let go of my feelings of guilt, heartache, loneliness, and regret. Regret is a bitter pill to swallow, no doubt, but I did.

Going through the motions gave me a purpose, a schedule of next steps. I might have been frightened of the next day, but I knew I could, at the very least, make it through my next class, then dinner with Cara, and then my shift at work. I checked off small increments of time each day. Eventually, I was completely each task without extended effort. I didn't check out although I can't say I was engaged either, but I made my actions appear as if I was.

With every passing day, the fog of lament clouding my brain lifted until I smiled one day, and I meant it. On a subsequent day, I laughed, and I felt it. That rumble of joy exploded, and I reveled in the pang of pain in my side from the force of my laugh. It was victory. It was life.

Finally, without notice, I was hit, obliterated by an emotion so strong that it had the ability to ward off all others. I felt gratitude, appreciation for all that I have been given and all that I have been able to experience.

With gratitude comes peace, and with peace comes acceptance. With that acceptance, I was able to find me, the person I have always wanted to be. Whole—I am a complete person, imperfections and all. I still have my cracks, but I am no longer broken, not by a long shot.

I feel happiness.

## Four Months Later

It is a rainy spring day in April, but it is absolutely glorious because I am done. I just finished my last exam. I have my student teaching left to do, but there are no more pointless classes, assignments, and tests. I am done. I am looking forward to the summer. Life for me is so uncomplicated at the moment, and I love it.

I stopped contacting Andres a month after I returned from my New Year's trip. He hasn't returned any of my calls, texts, or messages, and I am actually okay with it—for the most part. I am still madly in love with him, and I miss him every second of the day, but I can't turn back time and change what I did. If he can't take me back because of it, it is something I will have to live with.

I dream about Andres most nights, and I wake up happy. I am happy because I got to love and be loved by the most remarkable man in the world. It didn't end as I would have hoped, but it changed me in ways that I have yet to fully grasp.

I am not the same person as I was. I am strong, independent, and whole. I no longer doubt myself, but instead, I feel pride for how great I really am. I don't want to sound cocky…but if I am not my biggest fan, then who else will be? I don't need a man or a friend to hold me up. I am firmly planted on my own two feet.

Once I finally realized that my own insecurities were my biggest downfall, something happened. A switch flipped in my brain, and I was able to change. It turns out that I had the ability to change my perception all along. I simply needed the strength to do it.

I was able to experience a mind-blowing, marvelous connection with Andres, and now that I know that it is possible for me, I am not going to settle for less. I deserve it all—the rainbows, lollipops, and fireworks…every last blast. I really hope I find it again, but if I don't, I will be happy simply being me because I am enough.

Nolan and I are still friends. We're not as close as we once were, but I think that separation was inevitable. It took him a couple of months to heal his broken heart before he could bear to be around me as friends. He has turned into quite the make-out whore around campus, and to be honest…I think it is great. He was only with Abby and me previously, and he has always been such a flirt. He deserves to let loose and hook up with a bunch of gorgeous girls, right? I think he knew that our romantic relationship was finished when he told me about hooking up with one of my sorority sisters. I believe that he imagined me getting upset or at least showing signs of jealousy, but I didn't because I wasn't. I was happy for him. He isn't dating anyone seriously, but he is keeping his social life busy. I know that his perfect other half is out there, waiting to find him. She is going to be everything he needs, and she will give him what I couldn't—a happily ever after that he deserves, a forever.

We still hang out about twice a week, and even though it is not seven days a week, like before, I like it better. We have learned to establish new boundaries to our friendship. We are no longer flirty friends. That was too confusing and probably unhealthy, especially for Nolan, who is trying to move on.

I still love Nolan, and I always will. He played such an important role in this journey. He comforted me and made me feel secure when I wasn't. His love and friendship filled the void in my soul, quieted the doubting voice in my head, gave me courage when I needed it, and empowered me with strength to go on this journey that ultimately changed my life. I owe so much to him. Nolan's unconditional love held me up until I found myself. I will always be truly grateful for him. Nolan loves me enough to remain friends even though he might have wanted more, and for this, too, I am so thankful. A life without Nolan is not a life I can imagine, nor would I want to.

Cara has a new boyfriend, and she is quite enamored with him. His name is Dan, and she is in love—at least for now. She spends most of her time in his room at the frat house. We still go out together—sometimes with Dan and Nolan in tow—but not as much as before, and that is okay, too.

I like the alone time in our apartment. I am not lonely anymore.

Apparently, I am the walking poster child for finding oneself, and it rocks. This roller coaster of a year has taught me so much, and it made me a stronger person. I learned how to love, how to lose, and how to find peace with all the craziness that life will inevitably throw at me. I didn't need worrying parents or a doctor's psychoanalysis to find myself. I needed to find my once-in-a-lifetime love, to lose him, and to fall into the dark depths of depression. I needed two best friends to love and support me unconditionally throughout all my self-doubt and idiotic mistakes. Finally, I required the experience that came with this past year to discover the courage to keep going. I simply needed time to grow up and figure it out on my own, and in the end, I realized that I am enough, and I deserve it all.

I take in the warm, wet air as I pass several of my favorite spring trees lining the street to my apartment. I don't know what kind of trees they are, but every spring, they explode with pink flowers. Fragrant, bright pink flowers take over every branch. There are so many that I can't even see the leaves. It's just a ball of pinkness atop a tree trunk, and it's so lovely. The unfortunate thing is that these trees bloom for such a short time. There are only a couple of days before the flowers fall. I watch as the rain falls from the pink petals, carrying some of the petals to the puddles below. With this relentless rain, the divine pink petals will all be on the ground tomorrow.

Switching my gaze from the puddles with the floating petals to the view in front of me, I see someone sitting on the front porch of my house. I squint to make out the figure through the raindrops, but when he stands and faces me, I know exactly whom it is.

*Oh my Lord, he is here. He is really here, standing in front of me!*
*Why is he here? What does this mean?*
I need a moment to take this in.

*Deep breaths.*

I stop, frozen by indecision.

*Do I run up to him, jump in his arms, and kiss him senseless?*

*Or do I walk calmly to him and see why he is here?*

*Or do I stand still and wait for him to make a move?*

I go with my foremost thought. Andres being here can only mean one thing.

I run the block distance between us, and then I lunge myself into his arms when I am close enough. He catches me as my arms and legs circle around him. My pulse soars as he tightens his grip around my back, and my mouth finds his. I am not even thinking straight at this moment. My body takes over, and my body needs him. It is physically painful to be near him. My desire to touch and kiss every inch of his body is all-consuming. I want to devour him until I pass out. Our kiss is powerful and needy, extraordinary. I am helpless, completely riveted by this man. There is a light assault of raindrops on my skin, but all I can concentrate on is our kiss. Our tongues dance, twirling around each other, like two long-lost lovers starving for contact. We kiss for I don't know how long in my perfect bubble of happiness.

He eventually pulls his lips from mine and says in a husky whisper, "I couldn't live without you."

Tears pour down my cheeks, falling in line with the streams of rain falling down my face. "Thank God!"

Ravenously hungry for his sweet taste, I plunge my mouth onto his once more. My legs refuse to release from his waist, so he makes his way up the creaky stairs to my apartment, holding me the whole way. When my lips leave his, it is only so they can devour every inch of his face and neck. I can't resist him. He tastes divine and smells heavenly—all sexy, yummy Andres. God, my chest is about to explode. Joy, love, and lust are blasting from me like fireworks on the Fourth of July. The sensation of all these emotions renders my mind helpless, leaving my body to run on instinct and adrenaline. My mouth is consuming every inch of Andres it can reach, kissing his wet skin, as he reaches one of his arms out and opens the door.

We plow through the door, and the doorknob crashes into the drywall behind it. I wave my arm, attempting to indicate where my room is, and Andres seems to understand because he walks us down the hall toward it as my mouth ravishes his with immense intensity. After kicking my door closed behind us, Andres walks us to my bed and lays me down. I pull my lips away from his, so I can peel off my wet clothes in record speed, and Andres does the same.

I need to feel his body against mine.

He scans my naked body with his hooded eyes. "Fuck, Olivia, you are so amazing."

His lips find my neck, and I drag my fingers through his hair. His lips start working their way down my body, and I pull him up.

"No, Andres. I need you inside me now. I need to feel you. Right. Now."

He shifts back up, so his face is above mine. I spread my legs in anticipation. He is gazing at me with a mixture of fierceness and awe. He bites his lip as he plunges deep into me, burying himself as far as he can go.

"Ah!" I throw my head back into the pillow.

I grab Andres's strong biceps as he begins a frenzied rhythm in and out of me. I thought I remembered how incredible he felt, but my memories pale in comparison to this feeling right now. It's unreal. He feels so freaking fantastic that I can hardly stand it. It's so good that it is almost painful. It's a sweet, delicious pain that I want to feel over and over. It is so astonishing.

Andres interlocks our fingers, holding my hands above my head, as he watches me intently. Tears are falling from the corners of my eyes onto my pillow as our stares lock. In his eyes, I see passion, desperation, desire, and love...so much love.

"Tell me that you will never leave me again," Andres says through clenched teeth.

"I will never leave you again. I am so sorry, baby. I am so sorry."

"Promise me, Olivia."

"I promise, babe. I promise."

He bends his head down and kisses me, pulling my lips between his. "I can't live without you, Liv. You are mine. You. Are. Mine," he says with labored breaths.

"I am yours, Andres. I love you so much. Thank you for coming back to me." I moan, my chest shaking with a sob, as hot tears burn down my cheeks.

"Oh, baby," Andres groans before he crashes his mouth against mine.

He kisses me with so much passion as his tongue devours my mouth. I can feel all his desire, his hope, his determination, and his love for me. Pains of regret course through my mind. I can't believe I almost lost this all. I almost lost the best thing that has ever happened to me—all because I was afraid to lose it. I quickly turn off these thoughts and concentrate on his love, on him coming back to me, on our future of happiness.

Every one of my senses is on overload as I take everything in. The smell of his skin is a pure assault to my mind. I concentrate on the unforgettable smell of Andres—his sweet, savory manly smell, now with hint of saltiness as our bodies move together. The feeling of his smooth, firm skin as I run my hands up and down his back causes me to shiver with elated agony. I'm touching him again. I always hoped, but I never really knew if I would actually be able to touch his flawless body again. The sounds of our bodies coming together, of his labored breaths, and of the quiet, sensual moans that resonate into my mouth as he moves above me is enough to put me over the edge. All of this is coupled with the unforgettable taste of his mouth. The calming, satisfying taste of Andres is nothing short of heaven.

But it is when I open my eyes and see his face—the face that changed my life forever when I first saw it a year ago in the crowded club, the perfect face that I have dreamed about and prayed for all these months, the face that could fill any hole in my soul and make me complete—is when I lose all semblance of control, and my body is swallowed by sensation. My toes curl as the warm flood of ecstasy overtakes my body, and I scream my release into his mouth. My body is still convulsing when he shudders atop me with one more thrust, and then we still, his lips never leaving mine.

We lie on our sides, facing each other, with our legs entwined. Our hands are gently caressing one another—backs, chest, hair, face. The beautiful skin-on-skin therapy fills our vacant hearts until they beat, teeming with love, and they become whole again. Our eyes communicate with unspoken affirmations of love that have been building for months.

We spend the rest of the day in bed, slowly making love, and I cherish every second of it. Through it all, Andres whispers adorations of love, desire, and need into my ear, convincing me with his words and actions of how much he needs me.

Night falls, but desire to eat or do anything other than lie right where I am doesn't come. There are few words spoken between us as I lie with my head on his chest in the darkness, listening to his beating heart, until I fall asleep, my body humming with happiness.

I open my eyes, and I am looking directly into his striking dark blues, which appear almost gray in the morning light. "Hey," I whisper with a smile.

"Good morning, beautiful." He kisses my forehead. "I've missed you so much."

"Me, too." I run the back of my hand across his cheek. "I'm glad you came back to me."

"Me, too," he says with a grin. "I just wish I hadn't waited so long."

"We are destined to be together, Andres. You are it for me. I could never love anyone who wasn't you. Never."

"Me neither, babe. You are it for me."

I give him a soft kiss on the lips. "I wish we could have avoided all the jealousy, confusion, heartache, pain, and loneliness, but I think we needed to feel that torrent of emotions to be able to feel this right now...or at least, I did. I am in a better place now, a place where I can accept everything that comes with us and be happy with it."

"I can tell. You are different."

"Different good?"

"Yes, definitely good." He chuckles. "I don't see that lost look in your eyes anymore. You seem happy."

"I finally am, especially now that you are here." I lean in, giving him a chaste kiss.

"What are you feeling right now?" he asks as he rubs a strand of my hair behind my ear.

"Peace."

"Peace?"

"Yes, because I know that our love is forever. It's unbreakable. I am not afraid of losing you anymore. Before, I doubted everything. I doubted you and your true feelings for me. I questioned whether you would be faithful to me or leave me. I wondered whether or not I was truly good enough for you. I doubted my own feelings. I wasn't sure if what I felt was real or if I simply wanted it so badly to be real. Lying here with you now, I am a different person. I am happy. I don't fear losing you anymore because I know I won't. There is no one else on this planet for either of us, and I know in my heart that whatever else I face in my life, I will face it with you."

Andres pulls me in close and kisses my head. "I love you, Olivia Marshall, so much."

My heart smiles. "I love you, Andres Cruz."

He gives me his gorgeous wide smile and kisses me deeply. Pulling away, his beautiful blue eyes meet mine. "Promise?"

"Forever."

"Damn straight, baby. Forever."

# epilogue

*Green.* I peer down at my green robe as I walk in procession toward the stage. Eastern Michigan University could have better school colors. Despite my usual aversion to wearing anything of this shade, at this moment, it is the most awesome color in the world because it means that I am graduating. I am giddy with excitement to get my degree and start my official adult life.

Cara stands behind me, rocking her grassy-hued robe. She could be a model for the robe company. The gaudy color seems to highlight all her best features. My mouth breaks into a smile at the thought. I glance up into the stands where I know they will be. All five in a row are my people. Smiles grace the faces of my mom, dad, Max, Andres, and Nolan. My chest swells with my love for these people.

Today is definitely on my long list of perfect days. I get to graduate, side by side, with one of my best friends while my other one supports me from the stands. Nolan graduated in April, and he now works for a company in Ann Arbor. Cara and I needed another semester because of our student teaching requirement, making us December graduates. She will hopefully find an elementary teaching job nearby soon, but she isn't too worried about it at the moment. She has been promoted to manager at the restaurant, and she is happy about it. She is still with Dan, but she swears there are no serious plans in their immediate future.

Speaking of perfect days, I glance down to the diamond glittering back at me on my left ring finger. The platinum band is adorned with an oval diamond surrounded by a bed of smaller diamonds. The ring belonged to the other love of Andres's life—his mother. All that this ring symbolizes is perfection, pure and simple. I think back to the day that will always rank toward the top of my list of best days—when Andres asked me to be his wife on our beach in Cadiz this past summer.

Andres got on his knee during a stunning sunset, speaking words of love and unwavering commitment. These were not new words coming from his mouth as he had said them to me before, but they became all the more powerful when he said them while holding the breathtaking ring in his hand. I will never forget the love that radiated off of him as he asked me to officially be his forever.

Once again, my gaze finds Andres in the stands, and he gifts me with that smoldering smirk, letting me know that he knows exactly what I am thinking after looking up from my hand. He catches me dreamily admiring my ring quite often, and apparently, he finds it very endearing. Every time I see it, I still can't believe that I am here in this perfect life, graduating and going to marry the most amazing man I have ever known. I still don't know what I did to deserve so much happiness in this lifetime, but what I do know is that I'm not going to question it anymore.

My life has been a whirlwind of experiences since Andres showed up on my doorstep last April. He stayed in Ypsilanti with me for a week, so we could watch Nolan graduate. Then, Andres and I made our way back to Seville where I stayed with him until the end of August. Andres took some classes, and La Banda toured throughout Spain for most of the summer. They have developed quite a following, and they have started playing at bigger venues. I went to every show, and Nadia came along for many of them. My chest swells with pride for their accomplishments.

The time I spent with Andres this past summer was priceless. We had the opportunity to build our relationship on the knowledge of forever instead of the base of insecurity and doubt. Andres had some healing to do as a result of my betrayal. The experience brought back all the feelings of loss and rejection that he had gone through with his parents. Together, we were able to work through our shortcomings and come out stronger. Neither of us is flawless, nor will we ever be, but together, we are imperfect perfection. Our love is the one thing I will never doubt again, and it is the greatest gift of my life.

After the summer, I returned to Michigan to finish my last semester of student teaching, and Andres stayed behind to finish his degree. The separation was difficult, but it wasn't madness like the last time. I'd matured by then, and I didn't make the same mistakes again. Being separated from him was a calmer occurrence this time because I knew we would be together again forever. He graduated a week ago with a degree in art and music. I am so proud of him, and I wish that I could have been there to show my support, but I still had my final week of student teaching to finish.

Andres is here for the next couple of weeks to spend the holidays with my family and me, and then I am moving to Spain. I don't know if we will live there always, but for now, it is our best option. Andres has the band, and I am going to get a teaching job there. I have no complaints. Everything about Spain makes me happy. I will miss my family and friends, but we will have visits. Meanwhile, I will have my forever.

"Olivia Rose Marshall."

When my name is called, I walk across the stage and grab my diploma. I shake the university president's hand to the cheers of my five-person fan section.

As I exit the opposite side of the stage, I am overcome with a strong sense of gratitude. If I had to choose the three things that I am most thankful for in this very moment, they would be the support and love of the people in my life, the powers that be for putting me in a position to meet Andres and then giving us the opportunity to embark on this once-in-a-lifetime journey, and most of all, the strength to accept it all.

The End

# acknowledgments

My dream has come true, and I could not be more excited!

I have always wanted to be a writer, having a huge imagination and the love for telling a great story since I was very young. I'm an avid reader. There is nothing better than getting lost in a good book, falling in love with the characters, and having the message of the story mean something. As my childhood drifted away and the stresses of adult life took over, I pushed aside my love for writing in pursuit of stability. Life—work, school, and family— became priority, and I lost my dream of writing along the way.

No matter how many copies this book sells, I am blessed to have written it. This story and these characters have been in my head for a long time, and I am so happy to share this story with others. When I published this book, I accomplished a lifetime goal, and for that, I am so grateful. I want to thank my family and friends who have supported me in this journey and encouraged me along the way, always believing in me and lifting me up. You have my eternal gratitude.

To my children, the loves of my life, I want you to know how much joy you bring to me daily. I hope you always follow your dreams and find happiness in anything you do in this life. I am so blessed to be your mom. Mommy loves you forever and ever.

To my husband, thank you for loving me unconditionally, even when I am not always the easiest person to love. Your love and support lift me up when I need it most. I love you always.

To my family:

> My mom, who I suggested shouldn't read *Forever Baby* because she will be praying for me for weeks after, but who I know will read it anyway because she is always supportive of anything her children want to do—Thank you for always letting me be me and for making me feel awesome about it. The confidence you gave me has made my life what it is today, and I am so blessed to have had someone give me that. You have been my biggest fan from the beginning, and I love you so much.

> My sisters—You are my best friends, and I am so blessed to have you. You have always shown me unconditional love and have

been my biggest cheerleaders. Thank you for all your support and suggestions when I was writing this book. You have made this book and my life better just by being you. I love you.

My brothers—I love you tons. R—Thank you for writing a book first, reigniting my dream of writing a book myself, and for all your help with *Forever Baby*. You have also always supported me so much, and I am so grateful.

To my friends:

My cup runneth over with the amazing people in my life. To my forever friends who I trusted to beta-read *Forever Baby* first— Your suggestions made this book so much better, and I am so grateful. Thank you for taking the time to read it, in some cases multiple times, and for providing perfect, honest critiques. GN, LB, JJS, NR, JS—Thank you!

G—Your attention to detail rocks. You are so smart. Your comments made me laugh until I cried, and I still go back and look at them sometimes when I need a good laugh. You are tough and honest in your critiques, and my book is better because of you. You have been my constant my whole life and on my side always. You are one of the greatest blessings in my life. I love you forever.

L—I love you to the moon and back and then back again. Beta-reading might not be your calling, but thank you for loving and supporting me regardless. I've told you this many times, and I will tell you again—the day you were born, I was given one of the most amazing gifts this life has to offer. I love you forever.

JJ—Thank you for letting me know that I needed another BJ scene. The shower BJ is dedicated to you! Thank you for reading my book three times and for giving me great critiques each time. I love you forever.

N—My BBWFL! Thank you for setting me on the track for this genre in the first place. Your passion for reading reignited mine. Honestly, I started this book because of you, and I finished it because of your constant support. Our daily conversations, sometimes at two in the morning, about books are the best. Your suggestions for *Forever Baby* were perfect. Thank you for reading and rereading the book and many scenes multiple times! You haven't been in my life for very long, but I know you'll be in it always. I love you forever.

J—Thank you for loving and supporting me one hundred percent for more than a decade now. You are hands-down one of the most amazing people I know. My life is truly better because you are in it. Thank you for supporting me in this journey and in my life. #BFF #oneinamillion #beautifulinsideandout #iloveyouforever

S—You are my inspiration for Cara. Although you and Cara are very different in many ways, like her, you are the most loyal friend. You have always supported me and had my back. One of my beta readers said, "Everyone needs a friend like Cara." I agree, and my college years would have been way different without you as my partner in crime. I love you!

To my beta readers:

Christina, Debi, and Amy—Thank you for taking time out of your lives to read a novel by someone you have never even heard of. You ladies are so talented, and you gave invaluable insight into the story. It still boggles my mind that amazing people like you read books to just help authors like myself simply because you love reading. I know how much time and energy it takes, and I am in awe. Thank you! Amy—You are my BBFF! xoxo

To the bloggers:

I am new to this whole world, and I have yet to meet a lot of you, but to each and every one of you, thank you! Because of you, indie authors get their stories out. Thank you for supporting new authors and the great stories they write.

I want to especially thank Natasha from Natasha Is a Book Junkie. Her blog was the first one I started following, and because of her, I have read so many wonderful books. Her reviews are spot-on, and her passion for reading inspires others. She is the biggest supporter of great authors and their books. I don't even know her, but I adore her. When my books make it to her page, I will know that I have made it in this world!

I also want to thank Jodi from Butterflies, Books, and Dreams. She was the first person to reach out to me for no other reason than to be kind and supportive. She introduced me to the social media side of this business. She always responds to my questions right away, and I am so thankful for her. She is a true supporter of authors, and she has been an invaluable asset to me. Thank you, Jodi!

To my cover artist, Regina Wamba from Mae I Design and Photography—Thank you! Your work inspires me. You are extremely talented at what you do, and I am so grateful to have one of your covers. I love it so much!

To my editors:

> Jennifer Sommersby Young—You read only the first half of my first draft, but the insight and guidance you gave me was priceless. You are truly a talented editor and a class act! Thank you!

> Jovana Shirley from Unforeseen Editing—Thank you so much for the amazing work you did! I am so grateful for you and everything you have done to make this book the best it can be. I look forward to working with you in the future.

Finally and most importantly, to the readers—If you are reading this, thank you! From the bottom of my heart, thank you for helping my dream come true! I truly hope you enjoyed reading *Forever Baby*. I am so grateful for your support!

You can connect with me on several places, and I would love to hear from you.

Find me on Facebook: www.facebook.com/EllieWadeAuthor

Find me on Twitter: @authorelliewade

Visit my website: www.authorelliewade.com

Remember, the greatest gift you can give an author is a review. If you feel so inclined, please leave a review on the various sites. It doesn't have to be fancy. A couple of sentences would be awesome!

I could honestly write a whole book about everyone in this world that I am thankful for. I am blessed in so many ways, and I am beyond grateful for this beautiful life. xoxo

Forever,

Ellie ♥